ABBÉ PIERRE

ABBÉ PIERRE

BY

JAY WILLIAM HUDSON

D. APPLETON AND COMPANY
NEW YORK :: MCMXXII :: LONDON

PRINTED IN THE UNITED STATES OF AMERICA

To G.

Along the roads of Gascony
Is heard the sound of wooden shoes
Up the hills and down again;
Clatter, clatter,
Clack, clack,
The young, and the old with bended back,
Peasant women and peasant men,
With lives to live and little to choose
Along the roads of Gascony.

The sunny fields of Gascony
The peasants plow in wooden shoes,
Red sash, and black béret;
Plack, plack,
Plock, plock,
Wooden shoes and blue smock;
Hear them cry, "Ha! Mascaret!"
At the oxen that they use
Among the hills of Gascony.

Along the roads of Gascony
The blackbirds sing of fair to-morrows;
On happy vineyards the sunlight gleams;
Clack, clack,
Clop, clop,
The wooden shoes, they never stop!
Rhythmic with the peasant's dreams,
Rhyming with his joys and sorrows,
Down the roads of Gascony.

CONTENTS

CHAPTER   PAGE

I. How I Came to Write These Things 1

II. The Procession of the Crows   8

III. A Conjecture 15

IV. Why I Shook My Head . . 24

V. A Great Question . . . 27

VI. Our Village 35

VII. I Have Visitors 44

VIII. They Call Us Provincial . 52

IX. How I Went to Margouet . 59

X. How the Fête Began . . 70

XI. How the Fête Ended . . 83

XII. We Take Ourselves Seriously 90

XIII. The Little Doctor . . . 102

XIV. The House on the Road of the Madonna 108

XV. I Celebrate a Saint . . 118

XVI. Wooden Shoes 128

XVII. On Being Made Ridiculous 135

XVIII. Cabbage Plants and People 140

ix

CONTENTS

CHAPTER		PAGE
XIX.	GOSSIP	146
XX.	AT NIGHT	155
XXI.	ST. JOHN'S EVE	163
XXII.	OLD ABBÉ CASTEX	174
XXIII.	AUNT MADELEINE INSISTS	182
XXIV.	I GET A NEW PUPIL	193
XXV.	THE ROAD	206
XXVI.	IN GERMAINE'S GARDEN	217
XXVII.	MONSIEUR WARE TURNS POET	227
XXVIII.	I CALL FOR DAVID	230
XXIX.	A SINGER OF GASCONY	234
XXX.	THE LAST WOLVES OF AIGNAN	242
XXXI.	WHAT ONE GETS FOR A PAIR OF GLOVES	262
XXXII.	THE PIPES OF PAN	269
XXXIII.	MADAME SANCE ASKS ADVICE	277
XXXIV.	THE CHURCH ON THE HILL	284
XXXV.	I SEEK A PARISH	294
XXXVI.	HAVE PITY, O GOD!	305
XXXVII.	THE INEVITABLE	306
XXXVIII.	COMPROMISES	309
XXXIX.	THE WEDDING	316
XL.	SUNSETS	329

ABBÉ PIERRE

ABBÉ PIERRE

Chapter I: *How I Came to Write These Things*

I F one walks through our little village of Aignan northward by the Street of the Church, passing the covered poultry market, and the Duc d'Armagnac's house, and the shop of the sabot-maker (where the big, wooden shoe hangs high over the narrow sidewalk), he soon arrives at our ancient church with its Roman tower, discolored with age, mended and patched and re-mended by many generations. The church seems to lie abruptly in the way, but a second look shows that the street leads around it, past a broken bit of wall—the remnant of fortifications such as are found in so many of our Gascon villages. If one keeps straight on, by the long, gray cemetery wall, over which are seen the tall cypress trees, he comes to a sunny vineyard, and then to a rusty, iron gate, which creaks on its hinges. Just inside this gate, on the right, is my garden-house, with the door wide open. Anybody who calls, "Monsieur l'Abbé!" will soon see me at the door, extending him a real welcome. For I like my friends to come and visit me in my garden, although sometimes whole days go by, and no one comes, and the only human thing I hear is the clatter of wooden shoes on the hard, white road outside, or a peasant rattling by with his ox-cart, or children driving by their cows and geese.

I am here in my garden-house now, and very conveniently have I arranged it so that I can write the things I have long wanted to write. I wish that my old friend, the Abbé Rivoire, were not so far away, so that he could see it all, just as it is. I have made a sturdy table with some thick boards, nailed firmly on two boxes which Monsieur Rigot, the proprietor of the café, gave me. It is covered with a cloth, so that the boards do not show in the least. I have placed it so that, as I write, I look out the doorway, which frames the church tower against the sky like a clear-cut picture; only, this particular picture has the advantage of varying every hour with the moving clouds and the changing sun and the shadows that do not long remain the same. No one ever had a more beautiful place or a more quiet place in which to write. Sometimes, it is true, I become so interested in the thoughts that come to me that I forget to set them down; and, *hélas!* they are the best thoughts of all—the thoughts we have when we fall into long reveries on a summer's afternoon, and then awake with a start, somehow feeling that we have been near infinite things. But one cannot put such thoughts on paper. No, the words will not come soon enough, and, before we know it, the mood has passed.

I have just said that this is a beautiful place in which to write, and yet, I realize that it might not look entirely beautiful to everybody. For instance, these walls are not really beautiful; they are the same inside as outside, made in our rough Gascon way of a framework of wooden beams, filled in with much yellow clay and stones of many shapes and sizes. That work-bench of my father's by the door, covered with a disorderly miscellany of tools; that pannier of potatoes in the middle of the dirt floor; those two old, broken candelabra from the church lying in the corner; this box of tumbled books by my table—all these may belie the note of beauty. But, then, is it not all in the way one looks at it? My young friend, Henri, who is really an artist, came to see me lately, and he thought it was picturesque at any rate!

There is one thing here that is indeed beautiful. It is the silver crucifix on my table.

It is very old.

This hilltop of Gascony, where I was born! How strange it is and how good it is to be here again! Above all, to know that here I shall stay through the years that yet belong to me! The Abbé Rivoire used to ask me, knowing my love for the place, if I never had the ambition to be the curé of this, my native village. Well, the very old Abbé Castex is the priest of our parish. He is even older than I am, and leans upon a cane. At any time during the last forty years I might have been the curé of one of our Gascon villages; but there are many ways of serving the good God, and my way early led me far from my parents here to that great city which the whole world wonders at. Paris! It is close to that center

of things that I have been a professor in our ancient
Collège St. Thomas d'Aquin for these forty years
since I took priestly orders. How fast a man's life
goes! And every summer holiday when I could, I
have come back here to this village of my boyhood,
where my feeble old father still lives at the age of
eighty-six—my father, whose eyes are almost too
dim to see me any more, who lives only in my comings and goings, and who is very proud of his son—
it is not mine to say what for. If he is proud that
I could spend these years imparting philosophy (and
sometimes Latin) to the young minds that belong
to the to-morrow of France, well, it does him no
harm. And if he likes to talk of those two summers
long ago when, while yet a student, I actually took
the place of a priest in London, I shall not greatly
object, for my father admires nobody more than a
traveler—he, who has never left this part of Gascony in all his years. But these travels did help my
English, so that, at length, I could teach it to our
French boys, and could actually read with pleasure
such a poet as Wordsworth, and even such a novelist as Monsieur Hardy. I recall two of my favor-
ites, although I do not by any means approve of all
they write, especially when they touch upon theologi-
cal matters—concerning which I surely have a right
to say something!

But now I am getting along in years myself, and
if a man of sixty-five can be said to be old, why,
then, I am old. And always I have cherished in my
heart the day when I could come back to this little
village, yes, to this very garden, and spend the time

when life casts its longer, gentler shadows in this happiest of places. For I have been about the world considerably, having been to many places in France, besides those two journeys to London; I have also read about other countries and cities, and thought about the matter a good deal; and I have reason to know now that there is no place like this, our village of Aignan, here in the heart of Gascony!

There is one great disappointment, though; there is no longer any one here in my village to whom I can talk with any satisfaction. It was different when Jean-Louis Sance was alive! Our friendship began when we were boys at school, and was renewed through the many summers when I came back here. How many hours we spent together in his shady garden in the Road of the Madonna, speaking of the great things of life—things that ordinary men do not even try to understand! But he is gone now. Of course, there is the Abbé Castex; but he is so old that his mind is not all that it once was; and it never was a very great mind. So it is that already I doubly miss the Abbé Rivoire, my closest colleague at our dear school where I have taught all these years. With him I was intimate as with no other. Even when he became an invalid and could teach no more, I continued seeing him often, so that our precious comradeship ceased not. If only he were here, I could easily prove to him that this Gascony of ours is far above the things I used to tell him, although he always thought me extravagant in my

praise. Not only do I miss him, but I greatly fear
that he, too, will be lonely, now that I cannot visit
him any more in his sister's little house near Paris.

But if I cannot share my reflections with any one
else, it occurs to me that I can at least write them
down for my own pleasure. There is this much use
in it: the best part of one's life is the time one lives
with his thoughts; and, certainly, this is true—if
one does not express his thoughts, they are likely to
die. Then, if it should so happen that I write something worthy, something that I think would interest
the Abbé Rivoire, I shall not hesitate to send it to
him, to help him while away his tedious hours. It
will take the place of that journey to my village, of
which he has so often spoken, but which, alas, I now
suspect he will never accomplish!

More and more, during these later years, when I
have come back here for my holiday, I have noticed
things about my fellow villagers that I had never
observed before; things of which they themselves
are not aware, because they live here all the time
and take their lives as a matter of course. This time,
particularly, returning to this blessed place to wander
forth nevermore, I find myself looking upon this
most charming corner of the world in a way that
gives rise to a multitude of new thoughts. Truly, it
will be a novelty to be able to forget the sterner
things of the philosophers, and to set down my musings, just as they come, here in my garden-house,
which looks out not only on the church tower, but
over the red-tiled roofs of my village to the most

wonderful country the eyes of man ever saw—ending with the distant Pyrenees, on whose towering summits the snow gleams against the sky, even though it is the last of May, and the roses are in bloom.

Chapter II: *The Procession of the Crows*

NOT far away from my garden is the house where I live with my old father, in the Street of the Church. Last night, about nine o'clock, when it was quite dark, I was attracted to my upper window (the shutters of which were wide open) by a great medley of strange noises, which grew louder every moment. The first sound I was able clearly to distinguish above the hubbub was the monotonous rattle of a drum, and then a riot of confused shouts from the Place in the center of the village, which opens into my street. Soon I saw coming toward me, around the corner by Rigot's café, a disorderly procession of men, women, and children, whose faces, lighted by flaming torches, surged onward like the crests of countless waves gleaming on a restless sea. They bore with them numerous Japanese lanterns of all colors, hung high on poles. As they came nearer, I could see, toward the front of the procession, a large flag.

This is the way it was: First, there was the drum, never ceasing its strident rubadub; then the flambeaux, carried high above the bobbing heads of the crowd; then eager young men and women, many of

8

them arm in arm, and a host of children, laughing and shouting, amid which arose the brackets of gay paper lanterns; and then, at the rear, the older women, some with babies in their arms. As the procession approached, the ever-moving lights danced on the plastered fronts of the houses along our narrow street, making weird shadows, and the shouts and laughter and singing grew deafening, and there came from the crowd, above all other sounds, a confusion of raucous cries like the call of a multitude of crows, or *corbeaux,* as we popularly speak of them. At the very front of the procession, I could make out the stalwart form of Bajac, the butcher, just behind the drummer. I could also distinguish Sarrade, the sabot-maker (he is a very small, chubby man, with a rosy face and black hair and mustache), and the postman, and Victor Claverie, the village crier; then the janitor of the town hall; also the guardian of the forest, and many others whom I knew well. I had noticed that, occasionally, the whole procession would stop in front of a house and call out something; then they would proceed as before. When they arrived in front of my house, they stopped again, and this time I could discern what they were shouting. It was "Come out, all you blacks!" And then I knew at once what the procession was, as I should have guessed before, if I had not been dreaming; it was the annual "procession of the blacks," or, as we have long called it, the cortège of crows.

Now, so far as I know, such an interesting thing does not occur elsewhere in the whole world. (I shall have to inquire of the Abbé Rivoire; he, being a historian, may have heard of it in some other place.) Every year, at the very end of May, all people that are fortunate enough to have jet black hair and dark complexions, meet at night in the Place, in front of the town hall, to march in this procession, under the leadership of the chief of the crows, who just now happens to be Bajac, the butcher. Although his hair is now nearly white, he once had hair as black and a complexion as swarthy as any crow, so it does not matter; for after all, in this world it is what a man really is that counts, not the accidents of age; and I am glad that this is so, and it ought to be a rule more universally followed. Well, every year since the night of time (as the saying is) they have assembled this way from all the country round in our little village on the appointed night; and the procession is not all. As they stopped last night in front of the houses, loudly calling for recruits, the procession grew ever larger. Up the Street of the Church they went, past the church, down the Road of the Madonna, on by the large, iron cross, until they arrived at the fine house and garden of Dr. Dousset, who is our mayor, just on the outskirts of the village. The doctor came out and cheerfully put some coins in the hat passed around for money to pay for refreshments at the café afterwards. He even marched in the procession a little way, as it turned again toward the village by the back street. When the procession finally got back to the Place, having passed the old curé's house, and Madame Lacoste's, and the Hôtel Maulézun, and the post office, it was twice as large as when it started. In the meantime, one thing had occurred which showed the spirit of the crowd. There was a man last year who closed his door when the procession passed, and who defied the ancient custom, and would give nothing for refreshments. Last night, when they passed his home near the post office, they hissed him and his house, even though it is one of the grandest in the village, and he is a wealthy landowner, and belongs to the old family of Capéran. One cannot defy the ancient customs in our village, and one must be ever careful how he lightly treats things that are sanctified by time. There is too much of that these days.

When the procession, with still more torches and lanterns, had all assembled in the Place, near the village pump, with a goodly collection of money in the hat, so that everybody might quench his thirst, the real festivities began. First, the village crier, Victor Claverie, who considers himself quite a wit, and has a loud, oratorical sort of voice (as a village crier should have), got up in the middle of the crowd and announced that the next thing would be a grand ball, and then a bull-fight, with electricity, at midnight. One sees by this how good-natured the crowd felt, how like little children they were in their garrulous light-heartedness, for they all applauded him laughingly, although there is no electricity or electric lights in our village, and they knew there was to be no bull-fight, much as they would have liked to see one, or, at any rate, a cow-fight, such as we have on fête-days. But they did have what answered to a grand ball, as they always do, for, at that very moment, the solitary fiddler in front of the Café Ladouès struck up a lively tune, and the fun began.   Oh, it was a merry sight to see them, young and old, dancing the giddy quadrilles, with their maddening, care-free abandon; the vigorous rondos, that got the older people quite out of breath before they were over, so that they retired to the edge of the crowd, exhausted; and then, the milder polkas and waltzes, in which everybody joined, with much good-natured jostling, the Place all the while echoing to the multitudes of eager feet beating out their rough rhythm on the hard earth.   And round about, the fitful lights of the flambeaux flickering on the white walls of the surrounding buildings; and, overhead, the stars looking down from a clear sky— although I do not think that it occurred to anybody to notice them.

I had a glimpse of the dancing from my window at first; and later, while standing in my doorway to breathe the air before going to bed.   And while there, I saw something out of the ordinary.   It is rarely that strangers come to our village, since it is away from any railroad; so, it was with considerable surprise that I saw a tall, fair-haired, beardless young man, whom I had never seen before, and without doubt a foreigner of some sort, standing by himself somewhat beyond the circle of the crowd.   I could not see him very distinctly; but one moment, when the torches were flaring a little higher than usual and were shining on his face, I thought that he looked like an Englishman.   Suddenly, it occurred to me that he must be the American that has lately come to our village with his invalid sister, and about whom I have heard some interesting things, although I have not yet met him.

After I had stood in my doorway a short time, the butcher, Bajac, happened to stroll down the street. I ventured to ask him the reason why we have had this procession every year since the time when no man remembers, for I like to know the reason of things, possibly because I have been immersed in philosophy so much; and I had never heard the real explanation of this cortège. And he answered in these words:

"Why, don't you know? This is the anniversary of the day God painted the crows!"

The truth is, I had heard this reason given before, so it did not enlighten me in the least; and it did not seem sensible that a man with the white hair of Bajac, and with his dignity, and chief of the crows, too, should give such a reason. But he persisted in it, and looked perfectly serious when he said it, and would give no other explanation. So, I shook my head, and, happening to see the tall form of my young friend, Henri, whom I had noticed dancing with a number of the best-looking girls of the village—happening to see him passing, I took him to task and admonished him to ask of those whom he should meet the real reason. But he told me afterwards that they all said the same thing, as if they knew nothing else,

"It is the day God painted the crows!"

Although I went to bed fairly early, and could

hear the fiddling far into the night (even though I closed my shutters), I could not help thinking about that foolish account of the meaning of this custom. And it was only to-day that my old friend, Marius Fontan, solved the riddle for me. He likes to delve among old documents and papers hid away in the most unlikely places, and nothing interests him so much as to ferret out things of the ancient days, especially about our village. And he says that long, long ago the procession of the crows happened not at the end of May, as now, but about the middle of August, when the harvest is over, and the hay is cut and piled in stacks in the fields, and the wheat is all in, and the workers have grown swarthy in this southern sun, yes, black enough, as those who have seen them know! These were the "blacks" of those old days and this is why they were black; and so, their work all over, they sought relaxation and a rejoicing of some sort, and the result was this cortège of crows at harvest-time, and the dancing in the Place. Only, Marius could not tell me when or why the time of year was changed. I do not know surely if he is right about this matter, for to find the truth about ancient things is a sufficiently difficult task; but, undeniably, this account is better than that ridiculous one about God painting the crows!

At all events, the "procession of the crows" is well named, since it is a notorious fact that these birds, like some of our village folk, love to assemble together and engage in noisy demonstrations.

Chapter III: *A Conjecture*

TO-DAY, I arose later than usual, because the noise of the dancing kept me awake so long.
When I had said mass at the church, I came back to the breakfast prepared by my Aunt Madeleine, who lives with my old father and me. My Aunt Madeleine keeps house for us, and very efficient she is, if also somewhat exacting, the sharp corners of her disposition never having been rounded off by the attrition of matrimony.

Before going to my garden, I did something I should have done several days ago. I made a placard and hung it up in the window of our front door, downstairs:

> Leçons de Latin
> et d'Anglais

Anybody seeing this sign will know that the Abbé Pierre Clément is home again, and is ready to give instruction, just as he has done for a number of summers past, when any one has desired it, especially to the young boys in our village who have not done quite as well as they might at the lycées in the

15

neighboring towns. Probably every one is already aware that I am here, since it is difficult to keep anything secret in our small village, above all, the arrival of anybody, be he friend or stranger.

After placing this notice in the door, I went outside and glanced at it from the street to see if it was legible enough. Perhaps if a stranger were looking at the front of our house, he would be attracted less by this placard of mine than by two small ornaments of discolored brass, hung on the masonry each side of the doorway. They are the ancient insignia of my father's profession, each representing a dish, with a circle cut into one side, so that one being shaved could hold it closely fitted to his neck, to protect himself from the drippings of the lather. My father followed this art of the barber for many years; and, although the shaving dish is now becoming old-fashioned, and belongs to another age, like my father himself, he still keeps these emblems by our door. For he ever took a certain pride in his profession, knowing it to be an honorable one, it being mentioned even in the Holy Scriptures, where the prophet Ezekiel makes the use of the barber's razor a part of the preparation of the work of the Lord. My father loves to talk of the old times, which I myself remember, although I was then but a youth, when his salon was the place of resort for the best people of the village. Ah, many were the discussions that went on here, and many the great questions decided here, especially on Saturday nights, when there gathered together such important men as the notary, and the proprietor of the principal café, and the mayor. So it is but natural that my father likes to keep by his door these reminders of the good old days.

Musing on these things, I made my way up the hill, past the church, to my garden, speaking to several people who passed me on their way to the village pump or the baker's. I recollected that it was the first day of June; and such a June morning, with the sun shining bright on the white houses, making glorious the little gardens—a few fleecy clouds in the sky, and the air soft and balmy! Arrived at my garden, I walked by my garden-house without opening it, up the path by the fig tree with the wooden bench underneath, and then to the highest point, just beyond the roses, where I could view the country for miles around.

If my friend, the Abbé Rivoire, could but see our Gascony on a morning like this! A vast, rolling expanse of valley and hill, valley and hill—great waves of countless hills one after another, breaking into the spray of trees on the summits; and on every summit an ancient village with its church tower rising above the little, clustered houses, the good gray guardian of a long past, and the symbol of a dream! There are the fields, many of them vineyards, sloping in every direction and of every geometric pattern, bordered with hedges, dotted with white-walled houses, their red-tiled roofs mellowed brown by time; trees everywhere, none so conspicuous as the tall, upstanding poplars, following the devious ways of the little streams; everything green, green, green, except the winding, white roads, leading up hill, and down hill, and far away toward the lofty Pyrenees, just visible through the delicate, violet haze that floats along the southern edge of the world like a thin veil. And, over all, a fast-vanishing, dreamy mist, touching the hills and valleys like a timid caress! Those who made this Gascon landscape were unconsciously making poetry. It is like precious pages from an artist's sketch-book, made for his own heart, or pictures from some romance, old and fabled and forgotten. Or, one might say that, with its rolling hills all traced out into designs by the roads and hedges, it is like an undulating tapestry—the rare, old kind one sees in ancient castles.

Why, even the names of the villages that crown these hills make poetry, when pronounced in our robust, Gascon way. Castelnavet—is it not music?—there it is, yonder toward the south, with its tree-covered mound in its center, gleaming like a toy village; Sabazan, to the west, with its heavy tower against the sky like a donjon-keep, the spine of its roof so high that the whole impression is that of a cat humping its back! Castelnau, further toward the Pyrenees, with its picturesque, ruined fortress on a high hill, dominating the fertile valley of the Adour. Like poems are such names, I say, made thus eloquent to fit the glory of the landscape and the romance of the long, long years that brought these villages into being. And I am glad there has been given to these names such articulate music through which our villages may announce their existence to the world—not to speak of other villages in this same part of Gascony, the sound of whose names is ever beautiful to my ear, such as Plaisance, and Margouet, and Averon, and oh, so many more! Little villages which, if they could only live the music of their names, would be as happy as they look this morning, loved into new beauty by the June sun!

While I was quite lost in this sort of reverie, I heard a faint sound of footsteps on the road, and, looking through the trees toward the gate of my garden, I perceived a young girl passing. I have often envied the happy talent for describing people such as the novelists possess. But it would be hard, even for the best of novelists, to describe this girl, whom I have known from her infancy, just as she appeared this morning, transforming the commonplace roadway into a splendid picture. However, I have read a number of the best novels; and I suppose that a conscientious writer of that craft might describe her in somewhat the following way—that is, if he saw her as I came upon her in front of my garden gate; for she had heard my call, and had waited there in the sunlit road: A slender figure in white, her head immediately attracting attention because of its rich abundance of loosely arranged, black hair, dressed over the ears in the most charming way, under which looked out a face that held in it the colors of the most delicate, red roses. Large, black eyes, set wide apart, modest in their regard, and filled with a soft light; a high forehead, over which a wave or two of hair tumbled ever so gracefully; a strong nose; full, red lips, with a touch of sadness in them, but capable of the mood of joy,

too, when, suddenly, there is revealed a smile very
like the light one sees flashing over the snow of our
Pyrenees early in the morning. All in all, a face
not exactly beautiful, as formalists judge of beauty,
but better than merely beautiful; a face in which life
and health and high spirits and sweet, maidenly mod-
esty and good common sense shone forth as the suggestion of the temper of a soul. Her dress this
morning was a simple, white one, with sleeves short
enough to reveal an arm round and capable. Look
at the quiet glory of Gascony, then look at Germaine, and you would know at once that they somehow belonged to each other.

Although I, myself, would use soberer language,
I suppose a novelist would describe her in about
this manner; and, strange to say, he would not be
greatly erring on the side of over-praise, as novelists often do. She was carrying an armful of roses,
gathered in her garden on the other side of the village.

And well it is that I should speak of Germaine
Sance in this pleasant way, for her father, Jean-
Louis, was one of the best friends I ever had; one
of the stalwart, big-hearted, big-minded men of this
region, whose body, alas, has been lying these four
years in the little cemetery just beyond the south
boundary of my vineyard. Is it any wonder that I,
an old man, should feel like the spiritual father of
this splendid child (I call her "child," although she
is now nearly nineteen), when I myself helped to
teach her the catechism and shared in giving her her
first communion, and, with her father in the flesh,

watched her grow up, from the days when she first trudged to the convent school on the hill?

I had not seen Germaine since my return a few days ago. That is why I called to her as soon as I saw her.

"Leave your roses for a moment here in the shade of the chestnut tree," I said, "while you walk with me a little in my garden and tell me the news."

"How well your garden looks!" she exclaimed. And then I learned that her mother was getting the plowing done in her vineyard, and that her brother, Henri—what a man he is growing to be!—was very busy, which I can well believe, since it takes study to become a tax administrator, as I proceeded to remark.

"He not only studies, Monsieur l'Abbé, but at times he does his painting, too. Lately, he made a new water-color of the church from the Street of the Balustrade."

I must see that picture.

I had to ask Germaine if her garden was as beautiful as ever; and whether her mother still loved the jasmine as she used to; and if the hollyhocks were yet in bloom along the edge of the pond.

"I must go to your garden soon," I added, "for the sake of old times! You know your father and I had many a long talk in that garden of yours; and it is so much larger than mine, and has so many more flowers and trees."

"The grass is getting long; our kitchen-girl's father is to cut it for his cattle. And—oh, yes! the cherries are ripe; and we hear the nightingale when it is dark. You must come!"

Until lately, Germaine had been away to school at Bordeaux. I wondered how she managed to spend her time, now that she was back home for good.

"I am not idle, Monsieur l'Abbé! Besides helping in the house, I look after the garden—that is what I like best; and just now, too, I am making some filet lace for curtains; I do most of it on the bench by the pond."

Thus talking, we reached the height of my garden, where I had been drinking in that vast expanse of Gascony when she came along the road. I told her how I had been thinking about the music of the names of the villages round about.

"Yes, I love some of those names myself." And then I saw a mischievous smile as she added, "And away off there on that hill is Pouydraguin—not quite so musical!"

As she spoke, she pointed to an elevated place to the southwest, covered with trees, in the midst of which we could just discern a corner of an old château.

After awhile she said, "All these villages on the hills—I have sometimes thought that they almost grow to seem like persons. One wonders why Fromentas remains so quiet in its place yonder—why it does not go over and play with Castelnavet, when the sun is so jolly and each village so lonely on its little hill. But Fromentas turns its back on Castelnavet and forever thinks its own thoughts!"

Before long we went back to the chestnut tree by the gate, where Germaine had left her roses. I wondered where she was taking them; and then I wished I had not asked, for I suddenly knew they were for her father's grave.

"Father loved the roses," she said.

Just as Germaine was leaving, it came to me to mention last night's procession of the crows and to ascertain if she saw it, and especially to allude to the fair American whom I had noticed on the outskirts of the crowd at the dancing.

For already I had heard certain gossip.

But she said she had been at home, and had not come out at all.

As I turned slowly back to my garden-house, after having watched her walk away with that free, graceful manner she has, I thought to myself,

"She looked downward, and seemed a little confused when I mentioned the American."

And I could not help wondering; and I shook my head as I sometimes do when something does not entirely please me.

Chapter IV: *Why I Shook My Head*

O F course, one does not need any remarkable
endowment of wit to guess why I shook my
head. Germaine's manner, when I mentioned
the American, suggested to me, who am accustomed
to judging human motives, an interest in him of
which I had known nothing. For I had not even
seen this foreigner until the night before, and I knew
little about him; and this little came only through
such gossip of the village as my Aunt Madeleine had
heard.

I am sure that our village, for all that it has a
number of worthy young men, who can drive their
oxen or ply their trade as well as anybody, contains
not a single youth who would ever think seriously
of aspiring to the heart of Germaine Sance. Perhaps this is because the World War took away forever over fifty of the best young men of this commune. To some, this isolation of hers might seem
pathetic, but really, it is not pathetic in the least.
For, while Germaine never avoids the presence of
young men, she has never shown any preference for
their society, much less has she encouraged any one
of them to suppose that he was favored. For the

plain fact is that Germaine, with her social advantage as the daughter of Jean-Louis Sance, with her inborn refinement, her rare ideals of life, and her home-bred culture, broadened by several years at the excellent school at Bordeaux, is to these young men of Aignan as something entirely out of their realm—something to admire, but not to aspire toward. This does not mean that Germaine lives a lonely life—far from it. No one in our village has more friends; and, besides this, she is interested in many things, finding a lively joy in them all: her music, her garden, her reading, yes, and her delicate filet lace-making of which she so lately spoke.

So I had always felt that this spiritual child of mine was, for the time, safe from the disturbing influences of the romantic passion that changes so many people's lives, and, alas, not always for the best. And I had rejoiced in this. And I knew that if her life was ever to be disturbed in this way, it would be by some one from the great world outside her native village. So it is clear why I was disquieted when Germaine seemed embarrassed at the mention of this tall and handsome stranger, who, gossip told me, had already been seen at her house.

Now, if I were writing a story for people to read, instead of writing my reflections for my own pleasure, I would go right on and make a plot, in which Germaine and the American would be the principal characters. I would make them fall in love with one another, and write pages of conversation, and leave out tedious descriptions and all impertinent meditations, well knowing that when most people read a story, they skip such things to find out what is going to happen next. I wonder why authors are not more aware of this simple fact! I myself read a story lately, where the descriptions were beautiful enough, and the philosophic comments of the author were sufficiently profound, so far as I had the patience to peruse them; but I could not wait to consider them as much as I ought; I was too much interested to know the fate of the hero, Michael Henchard, and hurried through the tragedy of his rapid descent from riches and honor, as Mayor of Casterbridge, to that sad, sad ending of his in the pauper's grave. And then I tried to read the book over again for just those wonderful descriptions of Monsieur Hardy, and for his philosophy; but I had to hasten through them again because of the overpowering interest of the story itself, which still held me fast and would not let me linger by the way. I have no ambition to write such a story, for I know that I could neither construct a plot nor manage clever conversations with my pen—not in the least! Above all, I have not the worldly knowledge to write a story about love.—Love!—this mystery that moves through all the great stories of mankind and sings through its songs; this miracle that lives at the heart of the world's life and assumes such Protean guises —what is it?

Chapter V: *A Great Question*

THE entrance of love into a life greatly changes
that life, and, as I have said, not always for
the best.   There are so many kinds of love,
as anybody who knows human nature, or has read
more than a few romances, must admit.   And of all
the kinds of love there are, only two are worthy of
a human soul; and of these two, only one was meant
for me.   And that is why I am a priest.

I thought it all out when I was still a youth—a
sensitive youth, all on fire with the poetry of life,
and with a seriousness of purpose far beyond my
short acquaintance with the world.   And, at the age
of nineteen, I had definitely made up my mind that
I would never allow myself what most men cherish
as the dearest thing our good earth offers.   For, in
my mind, the thought of love had come to signify
more than the love that a man may have for the
woman of his heart—vastly more than that, beautiful as such a love may be and has been, times without number.

For it seemed to me that whatever one truly
loves, to this must he give his whole life, all that he
is or hopes to be.   Love, the more I thought of it,

27

meant the entire consecration of the spirit to the highest and greatest thing this world or any world may hold; truly, it meant nothing less than the adoration of the soul for that Something, of which all lesser loves are but faulty symbols and suggestions. In those days, I thought of mankind as treading a long, long road, a road that has no ending, urged on by the divine yearning that is within each and every heart; a yearning that was never meant to cease, yet which often wearies of its search, or is deluded, by the seductive cheer of the resting places along the way, to think that the search is over and that love has found its very own at last. Such a resting place is Art, where the poets and painters and sculptors and musicians tarry, to find their love fulfilled forevermore; they go no farther, because of their deep wonder and delight. Such a resting place is Truth, where the philosophers put down their staffs and lay their hearts upon that altar where Truth's candles burn unflickering lights. And such a resting place is Woman, where a man stops with a sudden glory in his soul, his speech turned into song; for now all Beauty, yea, and all Truth and Goodness are found in Her at last! Yes, some men stop at one of these places on the soul's long highway, and some at another, such as Wealth, or Fame; but most at that place where Woman waits and Romance sings.

But for me, the road seemed to stretch on and on, far beyond the glory of these things, into an infinite distance whither love still led, crying to me not to tarry at these lesser shrines. For I had learned to believe that what the soul is really seeking is much farther away than most men guess, much farther than any of these things men prize so highly. And what is this thing that the soul really seeks? It is that which contains within itself all the beauty of Woman, but purified of its dross; all the sweet thrill of music, but with its discords lost in harmonies too vast for ears of sense; all the dreams of the poets, but come to life in a dream that is a dream no more; it is nothing less than that Ideal in which live all things that Art ever meant in its longings, and all that Truth could have been to the ages that have sought it, and despaired of finding it, but kept seeking it, none the less. Verily, it is this infinite thing that the soul calls out for, desiring no other Beloved; the Ideal, to suggest whose beatific goal exist all dawns, and rivers, and peaks, and skies, and stars, yes, and the flowers that make death glorious with their dying! Love's Ideal, that contains all the precious rooms of all the inns that tempt to rest along life's highway, transfigured into that House of the Spirit whose towers are hid in blessed dimness and immortal mystery.

I remember that about this time of my life I happened upon some sentences written in the twelfth century, by Adam, of the Prémontré order:

In her trouble the spirit hath love abiding; but she knows no longer what it is she loves, what she ought to love. She addresseth herself to the stones and to the rocks, and saith to them, "What are ye?" And the stones and the rocks make answer, "We are creatures of the same even as thou art." To the like question the sun, the moon, and the stars make the like answer. The spirit doth interrogate the sand of the sea, the dust of the earth, the drops of rain, the days of the years, the hours of the days, the moments of the hours, the turf of the fields, the branches of the trees, the leaves of the branches, the scales of fish, the wings of birds, the utterances of men, the voices of animals, the movements of bodies, the thoughts of minds; and these things declare, all with one consent, unto the spirit, "We are not that which thou demandest; search up above us. . . ."

Thus it is that, a youth of nineteen, I heard the voice of the Ideal, and knew that to lose one's love in anything less meant the arrest and tragedy of the soul. Above all, to lose one's love in the adoration of an earthly being, however beautiful such a love might be, meant the betrayal of the spirit's quest. For a Woman, even more than Art and Truth, if loved truly, is ever thought of as the one compelling and absorbing goal of all one's love; yes, to the lover, his beloved seems ever absolute, "in herself complete," demanding all devotion, all sacrifice, to make the love of her that high and worthy thing he sings. To him there shall be, there can be, nothing further. She is all.

In those days, I did not say that there was no place at all for such a love. But from the first it was clearly not for me, and it has never been for me. Not that I may ever actually reach the white purity of that Ideal which out-glories all, and makes all else fade into nothingness beside it.

And that Ideal, what is it? I have come to know at last that it is what we timidly call God. Ah, love is indeed divine, to find its rest nowhere but in His infinite mystery; to say of each thing else, "Not this, not this, it is still beyond, its glory still awaits you, suffer a little longer, persevere through nights the darkest and days most dreary, through loneliness and tears, all for the love of God that calls and calls and will not let us rest!"

It was my conviction in those earlier days that every man has a supreme decision to make. He might choose the love which, however beautiful, ends its glory with the grave, and lives on only in the children and children's children one leaves behind; or, he might choose the love that makes one immortal by its own purifying fire, so that one need not live on in earthly children born of woman. Humanity would go on, I thought, losing itself in the earthly love until, slowly, through the generations, a few men, and then more men, would learn, one by one, the diviner love of which all earthly love is but the dim shadow.

These reasonings, I confess, were those of my dreamy boyhood, before I knew better what all these things truly signify. But my own great decision was made. I thereafter dedicated myself to God and His service. And here I am to-day, an old priest, treading that long, long road, keeping my eyes resolutely ahead, still seeking to find and be the dream of my boyhood's heart—which is the inner dream of the world!

But on one matter I have changed my mind.

There is more in the earthly love I spurned than I thought, when it is pure and true—oh, yes, when it is as pure and true as I have sometimes seen it! Divine love is a great and beautiful thing, and earthly love can also be a great and beautiful thing. They are both great; and I have learned that, in the logic of God, no great thing is utterly inconsistent with any other great thing. Knowing this, the Church blesses the true love of human hearts and makes of their marriage a holy sacrament. My own mother! When I remember thee and thy pure heart, I know that in thy tender love that brought me into life there is indeed more of heaven than of earth!

I now see that a man and woman, pure in heart, may tread together that long road toward the Ideal; hand in hand may they tread it, day on day, year on year, their love made stronger by its common yearning for the dream that each helps to keep alive within the other's soul; finding in one another's eyes something more than earthly light, in each other's speech something of the music that makes their steps keep rhythm with this vision that they share. Lost in each other they are—and yet not lost in each other; but, rather, saved through each other to the love that transcends both of them; finding each in each the dim suggestion of the goal each seeks, which somehow shines through one another's clay, rendering that clay beautiful and making earthly love partake of the divine. No, not alone must each man go, but blessed may he be with such companionship, his tears no longer bitter with their loneliness, but sweet as sorrow grows to be when understood and

shared. In Her he shall find, made secure through
nights and days, the far Ideal's search, since through
her very being it speaks to him and will not be denied. Oh, God is not merely at the end of the infinite journey—He is not so far away as that!—
He is sometimes found along the journey itself: in
Art in all its myriad forms; in Truth, yes, and in
Woman, too, if her love be pure and her heart given
to the holy things such purity may know.

But how many men and women find the glory of
such exalted love? I do not know. I only know
that thousands of desolated hearts, deceived by
earthly love, have come upon their bitter tragedies;
that for such love some men have broken every law
of God and man, and lost their souls, betraying generations yet unborn. For, such pure love as I have
written of is not so very common; and if a poet
needs rare genius to forge great and worthy verse,
and if a painter needs much genius to make of form
and color a thing of undying joy, so do lovers require great genius to live the love that God demands
of those who need such love. And in His wise design, there are some of us He sets apart for the love
of Him alone, our souls made single to His service
evermore.

So, now, it is evident why I shook my head about
Germaine. It was not merely that, knowing her innocent heart, I had always feared that tragedy might
some day enter it disguised in the gracious garments
that Love wears, be he good or bad; but, let it be
confessed that, long ago, ever since she had learned
her catechism with that sweet piety which I had

found to be her dearest grace, I had hoped that some day she would be led to give her life to that sisterhood of blessed women who present their souls to God alone and know no other love than that. Perhaps I may be a mistaken old man, but that is what I hoped, and still hope, for the soul of this child.

As I sit here in my garden-house, looking out the open door across the sunlit vineyard and down to where the slender cypress trees rise high beyond the cemetery wall, I can just see the top of a tombstone over which the roses climb. He who wanders there, as I sometimes do, reads there this name: "Geneviève Caussade." In my early youth I surmised, through her sweet soul, what pure, unsullied love might mean, if earthly love had been for me. But the long road stretched before me, and I made the great decision.

She has been lying in that grave for many years. She never married. The sunlight kisses her roses as I write.

Chapter VI: *Our Village*

THIS morning I heard the clear voice of a
neighbor of mine singing in his vineyard across
the road from my garden. It was a song about
a peasant girl and a king's son—a song that everybody knows. I could just catch the words as they
floated across the high hedge:

> *Jano Danoé, she goes to the spring, alone—*
> *Jano Danoé;*
> *Jano Danoé, she goes and fills her pitcher—*
> *Jano Danoé;*
> *The son of the king . . .*

I was waiting for the rest of it, because I like songs
that have passed from lip to lip these many centuries, but the singer had to stop to shout at his oxen,
which had gone amiss in their plowing.

Sometimes one's meditations, if they be of the
subtler sort, are irretrievably shattered by a little
thing like that—a song, the rattle of a cart, or the
clatter of a wooden shoe—and then it is no use to
go back to them, for one's thoughts have mysteri-
ously vanished, and try as one may, they will return

no more, unless by happy chance, long afterward. At such times, if one insists upon going on with his writing, from that moment it becomes artificial and poor. The inspiration is gone. That is the way it was with me this morning, when this song, with its abrupt ending, broke in on my musings. I remembered, too, that I had an errand which took me to the town hall and then to the post office, so I laid aside my writing, locked my garden-house, and started toward the village.

From the long, high ridge to the north, where the forest is, one can get a good view of Aignan on its lesser hill, across a stretch of vineyards. I have always had this view in mind when I have tried to describe our village to the Abbé Rivoire. At first sight, the village appears as a shapeless mass of roofs, huddled together from east to west, helter-skelter, sloping at all angles, their tiles, once red, discolored by lichens, with here and there the plastered walls gleaming in the sun. In the midst of this assemblage of little houses rises the old church with its rugged tower—not a very beautiful tower, but strong and defiant, its masonry covered with straggling ivy and hundreds of tiny, gray plants that cling to the countless crevices as though they were memories Time had given it to keep!

Often I look down from this very hill and dream how my village looked in the Middle Ages, that time which always enchants—who of us has not had a fleeting wish that he might have lived in those interesting and venturesome days of long ago! There was poetry in the world then, and nowhere more

than in these valleys of ours. Sometimes, as I stand
on this hill at the edge of the woods, the Aignan
that is to-day vanishes, and the Aignan that was hundreds of years ago magically takes its place. I then
see my village with its massive walls entirely surrounding the closely-built houses, assembled on one
short street, the castle and church rising above all.
There was the deep and wide moat following the
walls all around. One could enter only at the two
great gates at either end. The gate on the east was
guarded by the tower of the church, as if the strength
of the good God was added to the puny strength of
man; and the gate on the west by the heavy, square
tower of the donjon-keep, from whose belfry often
rang the signal that enemies were approaching, warn-
ing everybody to take refuge within the doughty ram-
parts. And when the inhabitants were all inside the
walls, and the drawbridges were up, and the great,
iron-studded, oak gates were swung shut, and the
enormous bolts were shot into place, and the four
heavy iron bars, fitting deep into the masonry on
each side, clanged into position—ah, then the people of my village were ready for any foe! Once the
Protestants got in by making a hole in the wall when
a great wedding was going on, and the vigilance was
relaxed, but they were frightened away in a hurry!

Well, those walls are gone now, but one can still
see remnants of them here and there. And although
the village has spread out a little more, it is not so
very different, after all. So, it is easy to imagine
it as it was in the old, old days, with its one narrow,
badly-paved, winding street, poorly lighted at night;

over which the upper stories projected so far that
(my grandfather used to say) one could reach out
and actually touch hands with his neighbor across
the way! The street was obstructed still more by
its cumbrous signs, which sometimes clattered down
in the wind, to the great peril of passing folk; then,
to complete the picture, there were the rows of arcades in front of the houses; and in the very center
of all, the irregularly-shaped Place, littered with
carts, and alive with chickens and geese, and long-
legged Gascon pigs, even as to-day!

Yes, to-day it is much the same as then. The village has added a street or two since the walls went;
but the same old houses still stand, bravely fronting
the same old, winding street; only, everything has
become neglected, and nothing is in repair. The
plaster on the houses has grown yellower, stained
with the buffetings of hundreds of winters and summers, and it has fallen off in places. What arcades
are left are rickety on their rough, wooden pillars,
eaten thin and propped up at the base here and
there by large stones. Even the church clock has
stopped since a time nobody quite remembers; its
hands forever point to twelve o'clock—noon or midnight, I know not which. And how quaint and interesting and beautiful our village is, as you see it in the
morning light of this new time! It is as if the waves
of the Middle Ages had washed up this relic of its
life here on Time's shores. I am glad, I am glad
that it is so little changed, and that the poetry of
another day speaks through the peace of our streets,
still so sequestered from the great world!

I was on the way to the village when I became lost
in these reflections. In our village, we do not walk
on the sidewalks; no, everybody walks in the street,
for where there are any sidewalks at all, they are
so very narrow, with the houses set right against
them, and are so encumbered with the wares of the
little shops set out for display, and with benches, and
pots of flowers, and piles of firewood, and even
wheelbarrows and carts, that one would tread a
very devious course if he attempted them. This
morning, as I stepped into the Street of the Church,
at the entrance of the village, I heard the loud rattle of the drum of the village crier, Victor Claverie,
and saw him, as I rounded the corner, standing im-
portantly in the space before the church, crying out
a proclamation that, by order of the mayor, the
price of meat and milk had been lowered, and that
all persons under twenty-two must be vaccinated.

I know Victor Claverie quite well. He is a stoop-
shouldered man. His round head is covered with
unruly hair surmounted by a little round cap, or
béret. His forehead is low, his face colorless, his
nose bulbous at the end, his ears standing out entirely too much for beauty, his eyes very near-
sighted. He always holds his head a little on one
side. I fear I have not made a flattering portrait of
him, but one could not do that and be truthful. I
doubt that his official eloquence, as he shouts forth
his proclamations, is very convincing; for he has a
manner of ever pausing to get his breath in the midst
of a sentence, which breaks it up so that it is some
effort to piece the fragments together again and

make sense. However, everybody is so used to him by this time, and he has seen such long service, that the authorities would never think of appointing any one else to this important office. Through him we learn all the significant local news, for, of course, our village has no such thing as a newspaper—never has had and never will have. They say it was an exciting time during the World War, when they heard the rattle of his drum nearly every day. But soon people grew tired of putting his broken sentences together, and were glad when the news was posted on the town hall, where everybody could see it and be sure what it was.

As I passed farther along the street, I called a hearty greeting to the pharmacist, with his long, white coat, just within his door, and to the baker, standing on the steps in front of his house, his big, blue apron splashed with flour; and to Fitte, the notary, just emerging from his home, the best-dressed man in our canton. He greets me with a high-pitched, husky voice, full of good will. And in the Place I meet the postman, just starting on his rounds, carrying the letters in his flat, leather box, suspended in front of him by straps from his shoulders.

"Good morning! Monsieur l'Abbé, I have a letter for you!"

When I was coming out from the post office, after having done my errand, I met my friend, Rigot, the owner of the café. I have always thought of Rigot as one of the big men of our village, big in body and big in mind. A village is made of houses and people; and one knows well which are the more important! This Rigot owns a great deal of land, and has always been the right-hand man of the mayor, although he has never been mayor himself. I like Rigot. He is massively built, big-boned, big-chested, with a large head. He looks like a judge. He is wearing a short, scraggly beard, but this is only because it is Saturday, and like many of our men, he does not shave during the week—only on Sunday mornings, when he appears a fine man indeed, with his black suit and starched collar. Nowadays he keeps his café open not as a business, but as a hobby; and only his chosen friends go there, as they would go to an exclusive club—his friends, such as the doctor, and the notary, and the butcher, Bajac, with whom he plays his game of bridge every Sunday afternoon. Any one entering his café sees a billiard table; but if one should ask to play, he would be told that there are no balls. Well, I happen to know that the missing balls are hidden behind the counter, whence they will never be produced again as long as Madame Rigot lives. For her son, who loved nothing so well as to play on this very table, never came home from the war, and sleeps far away, amid a forest of wooden crosses near Toul.

I left Monsieur Rigot in front of the village pump, which makes a tremendous noise and requires great effort for a little water. It is one of the sights of our village to see the young girls getting their water there—rosy-cheeked, buxom, laughing, *they* do not remind one of the Middle Ages in the least!

So this is our village, so shut away from the great

world that it is a world all its own. Is it any wonder that I love its peace? In coming here, one does
not feel so much that he has come to a different part
of our earth as that he has left it behind him. Why,
our village is so remote that even a letter may fail
to find us, unless the directions on the envelope are
very exact. The one the postman handed me this
morning had been wandering about France for over
a month, because the sender forgot to add this distant *département* to our village's name! We still
hold tenaciously to our ancient customs—our ancient
processions, and fêtes, and dances, and songs, and
dress, even our ancient speech. Here candles and
oil lamps still give a light good enough for any man
to see the faces of his loved ones, as he sits with
them about the fireplace of his fathers after night
has come; here the gentle gossip of the neighbors
takes the place of the theater; here oxen plow in the
fields or pull their two-wheeled carts along the road
as of yore; here one travels many steps and speaks
face to face with those for whom he has a message,
for there is only one telephone, that at the post
office, rarely used by common folk. So it is, the
Middle Ages are still here, as I said, peacefully de-
caying, yet very alive in good, old-fashioned ways.
For us who live here, even such universal things as
dawns and sunsets and moons and stars take on a
local character and seem to belong to us alone.

O little village of my birth! To you I have come
as a tired son comes back to his old, old mother
after futile wanderings. Your gentle peace, your
simple ways, sweet as an old-loved song, I would

choose to all the world outside. I would rather be poor here than rich there, for here are the riches of the soul's ineffable peace that money never buys! If cruelty sometimes visits the heart even here, it is not the cruelty that crushes utterly and makes of hope a ghastly mockery, as where great cities rise and human souls stamp each other out in agony and blood. Here even death seems kindlier, for those who from your humble doors pass into the valley of shadow are laid to rest not far away from human habitation, as is the wont in large cities, but within your very heart, beneath the gentle shelter of those cypress trees by the old church tower, to the tolling of the dear, familiar bell, there by their fathers and their fathers' fathers, never far from the thoughts of the living, who go often with the loving gift of flowers to kneel beside a blessed memory!

As I returned from the village and approached my garden, I noticed, standing in front of my gate, a manly young fellow, whom I took to be my young friend, Henri. With him was a tall man, whom I did not know.

Chapter VII: *I Have Visitors*

I WAS glad enough to greet Henri, as I always
am, but I cannot say that it pleased me especially to recognize that his companion was none
other than the fair-haired, beardless young man I
had discerned at the edge of the crowd at the dancing of the "crows" that night in the Place. I do
not know why I had conceived a prejudice against
this stranger from the first, any more than any one
can really tell just why he likes some people and dislikes others that are no worse. It was not because
he was an American, although I must admit that
Americans have often offended my instincts, princi-
pally because of what I feel as their aggressive ego-
tism, and a certain vociferousness of manner that
violates my milder mood and makes me retire within
myself. Also I, like most of my fellow villagers, am
suspicious of strangers, especially if they be foreigners; and to me this man was so far an utter stranger,
with nothing to recommend him to me, and that
foolish fancy of mine about Germaine to disturb me
in spite of myself—strengthened now that I perceived him so intimate with her brother, Henri.
Later, when I come to know more about David

Ware, I may revise my opinion of him. Indeed, even before he left my garden to-day, I knew that he was not so young as I thought, being twenty-seven years old; that his presence in Aignan was easily accounted for by an ailing sister, brought here to the south of France for her health by her English husband, who has actually purchased the ancient Château de Lasalle, hidden in the trees on a hill a short half mile from the village. It turns out that Monsieur Ware is with them for awhile; that he has been given his degree at the University of Harvard; and that he is this very autumn to start his teaching of English literature at a college in the middle west of America. It is true that I had heard some of these things as vague rumors before, but there is so much gossip in our village that one can never be sure.

But I did not know all this when I came up to Henri and his friend at my garden gate, and, as I frankly say, I was prejudiced, and was almost sorry that I had been the means of teaching Henri enough English that he would naturally be the one most likely to become acquainted with the first English-speaking person who should happen into our village, since no one else here except myself can manage that difficult tongue.

When I had unlocked my garden gate to let my visitors enter, Henri turned straight toward the garden-house, as was natural, for we have had many a talk together here, and I imagine that he had told his new friend about my study and wanted him to see it for himself. But somehow I could not bring myself to reveal to a stranger the privacy of this place, so intimately associated with my innermost life; and so, to Henri's surprise, I led right on, up the narrow path by the vineyard, to the bench under the fig tree, where I bade my guests be seated and enjoy the view. As for Monsieur Ware, he produced a cigarette and tried to light it with one of our French matches, remarking as he waited for the slow sulphur to sputter itself into a flame,

"Even the matches of your country are leisurely."

"That may be a symbol," I said, "of French and American ways—an American cigarette and a French match are hardly made for each other; and I suppose that there may be other incompatibilities, as between any peoples so different."

"We are not so different as you think," he replied good-naturedly. "For instance, Henri here has been apologizing all the way to your garden because I had come upon him wearing an old suit that had shrunk from much washing. You see the trousers *are* a little short. But when I told him that it is all the fad for American college students to wear their trousers that way, he seemed to think they were not so bad after all!"

I said nothing whatever to this, so he went on presently, clasping his hands about one knee and leaning back against the fig tree, puffing a cloud of smoke from his cigarette,

"I am not complaining of the leisureliness of the life here, Monsieur l'Abbé; I rather like it. I have felt since coming here somewhat as the lotus-eaters in Tennyson's poem. It is a land in which it seems always afternoon—where even the beating of one's heart makes music in one's ears; and I am almost tempted to the decision of those same lotus-eaters, to roam no longer, to return no more."

At this I said to myself, "Blessed be our ignorance, for it maketh conversation." For I do not agree that my Gascony, in spite of the soft air and the quiet, rolling hills, is such as induces the intellectual quiescence of the eaters of the lotus, whether they be Tennyson's or anybody else's. No, I hold that one has thoughts in Aignan, and very effective thoughts, too, not mere indolent dreams and lazy reveries such as I conceived Monsieur Ware to be making inseparable from our country. The peace of the spirit is here, indeed, but it is a peace that stimulates the thoughts that are the very soul of living, and living greatly. We Gascons do not merely dream our lives away here, leisurely as everything is, including our matches! But Americans always seem to think that unless one is bustling about all the time, one is doing nothing. I say that some of the best deeds that I have ever done have been the thoughts I have lived through in this same old garden by the white road, where wooden shoes go up and down.

But I said none of this to Monsieur Ware, confident that he would not understand it. While he was talking, I had been studying him, as is my wont. He looked well enough, I had to admit. He was tall, and athletic of frame. He was dressed in careless fashion, with a white negligée shirt, open at the throat, a loose-fitting, blue coat, and trousers of the same color. His face, surmounted by wayward hair that grew a little long, was undeniably strong and handsome in an intellectual way; and his blue eyes seemed to have two moods within them— one revealed when he looked straight at me with a frank and smiling candor, and the other when he narrowed them to a dreamy contemplation that looked beyond visible things to some distant purpose unconfessed. I began to put him down somewhat more of a poet than the Americans that I have so far met.

"You like our Aignan, then," I said, more to be polite than anything else.

"Immensely! Think of playing billiards in one of your little cafés with a real bull-fighter! 'Le Suisse' I believe he is called. I beat him, too, by three points. I must see him when he appears at one of the fêtes around here. By the way, these fêtes of yours!—and your market on Mondays, and your peasants that clatter around in their wooden shoes, with their red sashes and funny, little hats; and your religious processions, too, and your 'crows'— why, if some of my friends should get on to this, they would make a book of it!"

What Monsieur Ware said reminded me to ask him if he did any writing, though I well know that those who teach literature seldom produce any literature of their own.

Immediately he had answered, I knew that a previous surmise of mine was correct, for he said, laughingly,

"I have a volume of poems ready for the press; all I need now is one or two really good ones to make it go!" And then he added, "Perhaps I shall find those poems here. No wonder that your people have the note of beauty in them, living where there is so much beauty. In America, we lose the poet's mood—the mood that does not take anything for granted, but looks upon everything as though it were new."

After a pause, he went on, dreamily, "What is to be dreaded is the sight that becomes accustomed, and no longer wonders. The poet looks at that cloud, which hundreds perceive as well as he, but he sees it with the enraptured vision of a child. Here, in these valleys, shut away from civilization, my sense of wonder is coming back to me."

"What do you say, Henri?" I inquired, because Henri had been saying not one word, being puzzled by the English of our guest, which, I suspected, was a little too rapid for his ear; even I found it difficult, for I read English much more than I converse in it, lacking opportunities.

Finally, Henri found his tongue and diffidently remarked,

"Monsieur Ware has some unusual ideas about Gascony—I mean, our people."

"I talk too much, I guess! I know so little about your people! My sister agrees with me that your women—especially your young women—are wonderful. Now, in England, I saw many women to admire—tall, slender women of the willowy type, somewhat like those Burne-Jones idealizes; the spiritual kind, of whom one might say that their bodies are stems, and their faces are lilies. But your French girls, especially down here—well, they are more real, they are more human, they are more truly *women,* while yet seeming to possess all the spirituality that one can healthily have in a real world."

I wondered if Monsieur Ware was thinking of Germaine!

It was becoming cloudy, and my fig tree is no very great protection from rain, so we wandered back toward the garden gate.

I remarked that, down here in Gascony, we are used to the smiling side of nature; that the sunless days probably affect our moods more than they do the people of other countries.

I was surprised to hear Monsieur Ware remonstrate that we were wrong in that. He said that he himself was very fond of the cloudy, sunless days, because there seems to be more meaning and mystery in them. He thought that "a quantity of mere sunshine spread all around" seemed cheaper and more superficial. Besides, its gayety seemed to mock at the tragedy of life.

"It is inappropriate for God to throw a broad smile over the world, when people are suffering and dying."

I said nothing to this blasphemous remark.

It is a pleasant habit in our village to accompany one's visitors for a distance down the road before finally saying good-by. I have always considered it a beautiful walk from my garden down to the entrance of the village, and I was glad to see that Monsieur Ware was admiring the tall hedges, softly green, that border my road. Upon my remarking that Nature builds our fences for us, here in Gascony, he told about a man he knew in America who built a spite-fence between his house and that of his neighbor, whom he hated.

"He made it as ugly as he could. But Nature grew vines all over it, by and by. And now it is the most beautiful fence in the town!"

I am back in my garden-house, and the rain is playing a lively tune on the tiles over my head.

I must confess that this American is interesting.

What impassive faces Americans have, compared with us Frenchmen! For instance, Monsieur David Ware does not move his lips much when he talks.

I should say that Monsieur Ware has a kind face.

Chapter VIII: *They Call Us Provincial*

I HAVE written that I, like most of my fellow-villagers, am suspicious of strangers. There are several reasons for this, none of which may be justified. But the whole matter raises a question over which I have pondered considerably, and for which, at last, I have found a sort of answer.

Of course, for one thing, strangers do not happen among us very often, since we are remote from the chief highways of travel. The principal road near here is the one from Bayonne to Toulouse, just distant enough to make it negligible so far as our daily lives are concerned.

But the real reason for our attitude toward strangers is that when one of them does come among us, he is apt to make us feel that he looks down upon us as a people to be pitied, because we are so far removed from the larger world without, and know little about it, and seem to care less. I cheerfully admit that we are indeed shut away from what men call civilization, and I have spoken of the quiet peace of these hills and the old-fashioned ways of our ancient village as a glory and a joy. But this, which I have mentioned as a virtue, the strangers who visit us speak of as a positive demerit, and—in short—they call us provincial.

Rightly or wrongly, I felt this same attitude in Monsieur Ware. He compared us to eaters of the lotus, as if we lived only in a remote land of dreams, and were excluded from the pulsing life of real men and women, such as dwell in great places like London and Paris. There, people boast of that grand word, "cosmopolitan," which I am made to understand is the very opposite of being provincial, as we lesser folk in Aignan are!

I sometimes think that most of the arguments that human beings invent against their kind are not much more than calling one another opprobrious names, after the fashion of little children. And the trouble is that most of us so hate to be called a name that we get angry straightway, and merely use some other epithet, just as futile, on our enemies. When I was younger, I was very prone to do this myself. But I have since learned to look at things more dispassionately, and so, when people call us provincial, I simply ask myself what they mean, and if, after all, they are talking sense.

Because one has not traveled a great deal, and has not come in contact with many sorts of peoples and customs, does not necessarily make one provincial. Some of the narrowest and most opinionated people I have met are those who have dwelt in large cities, and have wandered to and fro over the earth's surface until it almost makes one giddy to think of their comings and goings! On the other hand, I have read about very great men whom no one would call provincial, and yet who never lived in great cities at all, and certainly never traveled far from the little village that gave them birth.

The fact is, there may be two very different kinds of provincialism; and any one with any discernment whatever can readily tell which is the worse. There is the provincialism of *outer experience,* on the one hand—the provincialism of the man who has been denied the opportunity of getting acquainted with the great world by actually roaming over it and coming in contact with its many-sided life; and, on the other hand, there is what I call the provincialism of the *spirit,* which means poverty, and littleness, and narrowness of the inner life. And one may have the first without having the second, and the second is more to be feared—far more—than the first, for the first is superficial, but the second reaches to the deepest currents of a man's very life! One's soul may be indeed narrow and provincial, although one has a cosmopolitan body that has traveled far and wide; and one may have a body whose eyes have never seen beyond the dawns and sunsets of his native valley, and yet have a soul whose home is no less than the infinite universe! The cosmopolitanism of the body, and the cosmopolitanism of the spirit— take your choice! Happy is he who can have both!

Here in Aignan, we do not have both. We are not "citizens of the world," nor are we free from local attachments, and even prejudices. Ours is the provincialism of the body, the provincialism of outer experience. And yet I sometimes wonder if even this is so. In a city like Paris, one indeed touches life in

its cosmopolitan many-sidedness, if one has a mind
to—but how many actually do it? How many,
rather, even in that great city, are compelled to in-
close their lives in the little, narrow routine of business, of shop, or office, or factory, from morning
to night, through year on year, only eating and sleeping the rest of the good time! How many Parisians
are really cosmopolites, citizens of the world, touching life in its breadth, in its infinite variety? How
provincial these Parisians are, after all—even in
their experiences! And all the more provincial,
because even the broadest of them tends to be ego-
tistically self-contained, and contemptuously excludes
the rest of the world as beneath his notice. Here
in the country, we are surely more humble and open-
minded, and so, really, the less provincial. We look
upon Paris with much respect, and some awe, and
listen for the echoes of its life; but who in Paris
thinks of our far-off Gascony with that same humility, or cares for the more subtle messages of its hills
and valleys? And, after all, is not provincialism just
such an attitude of mind, that shuts itself up in its
own little experiences, and considers all the rest as
if it were not? So I insist that the provincialism
of the Parisian is often worse than the provincialism
of us simple Gascon folk.

As I say, I am not sure that we here are so provincial even in our every-day breadth of experience.
Our life is not so narrow as one might think. True,
we do not come in contact with vast numbers of different people and customs along our quiet streets,
but we have the endless diversity of the nature that

surrounds us, which may well make up for it, and which the cosmopolite of the city knows little or nothing about. Can a man be said to be provincial who communes with the countless stars, with sunsets no two the same, with hills that speak, with winding roads that beckon, and with villages here, there, everywhere, each with its own past and its own intimate griefs and joys—and yonder the glory of the Pyrenees, loftier and grander than anything men ever build in cities? Our lives are not so narrow! And here, too, we have more time and the more likely mood for reflection upon the deeper realities no man sees, summed up in the blessed reality called God! City life easily disintegrates character; there are so few times when one can be still and think, comparing relentlessly and fearlessly to-day's deed with yesterday's ideal. There can be few sublime virtues without many sublime silences. I say we touch more points in the universe than do your boasted dwellers in cities. He is provincial indeed who knows not the wonder and the manifold beauty of the life that one can live here.

Of course we have our stubborn customs, handed down since the night of time; but if our usages are old, and hard to change—well, there is always the poetry that belongs to old things as to nought else. And, besides, because our customs are different from, say, those of Paris, does that make them any narrower? For instance, does one cease to be provincial merely because he uses an electric light? I can read the golden thoughts of Marcus Aurelius, or, better, the blessed reasonings of St. Thomas, just as well by my oil lamp as by any light that ever shone upon a page! Aignan is provincial—and yet, so different! So, how it divests one of provincialism for one who has never walked its streets to be here! I am tempted to say that if the veriest cosmopolite that has ever lived has left out my Gascony, he is still provincial! I do not say it, but I am tempted to say it.

The truth is, I think that one can be too much of a cosmopolite, in the sense in which people commonly speak of such things. Your citizen of the world, who is at home in every place, is likely to miss life's deeper loyalties. Having been weaned from any downright devotion to his native village, to his native customs, even to his native country, calling it the narrow patriotism of the circumscribed, he is in danger of losing also his loyalty to the right, as being a matter of mere place and circumstance— which finally may mean losing loyalty to oneself and to one's God. And the man who has lost the deep loyalties of the spirit in the cynical indifference that is so often bred by much contact with the world becomes a provincial of the spirit, touching no longer those boundless mysteries that are life indeed. That my fellow-villagers resent innovation may be an evidence of great strength, rather than of weakness. Such provincialism as is ours has its recompense: we do not lose our faith in the eternal verities so easily.

In what I have said, I do not mean to deny that many people in our village are in fact provincial. No, I admit it, and I admit it with regret. But I shouldn't wonder if such would be provincial, even if they lived in Paris, except in very superficial ways. I doubt if our village crier, Victor Claverie, would change much anywhere you put him, or even the old Abbé Castex, or, for that matter, my Aunt Madeleine. But I know of others who have lived in this village all their lives who were great cosmopolites of the spirit. Such was the father of Germaine Sance; such is old Marius Fontan, our dreamer and poet; such is Rigot, the proprietor of the café, and Bajac, the butcher; and certainly, such is Dr. Dousset, our genial mayor, whom a few of us who know him best affectionately call, "the little doctor."

As for myself, I have, of course, no right to say. I am not a provincial in experience, since I have been in Paris and London. But whether I am a provincial of the spirit, I leave that to my friends to judge —not to Monsieur Ware.

Chapter IX: *How I Went to Margouet*

THE next day after Monsieur Ware's visit to my garden, just after I was through mass at the church, I was walking slowly back to my house when I met Germaine's brother, Henri, coming from the center of the village. As he was hurrying towards me down the middle of the street, I thought what a fine-looking, stalwart lad he had grown to be—tall, broad-shouldered, his frank, boyish face suddenly brightened with a smile as he caught sight of me. We met just beneath the sabotmaker's sign, which is a big, wooden shoe jutting out over the street.

I noticed that Henri had a letter in his hand, and I exclaimed that surely the mail had not arrived yet.

And then he told me that the document he bore (it had a seal on it) had been brought by a postman from the neighboring village of Margouet. This postman has to come to Aignan every morning to get the mail for his village, so he sometimes serves his friends by bringing letters, which thereby escape the formality of going through the post office—which is useful, since it saves a stamp.

It happens that Henri is the proud correspondent

of a daily journal in Bordeaux, which, at long intervals, prints very brief news from our corner of the
world, if it is important enough. This explains why
the Margouet people had sent him the document,
which he hastened to show me:

MAIRIE
DE
MARGOUET-MEYMES

For the first time since the hostilities, the
Commune of Margouet-Meymes will celebrate
the fête of the anniversary of the patron saint
of the Commune, on the 12th and 13th of June.
We hope that henceforth it will be the same, and
we desire it with all our heart, for the mainte-
nance of the Sacred Union. If the good
weather is with us, the strangers, to whom the
best welcome will be reserved, will come in
great numbers, and they will be able to enjoy
themselves to their hearts' content.

And then followed the program of the fête, and
the approval of the *Maire,* with the impress of his
official seal.

Rightly to appreciate a document like this, one
remembers that Margouet is a little village, with
only a few houses clustered about its church on a
hill to the northeast. The whole commune, including several kilometers all around, contains at the
most only about five hundred souls. So I could readily understand why Henri was smiling when he
showed me this announcement; and I could not help

smiling a little myself to think that little Margouet-Meymes should put on airs in this way, as if it were an important village, say like Aignan, which has a real fête every year which people come to see from all the country round.   As if a fête like this had anything to do with the Sacred Union, by which name we called the union of our political parties during the World War!   The mayor must have smiled when he signed his *Vu et approuvé* to this document, for the mayor at Margouet is an intelligent man, with a good sense of proportion.

PROGRAM OF THE FÊTE
SATURDAY

6-7 P.M.   Artillery salutes, announcing the Fête.

SUNDAY

6:00 A.M.   Artillery salutes.
10:00 A.M.   Parade.
10:30 A.M.   Mass, with music by the Band.
11:30 A.M.   *Apéritif Concert*.   Salutes.
3:00 P.M.   Vespers, with music by the Band.
4:00 P.M.   Sports: Duck race; The Frying Pan Game; Sack Races; Bicycle Races.
5:30 P.M.   Ascension of a Superb Balloon, "Le Victorieux."
6:00 P.M.   Ball and *Apéritif Concert*.
8:00 P.M.   Illumination *a Giorno*.
9:00 P.M.   Fire-works.
10:00 P.M.   Grand Ball. Brilliant orchestra.

But it is when one reads this program which was appended to the announcement, and which I saw later on a large, red poster in front of our own town hall, that one's smile is very lucky if it remains only a smile. I came upon the apothecary's assistant as he was gazing at it, only half an hour after I left Henri. It must have been brought from Margouet by the same postman. I copied it to send to the Abbé Rivoire for his amusement.

Artillery salutes indeed! One knows that there are no cannon in Margouet, and that they will use merely *bombes,* or giant firecrackers, which, after all, will make enough noise to be heard quite a distance, if the wind is right. As for the "parade," that merely means that the band (probably four or five members), will walk up the road to the church, playing, together with any who happen to join them, which will not be many, since most of the villagers will have gone to the church already. And as for the *"Apéritif Concert,"* there is no café in Margouet, so I do not know how they will arrange that, though I am sure they will manage such an important matter somehow. Any one who knows the world would be likely to suspect that this ambitious program was copied outright from the fête of some large city like Tarbes; for Margouet to assume it is like a little wren trying to comport itself as an imperial eagle!

And yet I was soon to perceive that they were really trying to make something of the fête, for when the postman made his rounds down our street, he brought me a letter from the good old Abbé Préchac, the priest at Margouet, inviting me over to assist him at the mass and vespers on the Sunday of the fête, now only three days off. He also said that if I would only come, he would send the black-smith, Lartigue, with his cart to fetch me.

I hastened to accept this invitation for two reasons: first, because I like the old Abbé Préchac, who is a native of these parts, and knows much of the fascinating lore of Gascony; and, second, because I was curious to see what Margouet would really make of its fête in honor of its patron, St. Barnabé, whose accurate anniversary, by the way, is to-morrow, two days before the fête. Another reason, and perhaps the one that most moved me, is that the little church at Margouet is after my own heart, in spite of the fact that it is badly in need of repair. I admire its sturdy, square tower, windowless, and buttressed like a fortress; its low porch, with benches, out of whose broken stone floor the pink hollyhocks grow tall in summer, and which you brush as you would brush a fellow-worshiper as you enter; the long ferns, too, that flauntingly root themselves in the crevices of the gray masonry by the low Gothic portal; the little interior, with its two round, massive columns that fling graceful arches in all directions over the low vault. And it does not lessen one's appreciation of the little church to know that here, within these very walls, was found not many years ago a record of the birth of our famous D'Artagnan, whom the whole world knows as the dashing captain of the mousquetaires of the King!

People should remember that, and then call us provincial if they like!

We have a saying that when the Pyrenees can be seen, it is a sign of bad weather. For the next two days the Pyrenees could be seen from my garden, very dimly, it is true, yet there they were. So, when the Sunday of the fête came, and it was cloudy, I was not surprised. But we have another saying, from which I derived hope: "If it rains on St. Médard's day, it will rain for forty days, unless St. Barnabé comes and kicks him." I took hope from this second saying, for although it had rained on St. Médard's day—the day when Monsieur Ware visited me—it did *not* rain on the day of St. Barnabé, so there was the kick.

On the Sunday morning of the fête, Monsieur Lartigue rattled up in his cart to the front of my house, yelling, "Whoa, Coco!" at the top of his voice, just as I was finishing my breakfast.

"He has a spirited horse," thought I, and hastened down, as I was already a little late.

I had to revise my notions of Monsieur Lartigue's equipage. I found an old, rickety, two-wheeled cart, attached to a long-eared, white mule of considerable dimensions. Monsieur Lartigue turned out to be a large, big-boned, florid-faced man with a black mustache, from whose eyes, set near together, shone some shrewdness, more vanity, and still more good humor. He reached down his big hand, pulled me up to the seat beside him, and with a flourish of the whip we were off.

"Ah-eee! Coco!"

We pass the church at a gentle trot and are soon jolting eastward along the Road of the Madonna, past the blacksmith shop, kept by Lignac, who is lame, and who waves a jovial greeting. Straight on between the long rows of plane trees, past Germaine's great house and garden on the left, where, among the barns at the rear, one glimpses a pair of sturdy oxen hitched to a wagon piled high with hay. And then old Marinette's little house by the road— she was with Germaine's mother when Germaine first saw the light, nearly nineteen years ago! Good, hearty, big, red-faced Marinette, who answers a slow *"Bonjour, Monsieur l'Abbé,"* to our greeting, looking up from feeding her brood of little geese. Soon a turn to the left, and up the hill called the Bethau we go, at a slow walk now, for the hill is steep and Coco is tired already.

For my part, I am glad to go a little slower, for I much distrust these two-wheeled carts which, besides their motion of progress along the road, add other kinds of motion more distressing—a rocking motion backward and forward, and a twisting motion to right and left with every step. And since so many people are thrown out of these carts, especially when the horse is lively, a stranger might wonder why it is our custom to use them so much instead of sensible, four-wheeled carriages. Perhaps the secret why we have two-wheeled instead of four-wheeled vehicles is that then four wheels suffice to make two vehicles instead of one—and we are thrifty. One is tempted to think that if two-wheeled automobiles were possible, we would adopt them! Since it is impossible, we have few automobiles in our country.

Monsieur Lartigue's cart was even worse than

the ordinary cart, since it seemed to need repair at every point. The harness was mended with rough rope in half a dozen places, and the wheels had a way of wobbling back and forth in a very eccentric manner. At each turn of the road, I feared that one of them would forsake us—and there are many turnings on the road to Margouet. Why, our roads are so winding that what would be one kilometer in a straight line is often two by the road. But what does one care when the roads are so beautiful, with the high, uncut hedges on either side, often over-topped by waving crests of the graceful gorse—along whose edge I notice the dainty purple blossoms of the heather, the first I have seen this year!

And then the long rows of stately poplars casting their slender shadows, and the friendly grass crowd-ing as close to the road as it can; and wild flowers, gallant on their long stems, or peeping out mildly from their soft bed of green. And every little while a peasant's house, nestling very close to the road, a house to which the barn is attached more often than not, as if in hearty good will and companionship. On we went this Sunday morning through these scenes, made still more enchanting now that the sun had come out at last—only the sun was hot, and Coco insisted upon walking from one side of the road to the other in search of the shade, and even stopped to munch the long grass where the shade was thick-est.

"Ah-eee! Coco!"

At last we were on the summit of the long, wind-swept hill of the Bethau, whence we could look far down on my village, across fields newly stacked with the fresh-cut hay, whose scent is one of the delights of June.

"Hi! Coco!"

We dipped down the winding road toward Margouet, now visible on its lower hill in the valley beyond, from where we faintly heard the bells ringing.

"It will be a wonderful fête!" said Monsieur Lartigue, who up to now had been very busy managing Coco.

"It is a grand program," said I. "I saw it, printed in red, in front of our town hall. Has the balloon really arrived?"

"But yes! It will be a splendid sight! And the bakery has been turned into a café, so everybody may have refreshments.—But we must hurry, or we will be late for the procession."

"Coco!   Ah-eee!   Gently!   Gently!" cried Monsieur Lartigue, for, feeling the sting of the whip, Coco had made a sudden spurt forward that was so unexpected and violent that it nearly threw me backwards out of the cart, and would have done so had I not been holding very tightly to the side of the seat. But I consoled myself that we would soon be at our journey's end. We were already passing people bound for the fête, some on foot, some on bicycles, some riding in carts like our own, most of them with handkerchiefs suspended from their hats down over the backs of their necks to protect them from the hot sun, and every one of them with a cordial greeting for us and for every one else they met, as is our good Gascon custom.

Soon we were passing the windmill with its giant
arms, not far from the village—the old, stone windmill, through whose ruined roof one can look through
to the sky—and then the accident happened.

I had already noticed Monsieur Lartigue looking
back from time to time at our right wheel, and now
he pulled up Coco to a sudden stop, and cried out,

"Bou Diou! Arrè! Arrè!"—all of which means
in patois, "Good God! Back! Back!"

"What is the matter?" I asked with some concern.

"Milo Dits!" (A thousand fingers.) "The rim
has come off!"

To be sure it had. The iron rim had sprung away
from the wheel, and was hanging out from it in a
hopeless manner.

"I had better get down and walk the rest of the
way," said I.

"No! No! Monsieur l'Abbé, it shall all be arranged in one little moment! Here is rope. See!"
And Monsieur Lartigue tied the rim back in its place
on the wheel.

I was not much pleased with this arrangement, for
I was sure it would not last. Besides, we had to go
very slowly now, and the people whom we had passed
on the road were beginning to catch up with us,
every one of them anxious to ascertain the trouble,
until the crowd became so dense that we had to stop
and explain the whole matter and receive a thousand suggestions as to how to remedy the difficulty.
Just then, Coco suddenly started up, frightened at
the people, and the iron rim sprang loose again,
worse than before.

"*Animal!*" cried Monsieur Lartigue, and then we stopped again. I immediately embraced the opportunity to step down into the road.

"Thank you, ever so much, Monsieur Lartigue. It is not far now, and I can easily walk. I do not mind it in the least. Then you can lead Coco slowly to your house."

"I regret it, Monsieur l'Abbé! Coco is a fool!"

But I was not destined to walk, for just then my friend, Monsieur Capéran, came up with his fine new cart and insisted upon helping me up to the seat by his side; soon his good horse had out-distanced the crowd around Monsieur Lartigue and Coco, and the square tower of Margouet's church came full in sight around a turn of the road.

I am glad enough that Monsieur Capéran happened along. I had a distaste for entering the village with Coco and his dilapidated cart, even if it were fixed again by the rope. It was sure to be embarrassing, for every time the wheel went round and struck the thick rope, it made a jolting noise that no one could fail to observe, and I hate to attract attention like that. And it would hardly become the dignity of a priest on this occasion to be trudging along the dusty road and to be entering the waiting village on foot.

When we were approaching the curé's house, I heard the strains of the band. It was the procession starting for the church. And from the house an altar boy, clad in the customary red vestments, was running down the road toward the church with a censer swinging from his hand.

Chapter X: *How the Fête Began*

AS I look back over what I have been writing, I perceive that I am not really so old as I thought.

Why do I say this?

Because I have always noticed that a man that is really old has lost much of his interest in the happenings of the world that surrounds him. He has turned his eyes inward, so to speak, upon his own meditations. He is much more engrossed in the images of his memory and the phantoms of his speculations and dreams than in the real men and women with whom he lives, yet with whom he has, in a measure, ceased to live.

I used to wonder why it is that philosophers grow to be such old men; but now I am beginning to know. It is because a man has to grow old first before he can be a philosopher. Such men have actually begun that withdrawal from the world which ends at last in the utter withdrawal that we call death.

Now, if my observations are correct, it is clear that I am not in the least old. For everything that happens about me is still of living interest to me. Especially since coming back to my native village this time do I find that every detail of the daily events about me excite my curiosity and interest, so that I find myself really living in them with a somewhat eager zest about them. It is quite possible that I may lose this eagerness gradually as time goes on and custom grows stale; but just now, being freshly returned to these scenes, everything strikes me as though it had something of newness in it.

Well, there is no harm in that, and somehow I enjoy it; and, as I say, it proves that I am not so old as I thought—which is a great consolation when one remembers how short life is at the best.

Still, I had seen so many fêtes in my life that I fully expected that this fête at Margouet would seem dull enough. But because I had in my heart the gladness that greets old things as though something long lost were unexpectedly found again and thereby made doubly precious—because of this, I entered into the events of the fête with some of the eagerness I once had for such things when everything Gascon was dear to me—but never so dear as it is now.

By the middle of the afternoon, the road running through the little village was quite alive with crowds of people from the surrounding country. I was surprised to see so many; but, after all, there are people who never miss a fête anywhere, if it is at all possible to get to it, even if they have to walk many kilometers; and Margouet had seen to it that every village in the neighborhood knew about its great celebration. Up and down the road they thronged and jostled, greeting old friends, introducing new ones, standing in groups and talking and laughing, good-natured, eager, young and old, and all in their best clothes—many of the older women with the long, black Gascon hood over their heads, and many of the peasants with their red or blue sashes and their round, flat caps. I say it was a good-natured crowd—and why should they not be feeling at their best after such a wonderful dinner of course on course, always one of the great events of a fête-day, with food enough, yes, and wine enough to make the most unlikely disposition jovial and contented!

While I saw many strange faces, there were familiar ones, too, from Aignan and Averon, and even from farther off. The house of the Abbé Préchac is just across the road from the post office and the town hall, right in the center of things, so we both could look out upon the crowd whenever we wished, without being seen. Once I went to the garden gate long enough to greet my old friend, Marius Fontan, whom I had not seen for a year, and who, it seemed to me, was showing his age.

The crowd was largest in the great yard in front of the post office. There were plenty of reasons why it gathered here. In the first place, the band, standing under a tree, was playing a lively tune. In the second place, the bakery, this side the post office, and in the same building, had been turned into a café for the occasion, and men were constantly edging their way in and out. In front, long tables had been improvised by placing boards on sawhorses, and these all were full, and the garçons were hastening hither and thither, most of them with beer and lemonade-water. With the mixture of these one makes a *bière panaché,* which anybody will admit is an excellent thing on a hot day. If any one was so imprudent as to leave his bench for a moment, his seat was immediately taken. Everything about the café was lively indeed, except that just inside the door, in a corner, several very old men were playing piquet, using a saucer of white beans for counters.

But outside the café in the great yard was the sight to see. Everywhere booths covered with canvas, gayly decorated with streamers, under which, on boards, draped with bright red cloth, were spread all sorts of things intended to tempt centimes and francs. For the young men, wheels of fortune, whose spinning arrows would reward the sanguine with a package of tobacco, or a coffee cup, or nothing. For the ladies, hair-combs in great variety, and ribbons of all colors; for the children, gay horns and whistles and shiny, red, toy balloons, tugging lightly at their long strings; and for everybody, candy and cakes, which everybody bought sooner or later.

One might think that all this is a strange way for a village to honor its patron saint; but all our fêtes are like this, and one must recollect that the really important part of the fête is the religious part—at least, that is the way it is supposed to be. Even now it was nearing the time for vespers, and the band had ceased playing, and many of the crowd were moving away from the yard toward the church, whose bell was ringing. Perhaps more went to the church than otherwise would have gone, because the sky had become overcast and a few drops of rain were beginning to fall.

But the little church would not hold them all, even standing, much as most of them wanted to hear the band, which makes an immense noise in the tiny building, so voluminous that it threatens to burst the sturdy walls asunder—and the people like whole-souled music like that! And then the singing was better than usual, although the tenors were frequently out of tune, and the enthusiastic baritone of the blacksmith from a neighboring village rose too much like a discordant bray above the sweet voices of the choir boys. Still, he did his best, and was serious about it, and reverent perhaps, although I mentioned to the Abbé Préchac afterwards that his voice was not really adapted to singing the praises of the good God. Of course, God would forgive it, for He is ever pitiful for the frailty of His creatures; but there are some things it is hard for mere men to bear!

In the middle of the vespers, the sun came out again and shone, a riot of rose and gold, through the rich, narrow windows, so that people kept passing out the great, oak door, which creaked and rattled every time it was opened. Then others poured in, and so it went.

I think the most solemn thing about these fêtes of ours is the religious procession that occurs just after the vespers are over; and perhaps the patron saint is honored more beautifully by this than by anything else. Impressive it is to see the silver crucifix borne aloft on its tall staff at the front of the procession as it leaves the church; the priest with his sweeping, gold-embroidered cope flashing in the sun, chanting as he walks, an altar boy on each side of him, with his tunic of lace over red, carrying a censer; the women singing responses; and the men following two by two in the rear. Oh, it is a sight to inspire thoughts that reach far beyond this puny world!

The procession goes down the sloping path of the churchyard to the road, then up the road to the crossways, where stands the statue of the Madonna, garlanded with flowers; then slowly back around the other side of the church to the little cemetery at the rear, amid whose rows of pathetic mounds, newly covered with loving blossoms, rises high a rough, wooden crucifix, from which looks down the Son of God to pity and to bless. Blessed, blessed image, that transforms these graves of the sleeping dead into the vision of endless life!

Ah, he who would doubt God, let him only gaze at the crucifix for one moment with his heart in his eyes!

But some people do not have reverence for anything, no matter how sacred. How can that be? Even while the procession was passing from the church, bicycles were racing up and down the road, and people who ought to have known better, and who should have been in the procession themselves, were idly watching them. Although these did take off their hats as the procession passed, and called to the racers on the bicycles to stop, or they would run into the procession, that does not excuse them.

What the racers on the bicycles were getting ready for was the duck race, although at first thought one might wonder what a duck race has to do with bicycles. Truly, the matter can only be explained by one who is familiar with ancient customs. A real duck race is exciting enough. It is a game in the water where the best swimmers race after a duck and endeavor to capture it, which is a very difficult matter, as any one who is acquainted with the habits of ducks can attest; and the reward is the duck itself. But this popular game can be played only in the water; so where no water is to be had, they substitute a game with horses and rings. That is, small rings are suspended at intervals from a rope hung straight across the road, and then men on horseback, bearing long sticks in their hands, like javelins, try to put them through one of the rings as they race by. It requires a good eye and a steady hand. It resembles the jousting of knights in the Middle Ages, and is a splendid game.

Now, the duck race at this fête was just as I have described, only the racers used bicycles instead of horses, and their forefingers extended straight before them instead of poles. So the rings were hung low, just above the heads of the racers, and every time one put his finger through a ring as he sped by, the ring came off, being suspended only by paper, and there was much shouting and laughter, and he who succeeded in pulling down a ring that way was awarded fifty centimes and a great deal of applause.

All these exciting things I could view excellently from the Abbé Préchac's front window, in a room on the upper floor, where he has his books.

While they were preparing for the bicycle race, a young man appeared from the direction of the café, passing up and down the crowd with a large bowl of some yellow liquid that looked like custard, with the handles of two spoons emerging from it. Everybody was anxious to see the custard contest, and followed the bowl around, hoping it would begin at once. As every one knows, this game needs at least two persons, who are first blindfolded and then required to feed the custard into each other's mouths until the bowl is empty. In all such contests that I have seen, very little of the custard really got as far as the inside of the contestants' mouths, although much of it attained to some portion of their faces, and still more to their clothes. Undeniably, it is a hazardous game; but alas! since the only reward is the small amount of custard one succeeds in actually swallowing, and since no one seemed to be hungry enough for that to spoil his best garments, the crowd was cheated of what is a merry spectacle, and well worth seeing.

But everybody forgot this little disappointment at once, for immediately some one shouted that those who had entered the bicycle race were just starting for the crossroads half a mile away, where the stone windmill is, and where the race was to begin. There

was a great rush for the road to see them off and
to be ready in favorable positions when the racers
should come speeding back to the line where the
committee of awards even now stood, looking rather
self-important and disputing about some detail of
procedure.　There were three who had entered the
race, and these now were well on toward the starting place, all brawny youths, attired in what they
conceived to be athletic costumes, their arms and
legs bare.　There was one clad in a rough, red shirt,
who looked like a young giant, and whose muscles
stood out on his arms and legs in a way that impressed one with great strength.　I knew him for
the son of a peasant woman who lives in Mauser,
down behind the Forest of Aignan.

At last the signal for the great race was heard—
the firing of a gun down at the old mill.　It was
simply impossible to keep the eager crowd out of
the road, no matter how much the committee
shouted and warned and threatened and ran hither
and thither, for what is the good of a bicycle race
if one cannot see it?　On they came, up and down
the little hills of the smooth white road, the crowd
now eagerly silent, now breaking into murmurs and
exclamations, slowly becoming aware that the young
giant in red was rapidly out-distancing the other
two and was coming on as though nothing could stop
him.　The crowd was instinctively edging back toward the sides of the road to make room, when a
sudden shout went up,

"Look!　Ah!　He has broken down!"

The man in red had suddenly stopped, violently thrown from his bicycle.

Is he hurt?

No, he is picking himself up.

And now what is he doing? Not remounting—no, but running along with his broken bicycle by his side—running faster and faster, his competitors still behind him, but closing in on him—on he runs, straining every nerve, his trousers torn, his red shirt torn, his leg bleeding, his face grimy with dust and perspiration. He comes! He comes! *Bou Diou!* He is here! He and his bicycle have crossed the finishing line amid the tumultuous cheering and shouts and laughter, the winner!—one little yard ahead of the next man! As he limps by, one sees that the chain of his bicycle is broken.

But *is* he the winner? The committee solemnly consults. This is a *bicycle* race, and this man has run part of the race on foot. Here is a difficult point, requiring a judicial mind. One knows, surely, that it is all the more glory to have run part of the race on one's feet. Besides, he did not leave his bicycle behind, but brought it with him every step of the way, so it was a bicycle race, after all! And besides, again, the crowd is becoming impatient and demands loudly that the man in red shall receive the prize. And so, at last, it is awarded him—five francs, the highest prize offered for any of the events of the day, and the crowd applauds in great good humor.

For my part, I think to myself that it is of such

an indomitable spirit as this young peasant showed to-day that a great civilization is made—that France is made!

Even as I thought these things, I spied the widow Duprat, his mother, standing by the road, her round, plain face lighted up by the joy which her son's victory had brought to her simple heart. And seeing her there, my mind could not help reverting to the time, now three years ago, when she narrowly escaped death, in an event which was much talked of then by the people of these hills. It was a summer of terrible storms, when many of the vineyards were destroyed by hail, and when many a peasant lost all he had in the course of one tragic hour. But the worst storm of all was very early one memorable morning in August. The clouds covered all the sky and hung so low that they hovered almost over the roofs of the houses—and such ominous clouds they were, full of malignant threatening, livid with greens and yellows, with incessant sheets of lightning playing through them, and the constant rumble of angry thunder, gathering in volume and ending in crash on crash that rolled and echoed and reverberated among the hills with hoarse and inhuman cries. The hail rattled tumultuously in the distance and rushed nearer and nearer, louder and louder, like a cataclysm of certain doom. It was so bad that nobody dared ring the church bells to ward away the evil—it was too late and too dangerous for that!

Dieu! What a terrible storm!

It was about four o'clock in the morning. The woman Duprat, in her great alarm, knew of only one thing to do. Over the great fireplace in the kitchen, behind the picture of the Holy Virgin, on which her rosary was hanging, there was a piece of laurel, blessed by the priest on Palm Sunday—for, like every one else in this region, she had taken a branch of laurel to church to be blessed; and to burn it is a holy rite, which prevents calamity. To the kitchen, then, she hastened and, taking this branch of laurel from its place with her left hand, she was reaching up for the matches with her right, when there came a deafening crash greater than all the rest, and, hurtling through the roof, flashed a javelin of lightning which struck her uplifted hand, scorched its burning way down her arm, shot down her side clean to her wooden shoe, and shattered it into a hundred pieces, and cast her prone to the floor unconscious! Jean Duprat, her husband, who was in the stable attending to the oxen, heard the crash and rushed as fast as he could into the house to find his worst fears realized—ah, good God! she was dead! He called in the neighbors hurriedly and hastened his son to Aignan to bring back with him our Doctor Dousset. And blessed be God, he was able to revive her, and she lived! Since then, old Jean Duprat has passed away; but she herself was here to-day to see her stalwart son cheered and applauded. Surely, it was enough to warm her dear old heart!

I remember that old Abbé Castex, our curé at

Aignan, said that what saved her life that time was that she was engaged in touching holy things.

And who shall deny it? The invisible is much nearer than we think; and what we call miracles may well be the will of the good God reaching out to touch the things of this world, transfiguring them in ways we are too ignorant to understand.

Chapter XI: *How the Fête Ended*

L ATER in the afternoon, people were looking up anxiously at the sky; and well they might, for it was becoming cloudy, and rain threatened to spoil one of the most important happenings of the day, the ascension of the superb balloon, The Victorious. There they were, bringing it down the road, swinging from the end of a long, slender pole —somewhat shapeless yet, since it was not fully inflated; but any one could see how gorgeous it would look, with its generous stripes of pink and lavender and white. And such a large balloon, too, surely twelve feet from base to tip—what a thing it would be when it rose above the valleys so that in all the villages for miles around men, women, and children would be craning their necks to see, and would be exclaiming,

"That is the balloon from Margouet; they are celebrating their fête to-day!"

But the balloon is not up yet, and accidents may easily happen, as those who have attended fêtes are aware. One has to be very careful indeed how one inflates a paper balloon like this. Only last year at the fête at Sabazan the balloon caught fire when it was almost ready to ascend, and any one who was there remembers how the crowd was disappointed and went home, feeling that the fête was a failure.

But surely there will be no such accident to-day, for there are enough heads in this crowd that know how a balloon should be managed and who intend having some say in the matter. Everybody seems to feel some of the responsibility of it, for everybody has crowded now into the great yard, forming an anxious circle about the balloon, and many are excitedly engaged in giving advice to the men who have charge of it. A heap of straw has been made, and now a match is applied to it amid a sudden hush of voices, and the man bearing the balloon on the end of the pole, standing high in a cart, holds it over the flame, that the heated air may enter and swell it out.

"Closer to the flame!"

"No! Not so near, it's burning!"

"There!"

"Bravo!"

The balloon has expanded bravely, and now since it is bellied to its full proportions and its paper skin is taut, one may see the gay design of dancing devils printed over it. It has life, it struggles to free itself.

"Let it go!"

But not yet. The postman pushes his way through the crowd with a dish of paste in one hand and several long strips of paper in the other, and with a flourish attaches them to the balloon here and there. Each strip has "Margouet-Meymes" boldly lettered on it, and when the crowd sees the village's name, they cheer again.

"Let go! Let go!"

At last! The impatient creature is set free, and amid a generous clapping of hands, it rises high above the crowd, up, up, tipping ever so gently toward the west—higher and higher, growing ever smaller, as the band plays loudly the glorious strains of the Marseillaise. Long do they look at that far speck floating in the sky, until it is lost at last in the long sea of clouds that roll across the declining sun.

Symbol of victory indeed! If only our lives could rise to the freedom of the sky like that!

I was thinking that it was about time for me to start back home, for my Aunt Madeleine always has supper ready at seven, and I do not like to be late, for reasons that those who know my aunt would understand. But I do not blame her in the least, for she is getting old, and is entitled to some consideration. The question was, how I was to get home. I had seen my friend, Monsieur Capéran, with whom I had made my entrance into Margouet, standing near the balloon, and I decided that I would look him up and inquire how soon he expected to start. But I found as soon as I emerged from the Abbé Préchac's house that the crowd was already moving down the road to the large, open space in front of the little town hall, where the dancing was to take place immediately.

Here, on two sides of a rectangle, long boards had been put on old boxes to serve as seats. And all around, gay flags hung from strings stretched on poles; and there on a flat-topped wagon at the corner of the town hall was the band, comprising two clarinets, a bass horn, and a cornet, the latter played by the harness-maker from Aignan. The band had already started up a lilting tune, called *La Petite Nogentaise,* which invites readily to dancing steps—although the bass horn was ever off the key, and made the same monotonous grunts on exactly two notes, no matter what piece was played. All that one could say was that the player was persevering, which is a virtue much overvalued in this world. Facing each of the band was a kitchen chair, on the seat of which he propped up his music book, keeping it open with small rocks, for the wind was blowing. And on the wagon by the band was a gallon bottle of wine, glinting golden in a stray ray of sun. The village had furnished that, for it is universally admitted that one cannot play in a band without being abundantly refreshed from time to time!

There is no denying that the glimpses I obtained of the mazurkas and waltzes and schottisches were very pleasing, although the dancing green sloped so much that it required some skill to keep one's balance, especially during the merry quadrilles. Still, I was reminded of what little Renée, Madame Sance's kitchen girl, had said the day before,

"They know, they at Margouet, how to get up dances!"

I thought I had seen Monsieur Capéran go into the town hall a moment before, so I made my way

thither. The town hall at Margouet is only a small,
one-storied dwelling, now turned into an office for
the mayor and schoolrooms for the children of the
commune. As I was entering, I observed that the
last notice on the little, square bulletin-board by the
door was of a meeting of the municipal council seven
years ago. Time does not mean much at Margouet!

I could not find Monsieur Capéran anywhere in
the place. As I was coming out, it had started to
rain again, and the band was hurrying inside, the
dancers after them, as many as could enter. Immediately the band struck up again, and the dancing
was resumed in the small hallway, where it soon
became warm and stifling, the crowded couples bump-
ing against each other and making dancing exceedingly difficult.

I myself was sitting in a corner of a small room
off the hallway; and at the close of a dance, a young
peasant and his smiling partner came in; not seeing
me, he placed a kiss full on her cheek, and then they
quickly swept out into the hallway again to join in
the new dance which had just begun. I happen to
know these two to be engaged to be married, and
under the circumstances, I suppose there is some
excuse for such things; and they are young. I could
not avoid observing them; but even if I had not seen
the kiss, I would have heard it. This reminds me
that I picked up, in the Abbé Préchac's study, among
his old books, a volume printed in Toulouse in 1768,
which pretends to correct our Gascon ways of speech,
and which criticizes us for speaking of "making a

kiss,"—*faire un baiser*. But I think that this book is wrong, and I should like to tell the professor that wrote it that the Gascons literally do make a kiss; it is no merely casual thing; it has, as it were, an architecture—a foundation, superstructure, roof, towers, and flags!

Like Montaigne, I "speak my opinion freely of all things, even of those that, perhaps, exceed my capacity, and that I do not conceive to be, in any wise, under my jurisdiction."

The sun, now very low in the sky, was out again, and I was eager to travel back. And, very luckily, just as I went out-of-doors, I met the doctor of our village, Monsieur Dousset, who was very cordial with me, as he always is, and who insisted that I accompany him home in his automobile—the only one of which our village boasts. I had no great desire to wait for the fireworks, or the grand ball, or the illumination—it would be hard to illuminate Margouet with oil lamps and paper lanterns! So the little doctor helped me into his automobile under a tree, and with a brave blowing of the horn, we were on our way along the winding road to Aignan.

As I looked back, the last I saw of the great fête was the golden light of the setting sun on the heads of the dancers; and the last sound I heard was the monotonous rhythm of the bass horn, lost at the first turning of the road. Most of the merrymakers, especially the younger people, would not be moving homeward until after midnight. At two o'clock in the morning, and again at three or four, I was awakened by the boisterous singing of some youths of our village as they passed underneath my window.

What occupied me now, though, was the beautiful ride home along the hills in the twilight. Still— I may as well admit it—I did not think so much of the beauty of the evening as of one fact I have not yet put down; namely, at the dancing I had caught a glimpse of Monsieur Ware, the American; and with him was not only Germaine's sister, Madame Dousset, and Henri—but Germaine herself!

Chapter XII: *We Take Ourselves Seriously*

TO-DAY I copied and mailed to my devoted friend, the Abbé Rivoire, some of the things I had written about the fête at Margouet, thinking it might divert him. On my return from the post office, I was bending over my bed of strawberry plants just behind the garden-house, when I heard a peculiar sound from the direction of the gate. It was only one of our long-legged Gascon pigs, who was shaking his head so vigorously that his tremendous ears made a leathery, flapping noise. Our Gascon pigs are not exactly things of beauty; their legs are too long and ungainly, their hides are too offensively pink—hairless, too, and looking as if they had just been shaved and polished; and then, quite often, the rear portions of their anatomy are finished off in a jet black, with the astonishing effect of sleek-fitting breeches. They look better when they are fat, and still better when they have achieved their appointed destiny and hang in the cool doorway of some pork butcher. Then they do have decided elements of beauty, I suppose because then they appeal to a sense other than that of sight.

Immediately afterwards, I heard what I took to

be the faint rattle of a cart; but, looking up, I saw that it was Marinette, with her wheelbarrow piled high with wet clothes, on the way down the road to the public laundry to do her rinsing. One looking at dear old Marinette sees a good type of the older peasant women of my country—built on generous lines, strong, wide, and robust, with a large, round, florid face, high cheek bones, a vigorous chin, a determined mouth, and very straight, gray hair, if the cloth bound tightly around her head allowed one to see it. Our men are different; they are more bony and angular, probably from long hours of hard work and exposure in the fields. But both women and men of our peasant class have a look of seriousness, almost of stolidity, when their faces are in repose.

Coming from Paris so recently, I noticed this seriousness in the faces of the crowds at the fête at Margouet. It was inevitable to see that the people were taking even their pleasures gravely, very much as if they were part of a ceremony, or rite. True, some of the younger people were more light-hearted; but, even at the dancing, there was a certain earnestness about everything, as though dancing were not a thing to be lightly attempted in the mood of gayety, but, rather, in the spirit of a duty to be conscientiously performed. Between the dances, one might indeed relax and be more natural and smiling; but as soon as the dancing began again, a certain dignity automatically usurped any momentary lapse into the frivolous.

I suppose that a stranger would say that it is

natural for our peasants to be serious, even in their amusements, because they live such hard lives, with nothing but toil from the rising to the setting of the sun. How many millions are there of God's creatures who are compelled to make of life a tragedy, so that the lives of others may be less of one! And certainly, there is some truth in this explanation. Even our women of the common peasant class get old early; there is not that long and gentle interval between youth and old age which more fortunate women know, especially in cities. To-day our women are young, and lo! to-morrow they are old, and the roses have fled from their faces, the relentless lines chiseled into them by those cold sculptors—Pain and Toil. The children—they, too, tend to have an old look; pathetic it is to see the accusing sorrow that sometimes peers from their eyes, having learned the pitiless burdens of the world too soon, too soon!

But while many of our peasants remind one truthfully enough of Millet's famous painting of the stolid and hopeless figure wearily leaning on his hoe in the fields, many others are far from poor, and not a few are rich enough to be beyond the pity of such people as know no better than to suppose that all peasants are like that. Only a few days ago, I was invited to dinner at the house of one of these better peasants—he lives on the road near Fromentas—and I only wish I were able to eat such a dinner as Monsieur Fabre gave me, once a week for the rest of my life! Tapioca soup, clear and tempting; then sausage and butter; and after one had eaten of a delicious guinea-hen with wine sauce, the dinner had only just begun! String beans next, and goose-liver such as one seldom gets these days; then a wonderful leg of mutton, with just the right flavor of garlic; after that, lettuce salad, and cake with cream-sauce, not to mention coffee and fruits; and, after dinner, good old armagnac that warmed one's heart; and even now I have not mentioned the wine, fifty years old, besides the *vin ordinaire* all through the meal! I say I wish I were able to eat such a dinner often. But I am not, for one reason because my body is not fitted for such things. Even as it was, I enjoyed it so much that I was not at my best for two days afterwards, and wrote nothing at all in these pages!

Long live Monsieur and Madame Fabre, in their fine old home, surrounded by their cattle, and geese, and rabbits, and ducks, and pigs, and the great vine-yard rolling over the hill to the east towards Fro-mentas church!

Surely, such peasants are not to be pitied, with their large vineyards, and butter and eggs and milk to sell at the prices one pays now, since the war, when a pair of oxen that used to bring a thousand francs now brings ten times as much! Still, I am free to admit that even the richer peasants work hard enough, and acquire our Gascon habit of seri-ousness which is not easy to throw off.

Then, one must bear in mind that the people of these hills do not have many diversions, and when they do have them it is natural that they should take them more ceremoniously than do people in cities, who are used to amusing themselves in a thousand different ways. Then again, our Gascon people have a sense of dignity and independence, which comes of their living the lives they live, each on his own little plot of land, which he works with his own hands, getting his daily bread as the proud creation of his own will and effort. Yes, that sort of life gives a dignity to a man, crude as it may be, which it is difficult to deprive him of! And I suppose this dignity makes us self-conscious, even in our pleasures, and very sensitive to ridicule. One may call this sense of dignity a sort of vanity if one pleases; there probably is some vanity in us Gascons—we have been accused of it enough by unsympathetic strangers, who say that we love nothing better than to be looked at and admired; that we are even boastful and grandiloquent and fond of loud speaking, and that history is full of Gascon swashbucklers and swaggerers who apparently had never heard of the virtue called humility! It occurs to me that it all depends upon how one looks at things; and if one is a boaster, it depends upon whether he is boasting with or without reason. If one is a coward and boasts of his bravery, that is foolish and idle enough, and ought to be greatly discouraged; but if one is not a coward, but really strong and warlike and energetic and brave, then, just because he frankly proclaims the qualities he knows he possesses and can prove, being thankful for them and proud of them, it should not be called mere vanity or boasting, but a pardonable pride. Such are we Gascons.

Swashbucklers and swaggerers indeed! The faithful companions of Jeanne d'Arc, those who alone remained loyally by her side, despising danger and fighting for her from first to last, were Gascons; so that the English actually thought that she must be Gascon, too—for they made that very natural mistake! They called her "the little Gascon from Armagnac." And then, the renowned figure of D'Artagnan, brilliantly bold, splendidly valorous—where could the illustrious Dumas have found such a man save in this very Gascony, just over the hills, yonder to my left as I write! Is it any wonder that Napoleon said, "Give me an army of true Gascons, and I shall be able to charge through a hundred leagues of flame!"

No, and a mere boaster is not much use in the face of defeat, either; but I have noticed that Gascons ever keep a good heart in the midst of calamity, and greet misfortune more often with a smile than not, because they are brave and ever hopeful, and know how to make the best of even the worst situation. If one thinks he can get a Gascon into a place where he cannot help himself, he had better look out! For we Gascons are resourceful and we do not easily lose our presence of mind when we are in trying places. We Gascons, so prone to proverbs and sayings, like this one: "If the land is sterile, sow it with Gascons; they will grow anywhere." We like it, I suppose, because it does us justice. That is the way we are.

It is this intelligent resourcefulness, united with our boldness, that has enabled us to give France so many men who could conduct delicate affairs of state. Gascony gave even a king to France once, and I see no great reason to be ashamed of Henry IV—"our

Henry," as we call him—or of his court either, which was full of Gascons, just as was the court of Louis XIII after him—Gascons who had those superb qualities I mentioned as making notable men of affairs.

I think I have written down enough to prove to my own satisfaction that we are not mere boasters or vain, as people who do not know us say we are. Of course there are vain people among us, like Victor Claverie, for instance, our village crier, but then, there are vain people everywhere, and I am as much against them as anybody. The real proof that we are not vain is the way we Gascons condemn and ridicule each other's vanity, whenever it appears. If there is anything a Gascon does not like, it is to hear another Gascon boast about himself.

Say we are proud, if you please, and will not suffer humiliation from anybody. It is D'Artagnan who says to Aramis, "I come from Gascony, it is true: and since you are aware of it, there is no need to tell you that Gascons are not very patient, so that when they have asked pardon once, even for a folly, they think they have done at least as much again as they ought to have done."

Before making hasty generalizations about a people, one would do well to remember that, as Montaigne says, "man is a wonderful, vain, divers, and wavering subject; it is very hard to ground any directly-constant and uniform judgment upon him." We Gascons have our faults, as all peoples have, but there is no use in making little faults into big ones. I think the worst fault my fellow Gascons have is that they are not idealistic enough—they are too practical, too utilitarian; they live too close to the ground, they tend to be too materialistic. How much I have lamented this—I, who believe in the reality of spiritual things, and would lift men to the height of that vision which is not of this world. But I find it difficult. For, from the long stress of circumstances, I find my fellow-Gascons too insensible to the loftier ideals that would verily transfigure all their lives, if they would but let them! I suppose it is this practical spirit that blinds their eyes to beauty, when God has bestowed it upon them so plentifully in the wonder of our skies and hills. So, while we have had great men of affairs, we have had few great poets, and no great school of art; and they say that even our famous skill as narrators is spoiled by our want of artistic instinct, our vigorous disorder, our lack of form. I agree, that is one of our faults, surely.

And yet, not all Gascons are materialistic and utilitarian, and Gascony has given the world great idealists, artists also, in their way, that all mankind has been ready enough to honor. There was Fénelon—his fame, at least, is secure! Then, there was the Gascon Montesquieu, philosopher and profound satirist that he was, who, in spite of his disorderly style, transmuted such dry things as politics and jurisprudence into glowing literature. And then, greater than all, there was Montaigne—rather, let me say there *is* Montaigne, for he never dies. He, too, came from our Gascony! The great Montaigne! Explorer of the human soul, impartial reporter of the things of the mind! What clear intelligence! What exquisite feeling! What lively imagination! What paradoxes! All poured out in that inimitable style, whose easy disorder becomes the highest art! There was a man who loved Gascony, and who showed it by sometimes using our Gascon words because, he said, they had the flavor of his native place. "If French cannot say it, Gascon will say it." That is Montaigne. I say that he is really an artist, even though he is hardly an idealist in the usual sense of that word, and though I must differ with him on a great many serious matters. Still, I find that great man expressing my own thoughts so many times, that whole lines of his writings come to my pen's end without my knowing it.

But I do not have to go to these great men of our history to find our dreamers and idealists. Here they are and have been, right in my native village. There was my good friend, Jean-Louis Sance. There is old Marius Fontan, who has made himself poor by dreaming overmuch. Not to speak of Germaine, who knows the inner beauties of the spirit, possessing many of them within herself.

He who talks about a people, let him talk about their virtues; if they have no virtues, they are not worth talking about. And the many virtues of my fellow Gascons I see about me every day in the lives I have learned to love and to glorify by a sympathetic understanding. Can any one help finding joy in their amiability, their zest in living, their vivacity (despite their seriousness), which sometimes makes them quick-tempered, it is true—but, nevertheless, so likable; their courage, their persistence, their sociable humor, nowhere so evident as in their talkativeness. For we Gascons love talk, and are famed for the ease with which we accomplish it. I suppose the desire for self-expression is, after all, the beginning of all art—so there is hope for us yet! Our peasants in the fields even talk to their oxen and pigs and geese. I know a little lame girl that goes by my garden gate every day, driving her cows to and from the pasture, and she is always talking to them. Poor, lonely little Rosette!—it is about the only communion she has with any creature. Her father is cruel to her. He it is who beat her and made her lame.

If one wants to know what Gascons are really like at their best, one should see that wonderful play, *Cyrano de Bergerac*. I have very seldom gone to theaters, but I went to see this play several times in Paris, when the great Coquelin was alive. Once I took my colleague, the Abbé Rivoire, because, as I told him, the whole play is a celebration of good Gascon traits, but most of all, of good Gascon courage. Cyrano himself—ah, there is a tremendous Gascon for you, in spite of his nose, which is a little more Gascon than most Gascon noses really are. Cyrano!—poet, philosopher, musician, soldier, comrade of D'Artagnan, himself another D'Artagnan transfigured by a poet's soul! The very name—De Bergerac—robust and high-sounding, savors of Gascony.

I repeat, if one wants to find all the good Gascon

traits glorified, one should go and see that play.
Bravery worth boasting of? How Cyrano speaks of
the bold cadets of Gascony, swaggering boastfully,
with their eyes like eagles', their fierce mustaches,
their souls drunk with fame and glory! Readiness
for any situation? Cyrano knows well that in these
same cadets of his "the hero that sleeps in Gascon
blood is ever ready to awake!" Gascon strategy
against great odds? It is De Guiche who says to
Cyrano, "I know you love to fight against five-score."
Gascon presence of mind? Well, in this play, one
shall learn that there is "nothing more dangerous
than a rational Gascon." Gascon pride? Cyrano
speaks of his own as a matter of course, right at the
beginning of things. Idealism? That is in the play,
too, not only in Cyrano, valiantly generous, idealist
to the core; but if to dream of the poetry of home
and native land through the moving power of music
is a sort of idealism, those cadets of his are idealistic,
too; for when, in the forlorn and famished camp,
the old man plays on the flute the dear remembered
airs of Gascony, it seems to them the flute of the
woods that plays the love-song of the wandering
goatherds; through it speaks the valley, the wet
landes, the forest, the sunburned shepherd-boy with
scarlet *béret*, the dusk of evening on the gently-flow-
ing river—

"'*Tis Gascony! Hark, Gascons, to the music!*"

Beyond denial, Gascony is there in Edmond Ros-
tand's great play. Since Paris has seen it, it knows

at last the true qualities of Gascons as it never did before. I am glad of that, for it is a fine thing, not only for Parisians, but for the world.

Since I find myself writing in this way, I may as well put down that I sometimes think the poet Heine understood us better than many of our critics. He thought that we Gascons had all the great traits of our France carried to their highest, and once spoke of France itself as "the Gascony of Europe!"

What better praise is there for a Gascon, or indeed, for a Frenchman, than that?

Chapter XIII: *The Little Doctor*

I HAD just finished writing all this when I was disturbed by the tremendous blowing of a horn —three or four lusty blasts, reminding one of a ship in a fog, hoarse and insistent, and not to be denied. Then came a loud rattle and an ominous grinding noise, and all was quiet again. I emerged from my garden-house just in time to see my friend, Dr. Dousset, the mayor of our village, stepping down from his automobile in front of my gate.

That automobile of his makes so much noise that one might easily mistake it for a thing much larger than it is. Merely hearing it approaching, one's imagination gets ready for a large-proportioned car such as one sees in Paris; except that even these are very modest in their sounds, compared with this little, one-seated car of the doctor's. Along the country roads, everybody knows that he is coming when he is yet a long distance off; so, if anyone is sick, somebody can be by the road quite soon enough to stop him. After all, then, the noise has a value, as has everything in this world when truly understood.

When one says this car is little, even then it is hard to realize how little it is. And yet it is a brave little car, although it has only two cylinders—short, snub-nosed, with something of the effect of a bull-dog; marvelously compact, too, and gleaming with brass trimmings, for it was made before the war. The doctor is forever tinkering with it and takes it apart at least once a week in the wide doorway of the huge wine-cellar under his house, where he locks it up at night. Lately, he found something in the engine broken; well, he simply threw it away and then put what was left together again in his skillful manner, and all went as well as before, except for a rattling sound.

If one looks just below the wind-shield, he will see a brass medallion of St. Christophe; that is for good luck. If any symbol is capable of bringing good luck to travelers, this of St. Christophe should, con-sidering how strong this Saint was, and how he was wont to carry people over that dangerous stream without a bridge, once bearing the child Christ on his great shoulders, as the artists picture him.

But no one in our canton would think of ridiculing the doctor's car. We are really proud of it, as some-thing in which we have a personal interest. How often has it brought the little doctor with all good speed to the bedside of some suffering peasant miles away! So no one minds much if, as he drives through the village streets, the chickens and geese run in every direction for their lives, and the dogs, bark-ing excitedly at it, dodge out from the wheels just in time to avoid hasty death. Out in the country, they look upon it as a sort of miracle. Children are frightened by the approaching horn, which works with a crank, exactly like a coffee-mill—indeed, the children make way for it with alacrity, jumping to safe places behind hedges and trees.

To-day, the doctor wore his old military uniform of khaki, still looking neat and fresh. For the little doctor was in the war, and rose to be a *Médecin Major.* They say that Captain Dousset did valiant things at a hospital at the front. I have seen his *croix de guerre,* with a star on the ribbon. He looks well in that uniform of his, even if he is short in stature, for he is well-made and carries himself like a soldier.

As he was coming up my path, I thought that if there is any one in our village who best represents good Gascon traits, it is our doctor. No wonder that he understands our peasants and that they have an honest affection for him, often bringing him gifts of rabbits, or fish, or fruits, or brandy—or whatever choice thing they have on hand! For he himself comes of good peasant stock—not far away, either, since his father's farm is in Dému, just northeast of here, where they send for him frequently, which is a great triumph, considering that one's native place does not always have great regard for one's abilities. Pure Gascon the little doctor is, with our Gascon seriousness, but softened by a sense of humor. His vivacity shows itself in his quick, nervous manner and in his Gascon talent for talking, which is ever a rapid, decisive sort of talk—the kind that carries conviction with it.

Some faces one never sees too often. The doctor's is one of these, for one finds in it alert intelligence and kindness of heart. It is fine to see his brilliant smile, and the merry twinkle in his eyes! These same eyes are as black as night, as is also his unruly hair, brushed straight up from a low forehead; black, too, is his mustache, the ends turned up aggressively, but not carefully enough barbered to make a dandy of him. That large chin may signify his practical outlook, which also is Gascon. No, there is not much of the poet in our doctor, and I sometimes wonder if he is as religious as he should be. For he seldom is seen at mass; but this may be on account of the sick people. Still, I have always observed that however busy our little doctor may be on a Sunday morning, in the afternoon he is invariably at the café, playing his game of bridge— unless, indeed, he has gone fishing.

Such is the little doctor, respected and admired by everybody. Most of the peasants cheerfully pay him the fifteen francs in advance, which gives one his services for the whole year. For the last four years, he has been mayor of the commune, and it would be hard to elect any one else! There was Monsieur Capéran, who owns so much land; he thought he wanted to be mayor himself, and put up a rival ticket at the last election. But what good did it do? He did not get more than three or four votes. (Monsieur Capéran's house is the one the "crows" hissed on the night of their procession, because he would not contribute for refreshments.) So it is that one sees, and will see for some time, on a pole in front of the little doctor's house, a large, wooden shield, painted with laurel branches and a gold crown:

COMITE D'ACTION
REPUBLICAINE
DR. DOUSSET
MAIRE

Over it is a cluster of French flags. It was a sight worth while to see the two great May-poles they planted there after the last election.

"Good morning, Monsieur l'Abbé! I stop to ask if you will come to our house to dinner to-morrow?"

I made haste to accept.

While the doctor was rolling a cigarette, he was glancing about my garden. Finally, he looked beyond the fig tree, where the bench is, to the highest point.

"What are those boards you have lying over there, Monsieur l'Abbé? They look new."

I then told him how I was planning to make a little pavilion there, where I should have yet another place to study and write—especially when my father wants to tinker at that work-bench of his in the garden-house, when his noise disturbs me considerably. I added that the view is better there than anywhere else.

"There will be a little window, too," I said, "looking toward Sabazan."

"It will be very small, will it not?"

Very small, I told him—just large enough to sit

in and be protected from the sun and rain. Perhaps not even a door.

I do not think the little doctor thought it very practical, but he did not say so, as he is always polite, in spite of his brusqueness. He only started down the path to the gate, calling back,

"We shall expect you to-morrow—*a midi!*"

I was glad to be invited. To-morrow. It will be the fifteenth day of June, the day of St. Germaine— Germaine Sance's fête-day. Of course, the dinner is to celebrate that. They had thought of me as an old friend of the family.

Yes, I was glad they had not forgotten me!

Chapter XIV: *The House on the Road of the Madonna*

I FIND I sometimes write of the little doctor's house, and sometimes of Germaine's house, although, as a matter of fact, they are one and the same. I suppose that a well-ordered mind should ever have the same name for the same things—yet, language is made richer by variety, is it not? There are synonyms. One's imagination would be much narrowed if it were always restricted to the same words; and, like Montaigne, "I am one of those that feel a very great conflict and power of imagination."

It was perfectly natural that, fourteen years ago, our Doctor Dousset, then young and untried, fell in love with and married so attractive a girl as Marthe, the sister of Germaine; perfectly natural, too, that the young couple should start their lives together in the same great house with the parents, Monsieur and Madame Jean-Louis Sance; and perfectly natural that after Monsieur Sance was laid to rest in the cemetery on the hill, they all should continue living there. In those days, too, there was the other sister, Angèle—she who is now married and lives in Bordeaux.

Assuredly, there is plenty of room in that house for two or three families! Why, it must be as much as one hundred feet long—and then, continuing it, is the building for the grape-crusher and wine-press and the huge vats—a building at least as long as the house! And all made of stone faced with plaster, the house roofed with slate from the Pyrenees, and the rest with red tile. And that is not all. Back in the yard is the immense stone barn for cask-making and repairing; then another stone barn beside it for the carriages; and back of this, the stalls for the oxen and the horses, and even sleeping rooms for the drivers! And then one has not spoken of the extensive flower garden on the other side of the driveway, and the vegetable garden back of that, and the orchards back of that, and the vineyards all around!

The grandfather of Germaine, who built all these things, was a man of big ideas. Once he actually started a bank in Aignan; and he built a steam mill for grinding flour near the Château de Lasalle south of the village.

And Germaine's father was like him. But he has been gone now these four years, and things are not the same as they were. There are no horses any more, and the old carriages rest in the dark barn unused, and the cask-making has stopped, although one can still see some of the immense casks in the cellar underneath the house, where the deserted little office of the winery is overlaid with cobwebs and dust. Even the vineyards are most of them sold, for in the last days of Jean-Louis Sance, he lost nearly all he had, and his widow finds it hard to keep things going. And, of course, a doctor, who is a mayor as well, has not time to continue the great business of wine-making and attend to his patients also.

From the high ridge of the Margouet road to the east, one sees this cluster of buildings gleaming in the sunshine, at the edge of the village, by the Road of the Madonna, the six dormer windows of the house peeping above the trees, and high above all the two slender poplars in front of the garden. I have seen these two poplars clear from Sabazan.

I am glad that Germaine's house does not face the street, but the garden to the right, which I think is always the best arrangement. As one enters the generous wrought-iron gates, that swing upon high, stone pillars, one notices a long, rectangular pond between the garden and the road. Germaine fell in that pond when she was about seven years old, and was almost drowned. She had been watering the geraniums and had just started up the three stone steps that lead from the pond, after having filled her watering-can, when she slipped. Her grandmother, who was knitting on a bench near by, heard the splash and looked, and there was little Germaine, half sinking, half floating—oh, there was excitement enough! A cask-maker came from the barn, attracted by the cries, very leisurely, too, for that was his way, and waded into the pond up to his waist. Then, because he had heard that drowning people pull their rescuers down with them if they are not very careful, he extended merely his forefinger to

Germaine, who clasped it tightly, and thus she was saved; without doubt, it was a big, sturdy fore-finger, for Germaine remembers it very vividly. She also remembers that when she was being dried in the kitchen, it came to her to say that even if she had drowned, she was ready to appear before God, since she had only just then come from confession! Imagine that from a child of seven! And another memory, precious forever, is the frantic hug and kiss of her dear old grandmother, usually so grave and sedate, and not often given to expressing her emotions. Dear old lady! She, too, now lies in a sunny corner of the gray wall in the cemetery by my vineyard.

Then there are the Dorothy Perkins roses, simple-hearted and glad, blushing a rich pink, scrambling in mad disorder over the pillars of the gateway, and up the slender iron railings by the stone stairs to the wide entrance, over which the hospitable marquise casts its shade.

Strange to say, the most interesting part of the house for me is not the roomy hall, nor even the cool salon with its old Gaveau piano, nor the long dining room, with its windows looking out towards the sunsets—no, not these, but the great kitchen in the back. As a boy, I saw it fairly often. There it is one finds the most interesting things of all, although this may seem to stress the earthly side of life too much. But one can discover poetry anywhere if he looks for it, and for some reason I find it in this big kitchen more than anywhere else—unless it is the disused and dusty attic that runs the whole length of the house and contains the worn-out relics of several generations.

It seems incredible that one can get so many fascinating things in this one room of a kitchen, until one realizes that it is by far the largest room; the only room, indeed, that occupies the whole width of the house. It has not a stone floor, as has Monsieur Fabre's and many others around here; nor has it an earthen floor like old Marinette's and so many of the peasants'—no, this floor, built by Grandfather Sance, is of wood, being on the first story above the ground. Big? There is space for a massive table of thick boards running almost the full length of the room, with a row of benches beside it along the wall —a table so large that all the cask-makers and workers in the fields ate here in the old times. How the high rafters used to echo with their hearty jests and free laughter! Full-throated people they were— full-stomached, too, one can swear, when they arose from that table to clatter out down the stone steps back to their work.

For the rest, this kitchen is like most of our Gascon kitchens—I am sure that you, my dear Abbé Rivoire, never saw one like it about Paris! From the ceiling are suspended high in air two long, wide shelves, as long as the table; on one of them pot after pot made of yellow earthenware, big-bellied, with a handle on each side. They are filled with grease for the cooking; and side by side with these, pots of pickled goose, and other mysterious jars with goodness knows what. And on the other shelf, immense round loaves of bread in a long row, weigh-

ing at least ten pounds each! I have found that we
Gascons eat more bread than do Parisians—much
more. Bread in the soup—large quantities—that,
we think, lays a solid foundation for a meal, which
cannot be excelled! Then plenty of bread all
through the courses, and more bread with the fruit—
no wonder we Gascons are a sturdy race! Bread
between meals, too, rubbed with garlic, and sometimes seasoned with oil and salt and a little vinegar.
Eat that with a juicy pear or some grapes!

One can easily see why we make the sign of the
cross whenever a new loaf is cut.

But I find the real poetry of a kitchen like this
in the huge fireplace, blackened with use, before
which Dick, the hunting dog, likes to lie and dream
by the hour, although more often than not he is in
the way and invites many a vehement scolding for
stretching his long body on the busiest part of the
hearth. Such a fireplace! With its colossal, black
andirons; with its stout chains hanging over the
flame, with hooks for the kettles; and with its iron
bases of different shapes for the pots. In a corner
of the chimney, hams are suspended in winter; and
delectable they are when they come out fully smoked
and mellowed in the early spring! There in the
chimney, too, is the wooden salt-box, whose lid is
forever being lifted to flavor the seductive concoc-
tions simmering in the pots beneath. And there is
the spit, slowly revolving by means of an ingenious
spring wound up in one end, which supplants the old-
fashioned kind turned by hand—unless one has still
another sort I heard about the other day from the

little doctor himself, who visited an ancient house out in the country. There he found an old spit, no longer used, to be sure, which was turned by a revolving cage, in which a small dog tread everlasting steps, like a squirrel. The man that invented that had an active mind!

Next to the fireplace, I like to look at the shining array of pans of copper and brass, all in order, hanging on the wall over the charcoal stove. And then the red, earthen dishes, large and small; most interesting of all these, the heavy jugs with a spout attached, for drinking water, and holding ten quarts at least. Thick and cool they are; and it is a picturesque sight to see Marinette carrying one on her head from the well. But they are getting rare these days.

And what a miscellany of other romantic things all around! Yonder is the wire basket for shaking the salad; and there are the big scales; and beside them the coffee-roaster turned with a crank, and big baskets of all sorts hanging here and there, and the large goose wings for cleaning the hearth, and the tall clock, generations old, that is ever stopping and never keeps just the right time; and the odd-shaped, Gascon lamps of shining brass, hung on the chimney piece, not to speak of the strings of garlic hanging over in the corner; and, near the window where it is cool, the big piece of fat used to season soup—and add to this that in winter there are long rows of sausages suspended from the rafters in an enticing array!

And how one is reminded of chestnut time by that

long-handled pan over in the corner, with holes in the top! There is nothing better, to my thinking, along in October and November, than roasted chestnuts—unless, indeed, it is chestnuts boiled, that is, boiled with the leaf or twig of a fig tree, just to give them that subtle flavor which nothing else lends. A merry festivity it always is when the peasants gather in each other's kitchens or barns to husk the maize and eat boiled chestnuts and drink the wine that has just been made and has not yet had time to ferment! What stories one hears at such times! What gossip, too!

It is then getting near the time when one may have use for those bed-warmers hanging over there by the attic stairway. Both kinds are hanging in Madame Sance's kitchen; the kind with a long handle, an elegantly polished copper pan at the end, with a lid on it, which one fills with coals and passes over the sheets; and the kind which consists of a long, open oval frame, in the middle of which is suspended a pan for live coals, and which one covers up lengthwise in the bed until it is good and warm and inhabitable—the kind called a "monk"—I have often wondered just why, for what similitude there is between a monk and a bed-warmer it is at first hard to see! Still, it may be because the frame swells out in the middle like the portly figures of monks one sometimes sees in pictures. Yes, it must be because of the shape.

But the name is unfortunate, for it is related that over in the village of Nogaro many, many years ago—it might have been in the Middle Ages, for all

I am aware—a real monk came to the inn and asked for lodging for the night. He went to bed early in the front room. Soon after, another traveler came, and the landlord ordered the maid to put the "monk" in the back room, meaning, of course, to put the bed-warmer there in the bed. But the maid was a new one, and intensely ignorant, and so the real monk found himself awakened by this silly maid and put out of his bed into the back room, into a bed that was exceeding cold. Our monk had just ceased shivering and had settled down again for the night, when a third traveler came, at which the proprietor now bade the maid to put the "monk" in the yellow room. The wretched maid again awoke the real monk and insisted that he shift himself to this other cold bed, where he had need for much fortitude to retain his Christian charity and spiritual temper. And thus it went all the night long. But to me, this story uncovers a degree of meekness in this monk which I cannot imagine the most saintlike monk to possess. True, he unwittingly did a Christian deed and one worthy of all praise in well warming the beds of all these travelers in turn, but it was what one might call a work of supererogation. It shows the subtle dangers that lurk in language. It may be, as I said in the first place, a well-ordered mind should have the same name for the same things, even at the expense of that imagination for which I was pleading, having forgotten entirely about this monk.

Such, at any rate, is the kitchen of Germaine's house. When we were both boys, Germaine's father and I sometimes warmed ourselves there by the roaring fire on bitterly cold days. So there are things in this kitchen besides the things one sees! I was thinking of them much to-day as I looked forward to the dinner to-morrow.

As I said, I am glad they asked me to come.

Chapter XV: *I Celebrate a Saint*

WHAT a big bouquet of roses it was! Yellow roses brought that morning by Renée, the little kitchen girl, fresh from Marinette's garden down the road. We were getting ready to sit down to dinner, when Germaine's mother presented them to her, saying as she did so,

"*Bonne fête,* my little Maimaine!"

"Maimaine" is the pretty diminutive adopted for Germaine when she was a baby. I think that there was something suspiciously like tears in the mother's eyes, in spite of their happy light, as she bestowed upon her daughter a warm kiss. Then more kisses and embraces and a "*Bonne fête!*" from everybody else, and we all seated ourselves at the long table, where the savory soup was already steaming in the large tureen.

When I write "savory" about the soup, I am using the best word imaginable. When you make soup in Gascony, you go into the garden and gather some hysop, and marjoram, and thyme, and parsley, and celery-tops, and oh, so many other things besides— all of which give it a flavor, you may be sure. In spite of the great chefs, one never gets such soup as that in Paris, at least according to my taste. Why, the soup in Gascony is such a memorable and characteristic thing that when the Gascons in Paris wanted to form a club, they actually named it after one of our soups, *La Garbure,* a winter soup made of green cabbage leaves and pickled pork or goose, and all the herbs I mentioned, too!

I was the only guest—one would hardly call Germaine's sister, Angèle, from Bordeaux, a guest!— and they put me by Germaine at one end of the table, where I could fully enjoy those wonderful roses, for Germaine had placed the vase right in front of us. At the other end of the table was the little doctor's wife, between her boy, Robert (a splendid little fellow of twelve), and Henri, Germaine's brother. Then, on opposite sides of the table, facing each other, were Germaine's mother and the doctor, on whose right was Angèle. The doctor had arrived just in time for dinner from a visit to a peasant who had fallen from a cherry tree. Then he had been stopped on his way home by an urgent summons to the house of our curé, who had met with an accident, the nature of which I hastened to inquire.

"Nothing serious," answered the doctor, as he poured me out some white wine; "only he is growing infirm and needs some one to watch over him. This morning he was walking in his little garden and stepped on some old boards that covered his cistern. They broke, and he fell in. That is the second time this summer he has fallen in the water."

I had heard about the other time when I first came home. It had rained a great deal, and the ditches by the roadside were full of water. The Abbé Castex was sent for to take the Sacrament to a dying man in the country. He started out on foot, why, I don't know. They say a peasant found him, struggling in a flooded ditch by the road to Plaisance, holding the Sacred Host high above his head to keep it dry.

I suppose Robert, for some inexplicable reason, found something humorous in all this, for glancing up at his end of the table, I saw that he was laughing. One can hardly blame the boy for his lack of reverence, when even Madame Lacoste, pious as she is, has been heard to say,

"The priest is getting old and foolish!"

As for myself, I reserve judgment. I think he is more sensible than many men, though perhaps not so sensible as most men ought to be.

While the radishes and the butter were being passed around, Angèle told Robert that she had a rare postage stamp for him.

This Robert is a small edition of his father, the doctor, and looks wonderfully well in his blue, lycée uniform, with its double row of brass buttons.

"He got a stamp the other day from his cousin, Raoul, in Tunis," remarked Germaine's mother.

I asked if he was still with his regiment there.

She replied that he was. The doctor added that he was as rough and profane and as much of a daredevil as ever, from all he could learn.

"But," remonstrated Germaine, "he is not so bad as people say. Every night he prays that little

prayer mother always repeats before she goes to sleep."

"Yes," agreed Madame Sance. "You see," she went on, turning to me, "I learned this prayer when I was a little girl. I suppose I should have outgrown it long ago, and I was ashamed for people to know I still said it, until I heard Raoul mention that he, too, repeated it every night."

I asked how the prayer went. So, while we waited for little Renée to clear the table for the chicken, Germaine's mother said it for me slowly; and I did not mention that I myself was taught it when a boy, and often said it even now in memory of my mother. Here is the way it goes:

> *In my bed I place myself,*
> *In my bed I lay me down;*
> *Should death come to me this night,*
> *God be to me my sacrament.*
> *St. John, St. Luke, and St. Matthew!*
> *Accept the good God for my father,*
> *And the Virgin for my mother,*
> *And the Angels for my brothers,*
> *The Archangels for my friends.*
> *Good night, little Jesus, I go to sleep!*

I think that no one need become so old as to be ashamed of it. It always brings a lump to my throat when I say it, and tears are never far away, I know not why. It is often that way with the simple, beautiful things of this world; and this prayer does not belong only to this world, if it comes from a heart as sweet and pure as that of Germaine's mother!

At this point, little Renée, clad in her new, red dress, brought in the chicken. She belongs to a poor peasant family that lives on the side of the hill near the forest. She is only fourteen years old, but very capable for all that. Her face is pinched, and her eyes are large and sad, but I think she will be beautiful some day. Now that she is with the doctor's family, she will have enough to eat for the first time in her life! For all the doctor's skill, it is little Renée that knows best how to cure chickens of the pip. Lately, she had two tiny patients in the kitchen for over a week. They made their home in the warm ashes by the fireplace, and she tenderly nursed them through their ailments until they could rejoin their noisy family by the garden wall.

I mentioned that at Margouet I saw my old friend, Marius Fontan, and that he was looking worn and ill.

"Poorer than ever," responded the doctor. "If he would only write less poetry and attend to his farm, it would be better for him."

"Is it true—that about the snake?" asked Robert.

"I should not wonder at all," I replied. "It is like him."

"What is all this about a snake?" inquired Angèle.

And then I explained how Marius was walking along the road the other day, dreaming, as usual, and not looking where he was going, when he stepped with his left foot upon a snake, and was stung. Without a single moment's hesitation, he stamped his right foot upon the snake's head and ground it into the earth.

"That," interjected Henri, "is like the time the bear got loose from the gipsy camp beyond the Château de Lasalle. Marius was going down the road, dreaming, as you say, when he bumped straight into it. All he said was, 'What is this damned beast doing here?' and went on, mumbling some patois poetry that was in his head."

"I don't know what will become of the old man," remarked the doctor, as he refilled my glass with wine and water. "He asked to be placed upon the list of destitutes, so that he could get an allowance of bread. I told him to go to Castelnavet and get his birth certificate, in order to make out the papers. But it is five months now, and he has been too shiftless to go. And there he is, living all alone in that tumble-down house of his, with nobody in the world to look after him."

"They say he was handsome in his youth," put in Germaine's mother. "Grandmother knew of him then and used to think he had a future."

I had just been thinking of this woman, Germaine's grandmother, for, as I had passed along the hallway, I had seen an old, red shawl, with fringe on it, that used to belong to her. Religious was old Grandmother Sance, and very strict. Into this very dining room every night of her life the servants were assembled at nine o'clock to kneel down on the hard floor and listen to a prayer. If there was company in the house, they, too, had to join in these devotions—an ordeal they were not likely to forget soon, for the prayer always took half an hour at least, and the knees of even the most pious became impatient!

While the pancakes were being served, Henri mentioned his friend, Monsieur Ware, the American, who was to call later in the afternoon. This gave an opportunity for Robert, little scamp that he is, to cast sly glances at Germaine across the table, and for Henri to hint that Germaine had arrived at the age when girls get married. I was glad that the doctor silenced him by exclaiming, "Bo-bo-bo-bo-bo!" which is his usual way of expressing incredulity at any matter. When he says, "Bo-bo-bo-bo-bo!" very rapidly and decisively like that, the question is closed.

With the pancakes, we were drinking some excellent sweet wine, something like champagne, only without the sparkle, and I thought that it was about time to propose a toast to Germaine in honor of her fête. I was sure that I was the proper one to do it, being used to speaking in public. So I arose in my place and, lifting up my glass, I said,

"Why do we celebrate the day of anybody's Saint? It occurs to me that it is for the same motives by which we celebrate a birthday. And why is that? There are several reasons. In some cases, it is to cheer one who is approaching nearer the end of life—to say to such a person, 'How young you are!' Or, it may be because he has come so far so well. Or, it may be that it furnishes an occasion when one may express wishes for welfare during all the future years. But best of all, we celebrate this fête because in Germaine, Madame Sance here gave to the world a priceless gift, for which we all are thankful."

I had bowed to Germaine's mother here, as was proper; and now, raising my glass, I turned to Germaine, and continued,

"Montaigne says somewhere that 'our minds are as full-grown and perfectly jointed at twenty years as they should be, and promise as much as they can,' and that 'natural qualities and virtues, if they have any vigorous or beauteous thing in them, will produce and show the same within that time, or never.' Our Germaine, here, even if she had not one whole year more before the age Montaigne mentions, would not need to be ashamed."

Then we clinked our glasses and drank in silence, Germaine blushing modestly behind her roses, but deserving all I said, none the less.

I heard young Robert, who is interested in everything, ask his mother about the St. Germaine whose fête we were observing; and I overheard her telling him how she was a shepherdess, and how she is always represented in statues with a lamb at her feet and her apron full of roses.

"She was one of our Gascon saints," I remarked.

And then I reminded everybody (for here was my chance) how very poor she was, and yet how generous; and of the time she took her own small portion of bread to some needy peasants, and how her cruel stepmother saw her and was going to beat her, and demanded to know what she had in her apron. Then the shepherdess unfolded her apron,

and lo! from it came tumbling the most beautiful
roses!

All good deeds are like that.

A great plate of cherries from the orchard had
been passed around, and the coffee had been served;
and now Renée appeared with liqueur glasses and
a gold-topped bottle of *crême d'Armagnac*. The
label had the name of Germaine's father printed on
it. This liqueur was of his own invention, and so
exquisite that I think no other quite attains to it. I
must have praised it very highly, for Madame Sance
said she would present me with one of the few bottles left.

As I was sipping it slowly, its golden seduction
brought reflections upon the man with whom the
secret of this delicious elixir had perished. Jean-
Louis Sance! How I am forever missing his beloved
figure from our village! On the wall was the picture of his strong, sincere, generous face looking
down on us all; and out the window, across the roofs
to the west, I could clearly see the slender, sunlit
cypress trees that mark the place where he sleeps
now. How often would he sit in the very chair
where the doctor now presides at table and look at
the sunsets that cast their ineffable glory on our
hills! I could not avoid thinking of these things,
and of the song he used to like to sing at cherry time,
when the luscious cherries from his own orchards
were passed around the table, even as to-day. He
taught it to Angèle, and she sometimes sings it, oh,
so beautifully!

When the song of the time of the cherries we sing,
Gay nightingales trill, and the blackbirds are whist-
*   ling,*
All making merry!
In the heads of the girls there is madness and folly,
In the hearts of their lovers, the sunshine is bright.
When the song of the time of the cherries we sing,
Sweeter than ever the blackbirds are whistling!

Ah, it is brief, the time of the cherries!
When, two by two, we dreamingly gather
Pendants of coral;
Symbols of love they are, looking like roses,
Like drops of blood as they fall on the grasses!
But brief, oh, so brief, the time of the cherries,
When pendants of coral we dreamingly gather.

I remember that, although some of the words are happy enough, the melody is sad, sad, as of something gone that will nevermore return.

Even after we had left the dinner table and had gone into the salon, where the shutters were opened wide, and where Angèle sang to Germaine's accompaniment, I was still thinking of my old friend, and of what a vacancy the passing away of a strong man like that makes in our lives. Yes, in spite of the fact that it was Germaine's fête-day and that I ought to have been cheerful and talkative, I became silent and sad, and the big house suddenly seemed to my poor heart empty and forsaken, and the sun no longer shone.

Chapter XVI: *Wooden Shoes*

I WAS thinking this afternoon as I walked up and
down one of my garden paths, lamenting that
the petals from the last roses were already
strewn on the grass (though it is only the middle
of June), I was thinking, I say, of what Henri said
at the dinner the other day, that Germaine had arrived at the age when girls think of marrying. I
remembered that some one had said that Monsieur
Ware, the American, was to call that very afternoon at Germaine's house, and I could not but wonder if it was his new friend, Henri, who was the
attraction—or somebody else! Already, I am sorry
to say, the women of our village are gossiping about
Monsieur Ware's frequent calls, and are wondering
what he can have to say with that broken French of
his.

Then, after I had said my breviary, I was tying
some sweet peas to some poles I had newly placed
for them this very morning, when who should I see
coming through the gate but Monsieur Ware himself, covering the ground very quickly with his bold
step, so that he was up to me almost before I could
adjust my thoughts for the occasion. He had a

bundle under his arm, tied up in an old copy of *La France,* and after our greetings were over, he hastened to show it to me.

It proved to be a pair of wooden shoes.

"I bought them down there in the Street of the Church from the man that made them," he said; "Paul Sarrade, I believe you call him. What do you think of them?"

I took one of them and looked it over and told him that they were very prettily carved. For they were done exceptionally well, and by hand, too, as Paul always does them. The toes turned up at the end very gracefully, and there was a wide, black, glossy strap tacked on at the middle to hold them on the foot.

"They are not made for work-shoes," I remarked. "They are too low for that, and much too fancy. They are the kind the peasant women wear for their best. You sometimes see them coming in on market-day with sabots like these. They wear them over their felt slippers."

"I doubt if I can wear them about here," he said laughingly. "The peasants might think I was making fun of a sacred institution! I think I shall wear them, though, when I get back home in America—in my study, for instance."

I asked him why he should carry these all the way from France, when he could surely get just as good sabots in America.

This seemed to amuse Monsieur David Ware very much, for he looked at me in great surprise, and then burst out in a fit of merriment which I did

not entirely like, for it dawned upon me that perhaps he was taking these sabots home to show to the
sabot-makers there and to ridicule the kind poor
Paul makes in our little village as being inferior
for some reason.

It was then I learned that the peasants in America do not wear wooden shoes at all, even in the
fields! No, the peasants there wear shoes of leather,
although I should think that sabots would be much
more serviceable, not only on the roads, but plowing with the oxen. Our peasants would not wear
leather, even if they could afford it. And wooden
shoes are far less expensive.

Ah, that America is an extravagant country!

So Paul's handiwork was going there as a curiosity! I did not quite like that, either, for it seemed
to me that, in their ignorance, the Americans might
make fun of us. My resentment was increased by
what Monsieur Ware said next.

"I think these wooden shoes are what keep your
peasants from rising to the higher classes. They
literally weigh them down, so they cannot get above
being peasants at all."

I ventured to ask how.

"I have watched your people wearing them. They
have a decided effect upon one's walk and carriage.
They are so big that one gets to walk with his legs
spread a little apart; being heavy and loose, too,
you cannot raise your feet much from the ground,
and you can't bend them, so that you acquire a
shambling, shuffling walk that dooms a man to remain a peasant for life. Oh, I have made quite a

study of the matter. There is no doubt about it at all—these sabots are a symbol of your Gascon peasant and his unchangeable ways."

It always makes me indignant when foreigners, unsympathetic with our customs, speak of our great peasant class in that way. If one understood the least thing about our class distinctions in France, one would not be so free in finding fault with our peasants for not rising easily above their station. I do not know how it is in America; but here in France such criticisms of our people merely betray an ignorance of our French ways. You cannot shatter the traditions of centuries in a day, nor is it well to do so.

I said nothing of all this, however, because I knew it would be of no use. I only remarked,

"Then these sabots of yours will be merely a reminder of our unfortunate condition, will they not?"

"Oh, no," he protested, seeing that he had really hurt me. "Don't you remember I said when I first visited your garden that I was looking for something worth writing a poem about? Well, here it is, that something, in these self-same sabots."

This aroused my curiosity, and I said, perhaps rather boldly,

"Just what are you going to say about our wooden shoes in that poem of yours?"

We had been walking slowly along the path that leads to a large pine tree on the summit of my garden, and we sat down in the shade on those boards out of which I intend building my little pavilion.

Monsieur Ware did not speak for several moments, and then he answered musingly,

"I shall write of how one forever hears along these Gascon roads the clatter of wooden shoes—of how one sees the peasants, young and old, men and women, plodding along through their narrow lives in their wooden shoes, plowing the fields in wooden shoes—wearing away the flagstones of their houses with their wooden shoes—I have in mind a sort of lyric of wooden shoes, whose clack, clack, never ceases, beating a rhythm with the peasant's life, from the cradle to the time when he leaves his wooden shoes forever!"

What Monsieur Ware had just said was better, much better, and I began to think less harshly of him, for I perceived that, after all, he could see something of the poetry of things, mistaken as he was about some matters.

Badly mistaken, as his very next remark showed. For he began to say with all confidence that wooden shoes must be cold in winter, since they do not fit snugly about the feet and so would let in the cold air.

"You must study our wooden shoes still more," I rejoined. "They are very warm in winter. Of course, then you do not see the peasants going about in them bare of foot as you do now; and besides, they warm them before they venture out by putting hot coals in them and rolling them around, and then they stuff them with straw, too. No, they are not so cold as you think."

I would gladly have gone on telling Monsieur

Ware many other things worth while for his poem, only just then he happened to look at his watch and remembered he had agreed to go to the pharmacist's to fetch some medicine to the château for his sister —and the afternoon was near spent, and she might worry at his long absence.

Indeed, I could have given many valuable hints for that poem of Monsieur Ware. For often and often have I thought of these wooden shoes of ours that clatter up the hills and down again; that beat out their rhythm on barren floors without surcease; that, worn by little children's feet, go pattle-pat, pod-poddle, after the geese and cows, as they drive them along the winding roads to the red-roofed barns. What visions they do indeed bring, these wooden shoes! The peasant woman with a loaf of bread upon her head, returning from market in her wooden shoes, knitting as she goes plack-plack along the hard road. The poor father, burdened with his sorrow, climbing slowly, plock-plock, up the hard, stone stairs of the little doctor's house, with the fear of the death of his loved one in his eyes so tired with vigil. And so the visions come one after another, without end.

It was not so long ago when, over the hills of Gascony, came a cry from the north, "To arms for France!" Ah, then the sound of the wooden shoes was heard, an eager army of hurrying feet! These humble peasants of Gascony—they left their wooden shoes at a word for the poilu's boots and the sword of France! Chemin des Dames, and Rheims, Verdun! They were there, Gascons brave as in the old days when they fought the battles of kings! Deep in the trenches, there they were, a belt of shells for the old red sash; a hat of tin for the old *béret*— dreaming of home and their wooden shoes, down in these valleys of Gascony! At Fate's behest, for the glory of France, they laid them prone. And now, in their wooden shoes, bowed forms of women go under the cypress trees alone, to kneel where the crosses rise over the heroic dead, who will wear their wooden shoes no more, no more!

Let the wooden shoes be the symbol of our peasants if you will, just as Monsieur Ware says. Like our peasants, they speak of ancient customs and respect for long, long tradition; like them, they are stout and strong; like them, they are simple and primitive; like them, too, they have their note of beauty and make a music that is precious to the souls that understand it, and that wait for the echo of the dear remembered step when evening comes, and the wooden shoes wend homeward over twilight roads to the rest and peace of hearts that care.

I have a pair of wooden shoes myself, which I sometimes use when it is muddy in my garden, although they are too small to get on over my leather ones.

They belonged to my mother, who walks this earth no more.

Chapter XVII: *On Being Made Ridiculous*

IT becomes increasingly clear to me that I am very sensitive to ridicule, especially when it touches this Gascony of ours and the sturdy people who toil among its hills. I suppose that is why I so disliked to have our wooden shoes made fun of by Monsieur Ware, or by any of his friends in far-away America.

And this reminds me that I did not give all the reasons why our Gascon folk take themselves so seriously at a public fête like that at Margouet. Another reason for our grave decorum on such occasions is that, while we Gascons are fond of ridiculing others, and are really adepts at that sort of thing, we are very self-conscious, and not one of us likes to be ridiculed himself. Perhaps this is one of our faults. I have been wondering.

Isn't it surprising how a little thing like a pair of sabots can stir one up and set one to thinking?

I have noticed that there are two kinds of people in our world; the kind that thinks of everything in relation to their little selves—the self-centered people, they are; and the kind that do just the other thing, that is, relate themselves to all the great world outside them, looking not inward, but outward, and realizing that they are but very little portions of a very large universe. The great philosophers belong to this last kind of people, the great philosophers, who try to see all things in their just proportions, and who do not contort everything by thinking how it affects their own puny persons; and, avoiding this very lamentable trait, they are kept from being as puny as a human being otherwise is.

Now, it is just possible that it is this very philosophic temper that gives us what we call the sense of humor. That is, both the humorist and the philosopher are at one in this—they see things in their bigness, and can afford to laugh when one little part of the world sets itself up as if it were the whole world, as some people do who know no better. And people who see things in the large like that find much in life to laugh at, because, as I said, they perceive life with a generous vision, and notice when things get ridiculously disproportionate one with another. I repeat, philosophers and humorists are very much alike. When the humorist laughs, he is, as it were, philosophizing through his laughter; and when the philosopher criticizes our fragmentary world, he is a humorist whose laughter has turned into logic.

So it is that when you find a person who not only sees the ridiculous in other people, but can himself accept ridicule when it is deserved, and can laugh at it as heartily as anybody—I say then you have found a rare mind, a mind that views things in the large, as do the great thinkers and dreamers and artists, whose splendid vision the world is never

tired of glorifying, especially after they have been
dead awhile.

This is the reason, I suppose, why all great nations have been nations that knew how to laugh.
There was Greece, through whose happy, whole-
hearted laughter, which echoes even now, emerged
the large-souled philosophies of Plato and Aristotle,
and the art of a Phidias and a Euripides. There is
France—has she not also learned the splendid art of
laughter, and does she not teach it to the world, together with such other arts and such philosophies as
the whole earth is glad to know? Show me a man
who is acquainted with rational laughter—I don't
mean the silly laughter of school girls, but the laughter that comes of a deep sense of humor—show me
such a man, I say, who can laugh even when the jest
is about himself, and I will show you a man, too, who
has learned one of the greatest secrets of living un-
selfishly, of living so that he perceives events in such
good proportion that he knows well enough that he
counts for only one; a man that does not emphasize
his own little rights over those of his fellowmen,
and who is truly on the way to loving his neighbor
as himself. Even good morals and a mind attuned
to the humor of things are not far apart!

Perhaps it would be better, then, if we Gascons
were not so sensitive to ridicule, for I am afraid it
does not show as exalted a quality of humor as we
should have, and reveals us as a little too self-centered and lacking in large outlooks. It may be,
though, that we are no worse than other people.
And anyway, I have mostly in mind our uneducated

peasants, among whom, however, one will find many exceptions.

Montaigne has written a whole essay on the fact that we weep and laugh at the same things. How easy it is to pass from laughter to tears, from tears to laughter! Sometimes we are at a loss to know which to do. I wonder why this is so. I think our laughter and tears are thus near together because each expresses the same thing from a different point of view. For instance, look at Joseph Lignac, our lame blacksmith, who sings so baldly and loudly, following the priest in our religious processions. One might easily laugh at him because it is so incongruous to see his awkwardness as he lumbers along ungracefully, bawling at the top of his unmusical voice. But that is because we then see him from the outside; we have not entered into his soul, or perhaps do not realize that he has a soul. The sight of him might just as easily bring tears; but that is when one puts oneself in his place and enters into his good, honest heart and feels the deep pathos of his poor life—his crooked legs, his hard toil at the forge, and oh, the soul of him that rises so bravely in song over all his misfortunes and reaches—I am sure—to the gates of the eternal ways, where angels listen and find his singing sweet, be his voice as crude and barren as it may! But whether you laugh or weep at him, if you do it sensibly, it requires vision, imagination, for either. Or, maybe it is this way: He who laughs is he who sees a stray fragment of life ludicrously unfitted to that large perfection of God's universe that our ideals demand; he sees the farce, and laughs. And he who weeps sees the same thing, only from the tragic side; he cannot get his soul away from the defeat that the finite years always bring as we dream of the distant goal. Thus it is that we can laugh and weep at the same things, for they have both the comic side and the tragic side, to suit our moods. But for us mortals, tears mean more.

Weeping is laughter's second thought.

The greatest geniuses among poets and dramatists and novelists and orators are they who can merge both humor and pathos in their art. They furnish both laughter and tears for all the ages.

Ah, but the good God, who sees all clearly, He neither laughs, nor does He weep. For He sees both sides at once, the ultimate triumph, yes, and the endless defeat, too, of our poor hearts; He sees and understands, and although He laughs or weeps not, He ever sympathizes in His pervasive love with all our honest laughter and all our honest tears.

Still, when I thought Monsieur Ware was ridiculing us Gascons and our wooden shoes, and I became indignant about it, I was perfectly right to become indignant. For his was the ridicule of ignorance and not of understanding. And that makes all the difference in the world, as any one can see. However, it turned out that he did not mean to make fun of us in the way I at first supposed, so I will not make too great a point of the matter.

Chapter XVIII: *Cabbage Plants and People*

I HAVE been working on that little pavilion of mine at the top of my garden by the big pine tree. At least, little Renée's father—he is somewhat of a carpenter—has started it for me. He began this morning, and there has been an unwonted noise of sawing and hammering and slamming of boards and even snatches of song in patois, which broke in upon my usual quiet, so that I could neither write nor study. Besides, it was necessary that I stand about and direct things, else all would have gone wrong. One cannot trust matters of taste to others; moreover, I have no plan of this little pavilion, except in my own head, and even this plan has been a trifle vague in some particulars. I like to see such things grow naturally, without too much hurrying, like a tree.

However, Renée's father could not come back in the afternoon, as he had to attend to his vineyard, which needed spraying, so he said. So I went back to my garden after dinner, intending to spend some quiet hours in my garden-house, writing. But I could not write a word, having lost the mood, for somehow the noise of the carpentry still echoed in my head.

It was then that I recollected that it was Monday. And this gave me a happy thought. For Monday is market-day in our village, and I was reminded that I needed some cabbage plants for my garden. Then, too, there is nothing I like better than to go to the Place on market-days and mingle with the peasants that come in from miles around.

My stricken friend, the Abbé Rivoire, is like me in this. He lately wrote me that if he could have been at that fête at Margouet, he would have been more interested in the people than in their games. He ought to see our Place on market-days! Here I greet many old acquaintances from the country and talk with them about recent happenings and, perhaps, about old times. I hoped especially that to-day it might be my good fortune to see my old friend, Marius Fontan. He has a manuscript I wanted to ask him about.

As I made my way from my garden toward the Street of the Church, I noticed several teams of oxen hitched to their carts, standing peacefully in the shade by the cemetery wall. In some of the carts were chairs in which the peasants had brought their women folks. In the bottom of one of these carts, lying in the clean straw, there was a diminutive, rosy-cheeked girl, with a red ribbon in her hair, sleeping. What, I thought, is more sweetly mysterious than a little child, sleeping like that, with its tiny hands, half open and half shut, and its face full of that peace of God which only very little children or very old people know!

Our Place is at its very best on market-day. The merchants come from all the villages around, and like magic their white awnings spring up in every available space, with tempting merchandise spread under them on tables, or even on the ground for that matter, only then they put a canvas over the ground first. It is as though one had rubbed Aladdin's lamp and *voila!* our peaceful, prosaic square had suddenly become a great mart of trade, a city of tents! No wonder the more ambitious of our village have been bold enough to call our Place the "Place du Commerce!" It almost deserves that name on market-day!

And how genially the mild June sun shone down to-day on the canvas coverings placed at every rakish angle, on the plastered fronts of the two rows of shops, on the east side of the Place; on the old, rickety arcades, too, on the north side, venturing in under their weather-worn pillars and revealing the shop of the barber, and the grain store, and the courier's office, at other times of the day quite dark under the projecting upper stories! Here, there, and everywhere, peasant men and women and children threading their way hither and thither, greeting each other noisily, and chattering and bargaining without limit. And over the clatter of wooden shoes and buzzing of voices, one heard the calls of the more aggressive of the merchants, all mingled in one riotous hubbub.

"*Regardez! Regardez!*"

"Come and see these fine shirts, only five francs!"

"*Voyez, Messieurs et Dames!*"

"Nice kitchenware, quite cheap!"

"*Venez voir!* Look at these sashes!"

It is the merchant from Riscle who is making the most noise. His booth is just in front of the town hall, and he is selling all kinds of ready-made articles for the men—long, wide sashes, red and blue, work-shirts of a nondescript color, blue smocks, cotton trousers, and heavy socks. Oh, he has a fine assortment! The women are not forgotten either, for there is the man from Eauze with a long table filled with gay ribbons, laces by the yard (very cheap imitations, one may be sure), collars of lace, and fancy braids, and other things I do not even know the names of. Then, right beside him is a great giant of a fellow from Plaisance, with all sorts of materials for dresses, such as black satine, which the older country women like to wear in summer; and for the younger girls, ginghams, and voiles, and chambrays, all in bright colors. Do you need household linen, Madame? Well, here it is; and here, Monsieur, is heavy canvas of which Madame may make covers for your oxen.

If you want to get into the shade, you can wander over to the west side of the Place and find plenty to see as well. Under the cool arcades of the town hall is the grain market. Solid, well-to-do merchants you see here, displaying their maize and oats and wheat, and sack on sack of good, honest potatoes. And near by is the most interesting part of all, the long row of peasant women on the narrow sidewalk and along the curb, with vegetables and fruits, which make a man hungry just to contemplate them! Luscious, yellow plums and the last, lingering strawberries; and all these fresh vegetables were raised by these women in their own gardens—lettuce, and radishes, and onions, and string beans, and eggplants, and artichokes. Good old Marinette is here with the most attractive assortment of all, although she probably has the tiniest garden of any of them; but Marinette, after all is said and done, is a wonderful woman in her way! And here at a corner of the curb is the old gardener from Dému, with his garden-plants spread on the ground, all ready to set out. I shall see him about those winter cabbages before I go home.

I like to plant things in my garden. To place these living thoughts of nature in the fertile ground and see them grow—what is greater happiness than that?

I had turned the corner of the arcades and had just passed the barber's, when I came upon a group of girls, some seated and some standing, in front of Colette Rozies' grain store, just back of where the pastry-man from Nogaro had spread his table. There was Colette herself, talking in a most animated way with Yvonne, her cousin. Yvonne does not belong to our village. She comes to visit Colette from down on the coast, near Spain. Colette, by the way, is one of these bold, stately beauties, a pronounced brunette, with large, languid eyes, which are very conscious of their power over the young gallants.

I did not tarry near this group of young people

longer than to answer their greeting; for, as soon
as they saw me, their chattering ceased, and they
looked a little guilty, as if they had been saying things
they did not want me to hear. I passed on out of
the arcades, close by the stand of the pastry-man,
who was doing a thriving business in éclairs and
ring-cakes and those triangular tarts, filled with
cream, known as Jesuits.

I hold that a man who sells pastry should have
an inviting face, to match the fascinating quality of
his wares; but this man had a face that would rumple
with disgust the surface-calm of any soul. Perhaps, though, I was in no mood to judge faces just
then, for I had overheard Colette say something
that was not meant to reach my ears, and which
troubled me considerably, imperturbable as I try to
be, both as a priest and as a philosopher, in the
presence of idle talk.

Chapter XIX: *Gossip*

I WAS probably unjust to the pastry-man's face, since, I confess, I was angry. For what I overheard Colette saying was about Germaine Sance and the American, David Ware. She as much as hinted that it was no wonder that this foreigner lingered on in our part of the world, and that there would be a wedding before long that would surprise some people.

I have already expressed my thoughts about this subject. Ordinarily, I have not paid much attention to the gossip of the women of our village, which is mostly without foundation, anyway. But to hear Colette say such things was different. For Colette is supposed to be a great friend of Germaine's, and they talk over many things together, and anything that Colette says is likely to be believed. I was vexed with her that she should speak of such matters so publicly; besides, I knew what she said was not true. No, I could not and would not believe it.

As I turned away from the pastry-man, I happened to look over toward the bazaar-booth in the very middle of the Place, and there was Monsieur Ware himself, with his invalid sister leaning upon his arm, looking at the gay array of toys and the knickknacks for the ladies, which a man from Marciac always brings on market-day. I suppose Colette and the girls had seen the American there, which would account for their whisperings and covert glances in that direction. Somehow, I found myself moving that way. As I passed the booth of the shoe merchant from Maubourget, I heard a tremendous sneeze; looking up, I saw that it was the portly Aurignac from Riscle, who is a deputy and a red republican. Monsieur Fitte, the notary, who has a sense of humor, happened to greet me at that moment and remarked, noticing the direction of my glance,

"That is the great orator sneezing; even in his sneezing he is eloquent!"

"I prefer it to his speeches," said I, and passed on.

Although I had no great desire to talk to Monsieur Ware, I soon found myself quite near him. He and his sister, a pale, sweet-faced woman, with refinement and suffering written in every feature, were absorbed in looking at the little wooden horses, bisque dolls, pepper mills, combs, purses, school-bags, and pencil boxes—such an incredible miscellany of things as makes the bazaar-booth the most attractive of all.

The first thing I knew, Monsieur Ware had smilingly introduced me to his sister.

I ventured to say that he and his sister must find it rather dull here after the great cities, like New York and London and Paris.

"On the contrary! I don't know where in all the world I have ever seen just such a sight as this Place of yours on market-day!"

"Hardly a lyric, however," said I, thinking of the wooden shoes and Monsieur Ware's projected poem about them.

"No, not a lyric—but if I were a writer of plays, well, that would be different!—My sister and I are having the time of our lives!"

I noticed that Monsieur Ware had already bought something—at least he had a parcel in his hand. He saw my glance wandering toward it, and he at once began to unwrap it, and finally revealed a bright red sash and a *béret*.

"Another memento of your peasants," he remarked, while his sister laughed at his boyish eagerness. "Now I am all equipped—sabots, sash, *béret*. I shall show them what a Gascon peasant is like when I get home—what do you say, Emma?"

"I say, Monsieur l'Abbé, that my brother pays about twice as much as anybody else for the things he gets here. He just pays them what they ask— which shows what an impractical dreamer my big brother is!"

I had my own opinion of how much that same brother would look like a Gascon peasant, even if he put on a million sashes and *bérets*. It takes more than these things to make a Gascon, I can tell you!

I called the attention of Monsieur Ware and his sister to a tall, stalwart man from Vic-Fezensac, who stood by his display of hardware—skillets, iron

pots, earthenware dishes, and water jugs. He had a
rugged, weathered face, with something of nobility
in it. He wore the remnants of a uniform, and I
personally knew that he had received the *croix de
guerre* with a palm for great heroism, although he
was but an ordinary poilu in the war. His thoughts
seemed to be far away from his merchandise. Standing in the trenches, I thought, after a night of weary
vigil, he often dreamed of home and peace; but now,
home again—ah, is it not so?—he often pauses as
he does now, longing for those heroic and glamorous
days when he was a soldier of France!

That is the way life is.

Over on the sunny side of the Place, the shops
were doing a steady business. People were lounging
in and out of the tobacco shop; the Au Bon Marché
had its best goods displayed in its windows;
the cafés were full, especially the popular Café Ladouès, where the fair Élise serves at the tables.
Here a crowd was gathered about the one billiard
table, for two favorite toreadors were competing for
supremacy in a game much too mild for such swaggering champions of the arena. There was much
talking and laughter and good-natured bantering
about them, and incessant trays of drinks, from mild
orgeat and lemonade to cognac and armagnac.
Poor Élise will be weary enough by sunset, but you
would not think it, seeing her bustling hither and
thither with a smile for everybody.

A little farther on, emerging from the doorway of
a cheap barroom, I saw a girl of our village, her
cheeks rouged, and dressed in a flagrant way. The

effort to make her eyes look bold betrayed the guilt that weighed them down, for she is not yet entirely shameless. She lives with her lover at Toulouse, but sometimes visits her mother here.

In front of the big merchandise store, one always sees tiny Pauline, who has never grown up and is always strapped in her little chair by the doorway. Her mind is not quite right; but always she is smiling and greets everybody that comes with outstretched hand and eager eyes. She has been getting worse lately, and as I passed, I saw the doctor talking with the mother and writing a prescription for the pharmacist. I noticed that the little doctor had a new kind of prescription blank, with his name neatly typed in the corner. I saw this because the little doctor showed one to me, telling me at the same time that a number had been done for him by Monsieur Ware on his American typewriting machine.

We ought to have a printer in Aignan.

Monsieur Ware must be getting very friendly indeed with the Sance household.

Could there be anything at all—the least thing— in that foolish talk of Colette?

I had about come to the conclusion that I would not see Marius Fontan to-day, when I happened to look toward the tobacco shop, and there, by the wall, oblivious to the crowd moving about him, I saw Marius standing, his eyes on the ground and his hands behind his back. It was not until I was quite close to him and spoke to him that he saw me, and then with a start.

"You look as though you had just come from

Pampelune!" I said. And, indeed, Marius' mind is most of the time in Pampelune—that name we Gascons so often use for the place of dreams.

"Oh, it is you, Monsieur l'Abbé! Yes, I have been standing here quite awhile, I suppose. You see, Monsieur l'Abbé, as you know, I am writing a little something about our village as it was long ago. Pardon, Monsieur l'Abbé, I was thinking about that and forgot everything else for a few little moments here. No, I did not see you!"

I told him that it was about that very writing I wanted to talk with him.

"I am nearly done. If you will let me, I will fetch it to you in a few days, so you can see what I have put down. It will never be very complete; it is a calamity that the papers in the town hall were burned that time."

I like to hear Marius talk about old times, so I remarked something about the ancient market-hall that was torn down when I was a boy.

"Our Place was different in those days, Monsieur l'Abbé. There was the old tower of the dungeon, too. The market-hall stood just there.—It was built in the Middle Ages, although it was only of wood. A big, five-sided building it was, where the drapers and weavers displayed their goods on long rows of tables. The village made money out of it, too; it was rented every nine years to the highest bidder; he sold space to the merchants from all the towns."

"The arcades over there will be the next things to go," said I.

"It will be a pity. They are getting old. Well,

they will last as long as I will, Monsieur l'Abbé!"

About the old donjon-tower Marius mentioned, he and I have always had a quarrel. I maintain that the tower fell of itself, for the simple reason that it was too decrepit to stand any longer. Marius holds that it was demolished by the council because, they said, it had grown to be a menace; and Marius says the council was wrong and that it was no menace at all, but was strong enough to have stood for a long time. And he says this was proved by the great difficulty they had in tearing it down. But I know differently. I know that the tower had a big crevice in it that was growing wider every day, and that the grandfather of Germaine Sance proved how dangerous the tower was in the following way. One night he pasted a paper over the great crack, and the very next morning this crack had increased so much that the paper was torn in two, straight down the middle! Grandfather Sance had reason to be concerned, because his house was very near the tower —it was that one on the west side of the Place, in front of which the women now sell their vegetables.

But Marius will not listen to any of this. On one thing, however, we both agree. This is that the old tower should have been kept standing in some way, as a reminder of the ancient days. We are at one concerning that!

I told Marius that instead of waiting for him to bring his manuscript to me, I might walk out to his place soon to get it. Marius is becoming old, and the walk to Aignan is rather far from where he lives. Besides, I want to see for myself if he is in such a wretched condition as people say he is. I shall take him a package of tobacco. I must not forget that.

It was getting nearly five o'clock, so I parted from Marius to hunt up the gardener from Dému and get those winter cabbage plants I had set out for in the first place. While I was picking them out, I happened to look up, and there over by Marinette's display of vegetables, I saw Germaine and her mother doing their marketing, little Renée carrying the basket, almost as big as herself. Before I left, I saw Monsieur Ware and his sister join them. I observed that they were already engaged in a lively conversation, so I did not stop to speak with them. Instead, very thoughtfully, I made my way homeward.

While passing the covered poultry market, up the Street of the Church, I chanced to meet Henri, with his violin under his arm, going to practice with our young postmaster, who ought to be attending to his business instead. At almost any hour of the day you can hear the thin wail of a violin from the windows of the post office.

I suppose I should not have revealed what I had on my mind to Henri, but I could not help it. I even went so far as to ask him if there was anything between his sister Germaine and his good friend Monsieur Ware. I asked it carelessly, it is true, and not so directly as I write it here, but in a roundabout way, for I did not want to appear as if it was of much consequence, or that I was intruding into what was really not my concern.

Henri is very open and frank with me, and he merely said,

"I asked Germaine the other day if she liked Monsieur Ware, and she said, 'Yes.' She did not say anything more."

Later, I started out into the country to take dinner with my sister. On the road were many people going home from market—some on foot, some in ox carts, some with loaves of bread on their heads, some with live geese and ducks and chickens from the poultry market, and one man with more liquid in his stomach than was good for his legs. All the way I was vexed to find myself meditating on what Germaine had replied to that question of Henri's concerning Monsieur Ware.

She had said, "Yes." Still, that might not mean much. There are so many ways of saying, "Yes." One may say, "Yes," with a rising or falling inflection; with a sigh, or with clear downrightness; with tears or with laughter; lingeringly or decisively; curtly or caressingly.

"Henri did not tell me much," I said to myself.

I sometimes think that I am getting old and meddlesome. Yet what are our lives save as they are caught in the drama of the lives about us—the lives of those that are dear to us?

Chapter XX: *At Night*

IT was late when I came home from my sister's farm. As I was crossing the Place, lighted only by the stars, every footstep of mine echoed loudly, and I thought how different everything looked as compared with a few hours before, when this same Place was thronged with people, and the sun shone bright on the busy scene. Now all this riot of life was gone, and our public square was a place of dreams and shadows and a brooding peace.

How dark it was under the arcades where the sun was so lately streaming, and how mysterious the black shadows under the starlit pillars! In the daytime, these pillars were of ordinary wood, eaten away by time and weather-stained; but now, under the dim light of the stars, they might be of fairest marble!

I stood for a moment in the darkness in front of Grandfather Sance's old house—the same house that was once in danger from the ancient tower—the very house in which Germaine was born—and contemplated the quiet scene. The bell of the *mairie,* thin-toned, shallow, and unresonant, startled the silence with the stroke of the half hour. It was half-past nine, then. From a distant street came the bark of a dog. Once or twice a scarcely distinguishable form glided across the Place to the village pump, which suddenly raised a thousand echoes with its creaking and rattling. Then vanishing footsteps and silence, deeper than before.

From the windows of Rigot's café shine dim lights. And from the dark bench in front come the subdued voices of three or four men. One of them strikes a match, and I can see his face; it is Bajac, the butcher.

Now the moon has risen high enough so that the heavy wooden shutters of the houses, some closed, some half open, reflect the gray light on their blank surfaces. Above the low roofs, the church tower is a thing of silver gleams and vague shadows. Down the dark walls of the Duc d'Armagnac's ancient house the moonlight slowly feels its way until it strikes the ornate outlines of the window in which legend says the Duc de Bouillon lost his life.

A muffled sound of footsteps comes from the Street of the Church toward the Place. It is the girls going back to the convent school, two by two. They have been to evening prayer, before the altar of the Sacred Heart of Jesus. They cross the Place and descend the road to the south.

Then silence again. The men in front of Rigot's café have gone home. No one will come to the pump again to-night. The silence broods. Suddenly, thin and clear, like a muffled dulcimer, is heard the staccato notes of the toads, each sounding its plaint on a different key, one after another, rhythmically, with a slight pause between. According to the children, they are saying to each other:

> *"Tioc! Tioc!*
> *Has esclops?"*
> *"Nou!"*
> *"Tu?"*
> *"Jou tapoc!"*

The toads carry on their conversation in patois, so only the peasant children understand them; but what they really say in plain English is:

> *"Tioc! Tioc!*
> *Have you sabots?"*
> *"No!"*
> *"And you?"*
> *"Neither have I!"*

So, having no sabots, they cannot go and visit each other—alas!

And now I move out from the darkness and cross the deserted Place homeward. I look up. How bright the stars are shining! And how many, how many there are to-night! They are never so many and never so bright as when they shine over this, my native village. I have looked at them in many places, and this I know.

I enter the narrow, winding street that leads to my house. It is darker here. There are mysterious shadows here. A few windows still send out the dim rays of oil lamps. A door opens on the other side of the street—a sudden patch of light—then darkness—but not until I have glanced within; the harness-maker is reading a newspaper by the rude table in his kitchen. What a huge shadow of him the lamplight casts on the rough walls! From one of the projecting upper stories is seen the glow of a cigarette. Some one is leaning out into the night, perhaps indulging in dreams like myself. I note that just under this is the dark outline of the sign of the wooden shoe in front of the sabot-maker's shop. So it is Paul Sarrade behind that tiny glow, for even a sabot-maker has his dreams, and the night can glorify the world for him, too!

If Monsieur Ware really wants a lyric, let him walk through our village streets on a night like this; or, better still, let him come to my garden. How often have I stood on the summit and looked out over the brooding hills in the starlight! Gray ghosts of hills they are, softly looming through a gentle haze—God's good hills that lie in quiet sleep; only, if you look at them long and long, their dim breasts seem slowly to move with the secret of a dream. How dark the great forest looks on its hills to the north! *It* sleeps not; it merely waits, like a thing of foreboding; yet through its dense trees, if we were there to see, some starlight surely sifts its silvery way to its ancient and gloomy heart.

But look through the darkness along that high ridge of hills to the east. A faint glow slowly burns along the far summits. It looks like the reflection of the Blessed City where there shall be no more tears and where former things shall have passed away. Lo, the golden light grows brighter and spreads like the wings of an archangel across the hill tops—and suddenly, to the thrill of all being, the tip of a golden sphere rises over the hills and, slowly lifting its blazing circle above the charmed valley, rolls majestically up the sky for the wonder of half a world!

It is moonrise in Gascony!

See this miracle of light floating up the sky with no support save the inexorable laws of nature—and what are they? Oh, the wonder of it all! On that same moon as the lantern of God, Moses looked as he wandered in the wilderness. From imperial roofs, kings have gazed upon it, marveling, suddenly aware of things that set at nought all glory, even such as theirs. Perhaps from Judea's desert places the Divine Savior raised His eyes to this same wonder, and then looked down in sadness, the shadows of our human sins mingling with the silver shadows at His feet. How many men have climbed the steep road of life since then! This same moon has seen the birth and death of every one; they have vanished— but still she conquers the night as of old.

If ever you are forsaken and homeless and no more friends are left you in this world, and your heart is sick with the sadness of it all, go forth into the night and look at the silent moon! The moon you looked at in boyhood through the poplar trees, or over the high-roofed barn, or from your bedroom window; the moon, under whose silver benediction you once walked with friends now haply dead; the moon, which shines over the graves of hopes and memories all the way back over those years that have brought you so far, so far! Look up to the sky and see her—she is the same old friend; she is watching over you yet!

Ah, the love of God, who gives such glories unto men that they may be mindful of Him and forget Him not.

Oh, the wonder of it all, the mystery of it all! Let us sometimes pause in our frantic efforts to explain. Let us sometimes cast aside our poor human philosophy, and stand under the pure white of the stars and simply wonder!

I hold that each day should be a great event in itself, even though nothing else but the day happen to you. But the night is more than an event. As you stand beneath the glory of such a night as this, some mysterious ecstasy, something of growth, is added to your soul. The sky is no longer a sky that in the daytime seemed to cover you—it is an endless space! To me, the night seems deeper than the day —richer, more vibrant, nearer to the reality that underlies all things, compared with which the sights and sounds of the brazen day are but superficial glamour. At night, the imagination is set free from her trammels. The soul is no longer the prisoner of a planet; it takes on wings, it soars. During the day, we were citizens of the world; at night, we are citizens of the universe. It is then that the eternal seems to draw us silently, tenderly, surely, into its awful presence. Is it not strange that night should have been considered the symbol of ignorance, when it is more truly the symbol of a deeper knowledge, to which it opens colossal gates? Yes, night swings ajar for us the doors of the infinite, so that we dimly see the shadows of God's purposes march by —all that has been and evermore shall be. Mysterious night! Symbol of the three mysteries: the Soul, Death, and God! No wonder that cathedrals imitate thy dim shadows and thy brooding silences; and their flickering altar lights thy stars!

Sometimes, on starlit nights, I walk from my house down the road, on past the church and the cemetery, to my garden, to muse before going to bed. As I pass the church, I hear the soft, cottony flight of the owls as they go from place to place among the ruined masonry. Most often, when I reach my garden, I do not enter, but stand on the silent road in front, thinking many things. The murmur of the poplars by the roadside is like a distant, summer sea. But the tall cypresses near by in the cemetery, they are motionless and still. When the moonlight caresses them, how lovely their soft lights and shadows! They sing to the sight.

As I walk back past the cemetery, I look within the high iron gates. The great wooden cross where hangs the life-size image of the Blessed Son of God is transfigured as it rises in the center of the graves. The moonlight falls obliquely upon the face of the Man of Sorrows; it gleams on His crown of thorns, on His widestretched arms that reach out over those who sleep beneath the long grasses.

At the turn of the road, a little farther on, is the tallest poplar tree of all. How stately it is! And never so stately as at night, when it moves its head majestically to the incantation of the winds, or answers the breeze like Æolus' harp in days of old, or sings in the moonlight like some giant minstrel in the palace-court of God. Often, as a boy, I guided my way home by the beckon of this same tree as it talked with the stars, its friends for lo, these many years.

Perhaps we, too, may yet be worthy to talk with stars.

Chapter XXI: *St. John's Eve*

M Y faithful friend, the Abbé Rivoire, writes me that he is no better; he cannot even be taken out in his wheel chair to his garden. And yet we are in the midst of that part of the summer whose mystery is most enchanting—when the days lengthen to the longest day of all; when the year, like a deep-flowing river, widens to its greatest glory, and pauses for a moment between Time's banks, as if listening for some ineffable secret. There is a saying I learned when a boy; it tells how the days gradually increase in length, beginning with St. Luce's Day, just before Christmas, until June 24, St. John's Day, the longest day. As I remember it, the days begin to get longer like this:

> *At the day of St. Luce,*
>   *The hop of a flea;*
> *At Christmas,*
>   *The leap of a calf;*
> *At New Year,*
>   *The flight of a cockerel;*
> *At St. Antoine's Day,*
>   *The length of a monk's dinner—*

163

Which, therefore, must be rather brief and frugal, since St. Antoine's Day comes early in the year. I perceive now that I can recollect only the commencement of this saying, which has a great deal more to it, since it ends not until St. John's Day is reached. But another thing I call to mind: They used to tell me as a boy that if I would put a bottle in the sun on St. John's Day, there would be a time in the middle of the day when the sun's rays would go straight down through the neck, perpendicularly, to the center of the bottom, and strike the silver coin that has been placed there. I tried it once, so I know that this is true, or almost true.

We pay much more attention to St. John's Day down here in Gascony than I could observe them doing up around Paris. It is an ancient habit to engage servants on St. John's Day. Soon they will be needed for the harvest. In the old time it was not infrequent that some one who was going on a journey would remark, "I will return on St. John's Day." In one of our patois ballads there is a Count who goes away to the wars:

"For St. John's Feast," Count Arnaud said,
"I shall come back, alive or dead."

Then, on the morn of St. John's Day, Count Arnaud's mother climbs to the tower window, watching for her brave son's return. There at last he comes!—but what is this?—ah, Mother of God! he rides slowly between two stranger knights, sorely hurt, yes, wounded unto death.

"Oh, make the pillows soft for me,
But do not let my lady see."

"O Count Arnaud, your lady true
Has borne a fair young son to you."

Alas, the ballad goes on to sing his bitter death;
and, just as his dear lady comes to mass, all unknow-
ing of her fate, the body of her lover is lowered into
his tomb. Grief-stricken, she flings herself into the
open grave with him, and over the lovers, forever
inseparable, the cruel earth closes.

It is a sad song, like so many of our Gascon ballads. To hear it at its best, one must hear Marius
Fontan sing it.

Market-day was Monday; and now it was Wed-
nesday. I happened to meet Monsieur Ware in the
morning on my way to the post office, and I
told him that if he and his sister cared about it, this
very evening would be St. John's Eve, when they
could see the procession from the church and the
ancient custom that is observed afterwards, which I
thought would appeal to Monsieur Ware's temperament, he being somewhat of a poet. I told him that
when it was dark, he should, by all means, be at the
ox-market on the south side of the village, not far
from the Château de Lasalle, where he lives.

This ox-market is a large space, used chiefly on
fair-days, about four times a year. There are
great, old trees there, and then a considerable open
place, too, somewhat elevated, from the edge of
which one can get a wide view of the rolling valleys

and hills to the east and south. It is there that the great event of St. John's Eve occurs.

One could tell that something unusual was going to happen by the fact that during the day a number of boys were going about everywhere gathering fagots and dry branches and everything else that would burn. To nearly all the houses of the village they went, asking everybody to contribute what they could. So that by sunset a huge pile of inflammable material had been heaped in the middle of the ox-market.

When the bell of the town hall was striking nine o'clock, the twilight was deepening into darkness, the moon was getting slowly brighter in a clear sky, and the stars were becoming gradually visible, first one by one, and then by countless multitudes. There was scarcely any breeze at all.

Then the deeper-toned bell from the church tower echoed over the quiet roofs and out over the valleys. Slowly from the church the procession came, winding down the Street of the Church toward the Place. Many children were in the procession, and at the end of it was our old priest, the Abbé Castex, with his white surplice over his cassock, walking as he always does, his head bent forward and a little on one side, and one hand behind his back. Following him was the lame blacksmith, loudly singing the responses.

At length the procession arrived at the ox-market, where the people of the whole commune—those not in the procession itself—were gathered, waiting in the dark. One knew that there were a great many there by the sounds of their voices, subdued to a low murmur as the procession approached. Back of them was the dense darkness of the trees, but the moonlight was strong enough to reveal the moving mass of human forms gathered in an irregular circle about the pile of fagots, now almost as high as the convent school, whose dim, white gables could be seen through the trees toward the village.

A tall figure moves out from the circling crowd, in which the procession has now lost itself. It is the priest. The faint, sputtering glow of a sulphur match—the priest bends low toward the fagots—a little flame springs up—the priest makes the sign of the cross and steps back—the flames spread rapidly, with a crackling noise—they speed hungrily up the dry branches—they race toward the top—the faces of the great crowd suddenly spring into sight, the dancing lights contorting them weirdly—the eager flames mount higher and higher, they roar, they leap, they exult, they reach for the sky! The crowd moves hastily back toward the fringe of trees, whose outermost leaves begin to writhe and curl in the heat, and whose far shades are transfigured by the dancing flames into a strange fairyland of lights and shadows.

After awhile, when the fire burns down a little, one will see some interesting sights. One will see old men and women move as close to the fire as they can. They are in groups of two or three. First, they face the fire; then, one will casually say to his neighbor,

"This old fire is getting pretty warm!"

This will serve as an excuse for them to turn their sides and then their backs to the fire. If one watches them for a time, one will notice that they go through this performance quite often. One will also observe that they move rather stiffly, and that some of them are quite crippled with rheumatism. These have come, several of them, from far away in the country, because they know that if one stands in front of the fire blessed by the priest on St. John's Eve, and exposes himself on all sides, he may be cured. Poor old men and women! Some have suffered much in walking so great a distance, but a faint hope and faith is in their hearts—and who knows what the good God may do for them in His divine pity?

Others, mostly women, take pains to warm their backs thoroughly so they will not get lame bending over to bind the sheaves at harvest time. Then, when the fire has burned very low indeed, so that the flames are only a meter or so high, it is the turn of the boys, to whom it is great sport to vie with each other in jumping over the fire without getting burned. Even this leaping through the fire has its origin in ancient custom, for it was once believed that boils could be prevented in this way. But the boys know nothing of this—for them it is merely a game, as with much bravado and shouting they leap through the flames, looking for all the world like little devils as they pass through, their legs held close under them and their faces twisted with eery lights.

And now, when the fire is almost out, and the

crowd is beginning to move homeward, a number approach and seize upon some of the charred branches, which they carry away with them. An ember from the fire of St. John's Eve is very potent to keep the lightning from one's house, if it is placed on the roof. From the night of time, this has been so.

I myself did not wait to watch all this, for just as the fire was beginning to burn brightly, it lighted up the tall form of Monsieur Ware as he stood somewhat apart from the crowd, over by the trees. He was alone. I went over to him and led him away from the fire some little distance into the darkness, until we stood on the far edge of the ox-market, and could look out on the hills and valleys to the east and south.

I am sure that Monsieur Ware did not anticipate in the least the strange sight that greeted his eyes; for, after uttering an exclamation of wonder, he kept silent for quite awhile, contemplating the great amphitheater of space inclosed by the wide sweep of the eastern horizon. On all the surrounding hills, far, far into the distance, great fires like our own had been kindled. On every hill where there was a village, there burned a fire; and down in the valleys, too, fires sprang up, for not all our villages are on hills. And even where there was no village—only a little neighborhood of houses, as on the high hill of the Bethaut—even there the flames were rising. And besides the fires, one could glimpse the glow and roseate smoke of other fires beyond the hills that hid them.

Those countless beacons, aspiring to the sky, dotting the landscape in all directions, with darkness in between them, and a veiled moon overhead, give one the impression of being suddenly translated to another world—the whole scene strikes one as incredible, unearthly, supernatural, something of a miracle.

As you watch, you begin to perceive the truth. To-night all these hills, these villages, are united in a common bond of sympathy. They are many, and yet they are one. It is their reunion. Through these fires, they are recognizing one another, they are fraternizing with one another; old differences are forgotten, and they speak. They are signaling each other, they are hailing each other.

Yes, that is the truth which gradually dawns on you as you look at these beacons that spread to the far horizon. These fires are not merely fires, they have something of intent and meaning. They are struggling for utterance. These villages are persons, calling to one another, attracting the attention of one another. This is what they say:

"I had a great fête this year. Never was a fête like mine this time!"

It is Lupiac, speaking from its high hill, straight across the valleys to the east.

A little fire signals feebly from a far hill to the south.

"I am lonely on my hill. My brother village across the valley is gone. The tower of its church was torn down the other day."

Another beacon springs suddenly into being toward the north. The wind sways it gracefully,

"I am more beautiful this year than ever I was before. Perhaps you will get a reflection of my new steeple from my splendid fire!"

All the rest of the year, these villages are silent, dreaming, brooding, morose, lost in the wide expanse, each in its own sequestered place. But now each is a comrade among comrades.

Some of them like to speak of the past:

"I was great once, but pestilence came."

"Henry IV stopped my way once; the very house still stands."

"There was a day when my grain helped feed the armies of France!"

"Nothing has ever happened to me. I am always peaceful on my little hill. My children love me."

You observe that each one of these countless fires has its individuality. Some, on the loftier hills, are blown by a gentle wind. Some burn steadily upward, calm and still. Some rise high and thin. Some flare up vigorously and quickly die down. There is the biggest fire and the smallest fire. And they are of all shades of red and yellow and orange and gold.

Sometimes they say sad things, such as:

"There is no longer a priest here. But maybe the good God will come again and rebuild His broken altar. I wait."

Or, "My forest has gone. They are burning the last of the old trees to-night."

Or, "My dead are neglected."

Gradually the fires waver and break. The farthest fires have diminished to dim, uncertain glows. Far Auriebat on its high hill—the farthest of all—signals that all is well in its great valley of the Adour and sinks into blackness.

One looks up from the dying fires on earth to the undying fires in the heavens. The stars—they have seen and answered, too; the stars, God's fires that burn there in His infinite valleys— they speak nightly to each other and never go out. They, too, have seen and answered, only theirs is an infinite pity; for they were here, oh, so long before these little villages came into being on their hills; long before there were forests, and wild gorse, and broom, and rivers singing their way to the sea. They saw these same villages when they were girt with walls and towers, beleaguered by strange armies; when heroic deeds were done; when the castles of the lords rose proudly and defiantly, and the bells of the churches first rang out their holy call. I say the stars feel pity (and I hope regret), for they will be here when these poor villages shall have vanished like their fires, and shall have joined their men and women in the dust.

I tried to say some of these things to Monsieur Ware; but he did not respond. He was no doubt thinking his own thoughts. Yet, although it was out of his way, he insisted upon walking with me as far as my house, smoking his pipe. On parting, we shook hands very warmly, and I could not but feel that somehow we were friends.

As I stood in my door for a moment before going up to bed, the moon came from behind its cloud, and a breeze whispered faintly along the shadows of our little street.

Chapter XXII: *Old Abbé Castex*

AS I write about the happenings of our village, I find myself mentioning the old Abbé Castex from time to time, as is natural, since the curé of a village is one of its most important and conspicuous personages. This forenoon, as I was going toward my house, Monsieur le Curé was toiling slowly up the road to the church. I stood for a moment, waiting to greet him, for he did not yet see me. As he labored up the Street of the Balustrade, it seemed to me that he looked older and more decrepit than usual. It even occurred to me that he, of all others, might have been tempted to warm himself by the great fire on St. John's Eve, for his rheumatism was so bad that only with great difficulty could he bend over to apply the match to the fagots.

Undeniably, our old curé was walking up the hill more slowly than usual this morning. His tall form was bent forward, his left hand held behind his back, his right resting on a stout cane, which was extended at an angle from his body the better to support his large frame. He was wearing that old, rusty hat of his, and a cassock almost green with age, especially where the sunlight struck it. As he came nearer, I thought that his face looked pale and weary.

The Abbé Castex has an interesting face, some would say a strong face. It is rugged in its outlines, somewhat long and angular, with high cheek-bones and a large chin. His head is quite flat at the back, and narrows up to a shape resembling the end of an egg. His sparse hair is long and straight and almost white, with ragged wisps that reach out from behind his ears and over his collar.

As the good curé came up at last to where I was, he nodded, and then rested a moment before he could get breath to greet me in words. Any one hearing him speak for the first time would remark how deep and rough his voice is, vibrating something like a loose drumhead; it is rather inarticulate, too, perhaps because so many of his teeth are gone. Nowadays, when the curé makes the announcements for the week, one must listen very closely to know what he is saying. As for his sermons, one usually catches only a word here and there, although sometimes a whole sentence becomes clear, since he is likely to repeat himself often.

It is plain that the Abbé Castex is about worn out, though, as Monsieur Rigot said the other day (intending to be humorous), what has worn him out it is hard to tell. After all, he is not so old as some priests around here, being only seventy.

In this connection, I am reminded of a remark of our Montaigne: "It is the body which sometimes yieldeth first unto age; and other times the mind: and I have seen many that have had their brains weakened before their stomach or legs."

Our curé still has a good appetite, so it is not his

stomach. As for the rest of him, it is hard to say which is yielding first. I doubt that it is one thing rather than another, much as I wish I could say that his mind is still as clear as ever.

Lately, they have got to telling many absurd stories about the old curé, none of which I am any too willing to believe. The one that I credit least is the one about his forgetfulness a few weeks ago when he was saying a mass.

The way they tell it is as follows:

Two of our well-known families, the Capérans and the Lacostes, each had made an arrangement with the curé to say a mass for the repose of its dead. One morning, both these families appeared at the church, each under the impression that this mass was the one it had arranged for. Naturally, the Capérans were surprised to see the Lacostes there, and the Lacostes were equally surprised to see the Capérans; for, besides Madame Lacoste herself, no one goes to early mass except the curé's old house-keeper and a certain Belgian refugee who has settled in our commune and who is very pious—and in addition, perhaps, Marie, the dressmaker. After the mass was all over, Monsieur Georges Capéran went up to the curé and asked him for the repose of whose soul the mass had been said. It is reported that he replied that he did not at that precise moment quite recollect, but that he would consult his book at home and find out.

"It is all in my calendar somewhere, so everything is all right, in any event."

It is not necessary to give credence to all that

people say, and nothing is gained by believing a story of this sort, so why believe it, and, above all, why repeat it?

But it is easy to see why people do repeat it. They have clearly lost some of their respect for their old curé and do not care much what they say—which is a shame, whether this particular story has some truth in it or not. I lament that our people do not treat the curé with more respect, not only for the sake of his holy office, but for his own sake, especially since he is so old and lame. I wonder if the people who gossip about him so lightly ever stop to think that there was a time when our venerable curé was young and straight and strong, with all his future before him; that, though only the son of a poor peasant in this very canton, he had it in him to lift his thoughts far beyond these hills to God! Would that they reminded themselves of the many, many years he has walked these same hills on God's holy errands, until, at last, the paths of his youth are getting too steep for him and his thoughts begin to wander often to those grassy mounds where he has helped to lay the dead to rest, and where he himself must soon lie down to sleep!

Old age like that demands reverence, not ridicule. If the mind has lost its vigor and the body its strength, let reverence be seasoned with a little pity, too. We stand in awe before the dead; well, he who has grown so old that his judgment and speech wander, and his eyes grow dim, and his feet falter— such a one has already moved a little into the enfolding shadows, and calls forth the same feeling of awe as death itself ever stirs within us. Consider him who, with face averted from this world, and increasingly deaf to its noises, has partly entered those gates beyond which men discern only darkness; whose eyes, just because they are dimming to things of earth, are becoming accustomed to the blessed mysteries we long to know; and then say whether such should breed in us a reverence accorded to nothing else merely human.

The trouble is that some of those who gossip most about the good Abbé Castex are as old as himself—upon whom, therefore, the reminder of the curé's age has no effect whatever; although it really should appeal to them because of the sympathy old people ought to have for one another—a sort of comradeship that belongs to those who walk together in the deepening twilight. To these I say, have reverence for the priest's holy office anyway, which, if it can gain or lose in sanctity with time, ought to increase its claims upon the heart as the priest grows old in service.

For, after all is said, what human being can possibly deserve that rare place in our thoughts which belongs to the venerable priest of one's own village? When you came into this world, he it was who christened you with that name by which all men call you; he it was that taught your tongue to lisp the first holy words of the catechism; he heard the first confession of your timid heart, uttered with lips that trembled in that awesome place where, many times since, you have unburdened your soul of sins that brought you tears of shame; he it is that placed your hand in the hand of her you loved, in holy marriage; no one, as he, has learned to know your inner life, your intimate hopes and fears; and he it is that will be at your bedside to give you the last comfort and blessing before the silent portals shut you out from this life forever.

To many in our commune, the old Abbé Castex has been like that.

Only the other day, he and I were coming from the cemetery together when our conversation happened upon these very matters. The curé was saying,

"The priest stands between this world and the next; so it is that he belongs to neither, but to a region of his own."

He did not say it quite in these words, but that is what he meant.

Then we talked about death—I think the old curé was feeling his age—and I remarked,

"It is easier for a priest to die, to pass into the next world. His vows have made him already dead to this world with respect to most of the things men prize. To the priest, this world is valuable only as a symbol and sign of what lies beyond."

I was thinking of how all of nature's panorama is a language that suggests things we cannot see, and that are much more real. For instance, these rivers flowing to the ocean tell me that all things flow at last, through devious windings, into the ocean of God's life; the flowers are God's words blossoming forth the story of his beautiful compassion; and the sunsets—who has not seen in them the prophetic glory that hovers over death, whether it be the death of suns, or stars, or flowers, or rivers falling toward the seas?

Such thoughts do we priests have, perhaps more frequently than other men whose lives are harshly bound to the business of this world.

Although our curé is old and worn out, as I have said, he wants to do everything himself. He will not let the young vicar, who was lately appointed to assist him, do anything at all if he can help it. Not he—though people say it would be far better if he did. No, the old curé walks in all the processions of our holy fête-days and in everything relegates the vicar to a secondary place. A little while ago, before I returned from Paris, our sacristy was burned. And now our curé is laboring hard to raise the money to rebuild it. Even in this, which the young vicar could do very well, the curé will allow no interference. It is he that will do it, or nobody will do it! Somehow this perseverance of the Abbé Castex, in spite of his growing infirmities, this reluctance of old age to let go of its time-honored tasks, has something admirable, something of greatness in it, however mistaken it may be.

Lately, when it was very warm in the sun, and the curé was perspiring as we were going up the street, I mentioned how other people were able to change to cool clothes, while we priests had to wear our rather warm cassocks, no matter what the weather was. I did not say it in a complaining way, but only mentioned it casually as one might any passing fact. He stopped in the middle of the street and said,

"We priests make many sacrifices." And then, with a dry smile, "But we look forward to something in the next world. It is thus that we priests are all idealists."

Old Abbé Castex lives in a square, two-storied house in the "back street," facing a new road that leads out into the country. There are three worn stone steps on each side of the entrance, with slender, iron balustrades. The double doors, once white, have the paint much worn off them, especially around the iron knocker. In the evening, the heavy wooden shutters of the upper windows are wide open, and frequently one can see the old curé slowly limping up and down in his study with his hand behind his back and his head bowed sideways. Once in awhile he pauses at the window and looks out over the hills at the afterglow reflected along the eastern sky.

From something he said to me this morning, I am certain that the Abbé Castex will not look out from his window over the hills many times more. He complained that lately he had strange sensations from the waist down. He said,

"Sometimes my legs feel as though they were melting, like snow."

Well, beyond the afterglows are the stars; and beyond the stars, there is something else. I sometimes fancy that the universe is much larger than we think. And that it has many doors!

Chapter XXIII: *Aunt Madeleine Insists*

THE pavilion at the top of my garden is finished, although it is not painted—and I doubt that it will be soon, for paint is very expensive these days. Perhaps later. It has turned out to be a little structure, five feet square and some ten feet high, with a gabled roof to shed the rain. The front is all open—it has no door yet, though I think it must have a door. The trouble is, there were not enough boards left. Within, I have put up a shelf along the back wall. In the center of that is an image of the Virgin between two small vases of flowers. On the wall, I have fastened two unframed water-colors made for me by Henri. One is a copy of a picture of St. Peter, and the other is a scene in the old city of Auch, showing its steep streets and red roofs, the cathedral and tower surmounting all. Henri made it while he was a pupil at the lycée there. Then, I have a board that can be supported next to the wall, so that I can write; although when the board is in place and I am seated, as I am now, there is no room to hold anybody or anything else. The front of the pavilion faces east, toward my garden. I have made a little window the height of my head when I am sitting, just large enough to look over the hills to the picturesque village of Sabazan, with the square tower of its high-backed church standing out against the sky.

Since I was in the business of arranging things, I thought it was a good occasion to clean up my garden-house; for no matter where I live, everything gradually becomes misplaced, so that it is hard to find what I want when I want it. Especially my many books had gotten themselves into great disorder, due to the fact that I kept carrying them back and forth from my father's house in the village to my garden, as I required them, until now it was difficult to tell the whereabouts of any particular book. Some were piled promiscuously into a big box by my table in the garden-house; some were heaped on various shelves there, meant for flower-pots; and some were even on the floor. As for my study at my father's house, it was a sight to see! My old Aunt Madeleine had become quite disagreeable about it, saying that one could no longer walk about in the back chamber, where my books lay scattered, without stumbling over some philosopher or saint or poet; and she threatened to burn them up straightway if I did not put them in some order. For that matter, to be consigned to the flames would be no new experience for some of these same philosophers and saints, for that is the very way several of them perished. Through the portals of fire they entered heaven! But I wished to save their tomes from any such fate. So, yesterday afternoon I set to work.

First, I got my Latin pupil (the only one I have been able to obtain so far) to abandon his lesson for the day and bring back a number of volumes from the garden-house in the wheelbarrow. He had to make several trips. I myself stayed in my study, busily endeavoring to achieve some order out of the confusion.

Of the five rooms over my father's old *salon de coiffure,* I have two; one at the front, which is my bedroom, and one at the back, which I sometimes dignify by calling my library. This summer I have not used it much, since I have found myself preferring the garden-house, except in bad weather. As I was trying to remedy the chaos into which my books had fallen here, I thought of what Montaigne said of his own library, which leads me to suspect that it was often in no better state than my own, since he confesses that without any order, without any method and piecemeal, he was in the habit of turning over and ransacking now one book and now another, musing and raving and walking up and down, inditing his conceits; for, plainly, Montaigne could not think so well if he was sitting. I am glad this last is not the case with me, for my library furnishes no space at all for walking. But then, perhaps, my thoughts are not worth inditing, either—which may prove that Montaigne's method is better.

As I call to mind the other interesting things that Montaigne says about his library, I am persuaded that it was sufficiently unlike my own in most particulars. His was large, and mine is small; his was round, and mine is square; his books were five shelves high, while mine reach to the ceiling. Montaigne's library was in a tower in the chief entry-way of his house, and mine is at the very back, away from the street; his had three bay windows, and mine has only one window, and that one of a very ordinary sort, by which is my table and chair. From his windows, Montaigne had a rich and unrestricted prospect, while from mine the view is shut out by the backs of houses that front the next street—except for a little slit of space between walls, where I get a tiny but precious glimpse of the far hills to the east, and through which the first sunlight of the morning strikes my window. But in one thing, at least, my library is like Montaigne's, namely, it is my seat, my throne, where my rule is absolute, where I am sequestered from all the things of this world, including even relatives and friends, save at rare intervals. Even my Aunt Madeleine does not enter here, except when she insists that her household duties require it. And then I warn her not to disturb anything.

The view from this back chamber of mine is not so bad as one might think. Just across the narrow, winding alley, which marks the line of the old fortification wall, is the little rectangular garden of Madame Lacoste, with a path straight down the middle of it, and another running completely around it, bordered with flowering shrubs of several kinds. Then, there are roses, and sweet peas, and some potted geraniums, and many other flowers, too—little beds of them; and an expanse of green grass; and over in the corner, by the wall, a dwarf pine tree. It is just the same as if it were my own garden; for, without leaving my chair, I can look out and enjoy it to my heart's content, under sunlight or starlight. Then, to the left of this charming garden, an ancient archway leads into the large courtyard of what used to be the Hôtel Maulézun. Through this arch, I get just a glimpse of the path running in under it, with the weeds along its border, and can see people entering, or coming out—only this is seldom, for the old hotel now lives mostly in its memories. I sometimes feel that its old, brown walls are trying to speak to me across the alley of what they saw and heard hundreds of years ago, when a branch of cedar or pine was hung over its door—the sign of an inn in this part of the world.

But while I was occupied in arranging my books, I regarded my window only as something to let light in on my task. From the middle of the chamber, where there was not much more than enough space on the floor for my two feet, I surveyed the disorderly scene. Books everywhere. How much of my life they did indeed represent! Great books—how they signify epochs in a man's growth! Are they not as milestones along the highway the mind travels?

"What a fascinating assemblage they are," I thought; "not one without a personality of its own, and each dressed in its own costume, whether shabby and worn, or decked out bravely in the latest fashion!"—although these last are in the minority in my library. They look out on every side from their shelves, from floor to ceiling; crowding one another, jostling one another, some standing staunch and upright, some wearily leaning against a neighbor for support, a few standing perversely on their heads. They all have semblances of faces, some smiling, some frowning; some sedate, some trivial; some inviting, some repelling. Large books and small; tall books and short; portly books, such as those stately tomes of canonical law on the top shelf, and thin ones such as that yonder—the discourse of Clemens Alexandrinus, exhorting the pagans to embrace the Christian religion. Arrayed in many moods of leather they are, the dark reds and browns predominating, many of them beautiful with stamped designs of faded gold; several with heraldic devices on the covers—these came from some noble's library, and are, no doubt, melancholy over departed greatness. Old books bound in white skins, too; their titles written in faded ink on their backs. Books with their leaves gilt-edged, and some rededged, and some plain-edged, and all alike mellowed with dust; books that speak their lore in diverse tongues, some in Latin, some in Greek, some few in English, and a great many in the French of two centuries ago, with their unfamiliar spellings, and always having on the title-page, *With the Permission of the King*. Books printed in big type, and in little type; with margins generous, and margins narrow. Books on all subjects, from gardening to theology, from romances to breviaries. Such is my library. My Aunt Madeleine was right; these cluttered shelves had to be straightened out and space made for the books on the floor.

Only, I have one trouble, and always have had: not more than a few of my shelves will accommodate the tall books; so that volumes have to be placed together according to their size, and not according to what they are about—which is ridiculous, and makes odd comrades now and then. For instance, one finds that infidel, Voltaire, rubbing elbows with the good St. Augustine!

I began with the books on the floor. There at my feet was that illustrious and eloquent Father of the Church, St. Ambrose. I got him out a few weeks ago to consult his interpretation of a passage of Holy Scripture; but the small print of those double columns of his made the task forbidding. I hope the priest of St. Geniez (that town of cloth-makers), whose name is written in the title page, had better eyes than I! I put this ancient writer of hymns over on the bottom shelf by St. Gregory the Great. There was a wonderful soul for music! I wish I owned his famous exposition of the Book of Job; but I am glad to have this commentary of his on the Gospels.

I have another large tome, not so old, though, as either St. Gregory or St. Ambrose; it is the works of St. Theresa, printed in Paris in 1676. What a woman, what a woman! One of her biographers speaks of her as being born at the very moment Luther was secreting the poison which he was to vomit out two years later! Such a holy servant of the Church is worth a million Luthers. What self-denial she showed the world, scourging her flesh, wearing garments of rough hair and sandals of rope —abstaining from all meat, too, and sleeping on a bed of straw. But through the denial of her body, her spirit grew toward unseen things until, at last, that heavenly voice came, telling her that no more would she speak with men, but with angels. There was one vision of hers that has always seemed to me exceptionally wonderful, significant of deep and ineffable things—the one in which she became, as it were, a frameless and infinite mirror, with the Holy Son of God radiant in its center, and yet the mirror at the same time within the Son of God Himself!

She, too, I placed by St. Ambrose and St. Gregory on the tall shelf.

My frayed volumes of ecclesiastical history—there are twenty of them—I climbed up and put them high on the top shelf. He who reads those books through will be learned in most things worth while, if he has the mind to grasp it all. And while I had the ladder convenient, I took St. Augustine away from Voltaire. "At the Sign of the Cross of Gold"—that is where my copy of St. Augustine's *Confessions* was printed in Paris, two hundred and fifty years ago. I put it next to the six tomes of St. Thomas d'Aquin, to make up for my carelessness.

Plutarch—ten volumes of him, translated into French by the learned Abbé Ricard of Toulouse; with these put in place, my floor was beginning to get cleared.

As I was putting St. Cyprian in place, my Latin pupil arrived from the garden, laboring up the stairs with more books. Among them were four well-built volumes under the seductive title *Critical History of Superstitious Practices that Mislead the People and Embarrass the Savants*. I bought them at one of those book-stalls on the quai St. Michel in Paris, and found them very interesting—all about talismans against rats and rain, and any number of other unusual things I never knew existed. Verily, the Lebrun that wrote it would know more now.

Along by St. Theresa I placed a book about St. Basil the Great, although he lived a good thousand years before her. But both were famous for self-denial. I read once how St. Basil journeyed to the hermit saints of Syria just to learn all the ways in which one should macerate his body!

They must have shown fascinating signs in front of the publishers' houses in the old days, judging by what one sees on the title pages of some of these books. I have one, a *Moral Theology* for priests and confessors, with the imprint, "Under the Tree of Jesse." Another of my books is published by one who is to be found, "At the Palace, in the Hall of the Haberdashers, under the Steps of the Court of the Aides of Justice." I would have gone far to find this Guillaume de Luyne, whoever he was, for he used most elegant type on his pages.

If any one should ask me which is my finest-looking tome, I should name a stately one of sumptuous red leather, with a gold coat of arms stamped in the center of the outer covers. It is a *Rerum Gallicorum* of 1625. I sometimes let my Latin pupil look at it.

That is my finest book. My oldest book is the

one that contains the works of St. Bernard. It was printed at Basle in 1552. It is very thick, having nearly three thousand pages. The mice once got at it—I observe that mice prefer very old books and papers, perhaps for the same reason that we human beings prefer old wine; and they have eaten a ragged semicircle into the margin and have even made away with part of the thick cover. But the text is still unharmed. When reading it, I do not marvel that when St. Bernard spoke, mothers concealed their sons, wives their husbands, and friends one another, so that they would not be persuaded to follow him. I put this famous crusader and silencer of Abelard up there where the mice will not be tempted further.

But neither my finest-looking book nor my oldest book is the book I prize most of all. No, my most treasured volume is a breviary given me by my old teacher in the seminary in Paris, to whom I owe my Latin. He was very old when I knew him, with most of life's hopes dead and laid away, oh, so deep, among the graves that sleep beneath the moonlight of memory. His patron saint was St. Bernard. He taught me to read him in the Latin text. He was wont to say that he himself, who longed to be like St. Bernard in many things, had become like him in only one particular: he, like the great Saint, had grown so old that nearly all his friends were gone before him.

The other night I saw this good, old man in my dreams, his hair white as snow; his pure, clear face molded by the loving hands of Pain. In my dream, he was smiling just as I used to see him smile at me.

His picture is the only picture I have in my study. It may be foolish, but I was glad this morning to notice that the first, narrow beam of sunshine that visited my window crept over gently and touched his dear, old face.

He it was who taught me to love books.

Chapter XXIV: *I Get a New Pupil*

I WAS pausing for a moment from arranging my books and was looking out my open window on Madame Lacoste's garden, where, in a sunbeam by the wall, a swarm of small flies was darting hither and thither, weaving the light into invisible tapestries —I was standing at this window, I say, when I heard a loud knock downstairs at the front door. If it were my Latin pupil with a load of books, he would not knock. So it was not he. I could hear my old father go to the door and open it, and a little later he called up the stairs that Monsieur Ware wished to see me.

Now, Monsieur Ware had never before called on me except at my garden-house, so I was surprised— a little inconvenienced, too, since I wished to finish my task before twilight, and so was in no mood for a visitor. Still, I thought it must be something urgent that brought Monsieur Ware to see me, so I told my father to invite him to come upstairs.

I waited at the head of the stairs, up which he started two steps at a time like a boy—I smiled in spite of myself at the ebullience of his humor, which, however, he hastily moderated when he saw me.

"It's dark up here, Monsieur l'Abbé!" he exclaimed laughingly, for I suppose the bright sunlight out-of-doors had blinded his eyes for the moment. "Your father said you were in your library up here. I'm interested to see what it's like—is this it?"

Monsieur Ware is so tall that on entering the door of my chamber he instinctively stooped, though I think he might have got through unharmed if he had walked upright.

I could hardly ask my visitor to be seated, for both my chairs were heaped with books that I had been sorting out. However, this did not seem to trouble my young friend in the least, for even while he continued talking (chiefly about how he had glimpsed the Pyrenees in the morning) he was clearing the books from my large chair—it is a heavy, wide one, like a throne, one which my grandfather once acquired, I don't know how. It must have come from some old château, stricken in its fortunes.

I suppose such an informal procedure in making oneself at home is the American way, and I may get used to it after a long time.

Monsieur Ware seemed to be in no great haste to mention his errand. Instead, he was looking curiously about him at my assemblage of books here, there, and everywhere. He got up from my grandfather's chair almost as soon as he sat down in it, picking up now one volume and now another with much more interest than any one has ever shown in my collection. Of course, I was pleased with this, although I wished he would state his business and let me finish my work. At length he spoke.

"Pardon me, Monsieur l'Abbé, I come to borrow that book on Gascony you promised to loan me."

Then I remembered I had mentioned *Propos Gascons,* by Xavier Cardallac, which tells many legends and customs. Madame Lacoste it was who presented it to me. I hastened to get it from its shelf.

But in the meantime, Monsieur Ware was turning the leaves of some of the books still cluttering the floor. He was looking at the woodcuts of several of the Popes in my book on the Council of Trent and I saw him curiously examining Bishop Lafitau's *Advice Concerning Conduct Suitable for People in Convents and Monasteries and People of the World.* It seemed strange to see a young, modern American looking at that!

I thought that Monsieur Ware might be interested to know how I obtained some of these older books of mine, so I told him how, years ago, they belonged to a learned and much-loved priest at Pouydraguin.

"Pouydraguin," I went on, "is a village you may have seen on the distant hill to the southwest of your château. When the old priest died, he left all his books to the village to dispose of as it saw fit. They packed them away in a little dark room in the town hall, where they accumulated the dust of many years. I happened to know the mayor, and one day he opened the little room and showed them to me. He said he did not know what to do with them. He offered them at so many centimes a kilo; I took as many as I could afford—and here they are! Some that weigh the most are worth the least; but, altogether, that day made an epoch in my life."

I then showed Monsieur Ware my six tomes of St. Thomas d'Aquin, remarking,

"Think of getting twelve kilos of the Angelic Doctor for a few francs—he, whose pages are worth their weight in gold!"

"Did you get this by the kilo, too, Monsieur l'Abbé?"

Monsieur Ware was turning the leaves of a small, thin volume which he had already taken up and laid down several times. I could not make out just what it was from across the room, so I asked him.

"It is *Questions of a Princess,* with answers by one Monsieur Pontier, a priest. Let me see—*At Paris, 1687,* it says."

I told him that this, also, was one of the books that belonged to the old curé of Pouydraguin.

While conversing, I had taken the liberty to resume the arranging of my books. Suddenly, Monsieur Ware laughed. It rather surprised me, for I don't know when I have ever heard laughter in this quiet library of mine before, especially such hearty, robust laughter as Monsieur Ware knows how to achieve. In fact, I nearly dropped the *Four Evangelists* of Maldonatius, which I was laboriously lifting to a shelf. I turned to Monsieur Ware. There was no doubt whatever that he was more than ordinarily amused by something he had found in the questions of Princesse Henriette, Duchesse d'Angoulême.

"I couldn't help laughing, Monsieur l'Abbé! The

author says that his princess is interested in many
sciences that seem to be beyond the reach of her sex
—one can readily believe it when one looks at these
questions of hers."

I did not like this tone of levity.

"She was really an exceptional woman, Monsieur
Ware," said I, perhaps rather severely. Then, hoping to impress him, I added, "Henry IV was her
godfather."

"There is nothing on earth or in heaven she
doesn't want to know. Listen to this one: 'Why do
birds not have teeth?' And look at this one: 'Do
the angels speak with one another, and in what
manner?' And here's another: 'Who was the in-
ventor of crowns and diadems?' She is insatiable!
—That old prothonotary of the Pope must have been
sorely pressed!"

Now, it had never occurred to me before that
those questions were so ridiculous; but suddenly they
did seem just a little absurd. I could see why, too.
For Monsieur Ware, belonging entirely to this twen-
tieth century, with its blind reason, afforded a violent contrast to the ideas of a princess, or a priest
of two hundred and thirty-three years ago. Such a
contrast might well yield laughter; but to me, who
can so easily put myself into the mood of other centuries, so that I see them with their own eyes, as it
were—well, I felt only pity for Monsieur Ware in
his narrowness. I began to feel that the presence of
this ultramodern American in my old library must
seem like an impertinent intrusion to many of my
beloved books.

"Have you seen the answers?" I asked. "They may not be so stupid as you think."

Monsieur Ware confessed that he could not read French very well, especially the French of this book, because some of the letters were in the old style, let alone the faded ink.

I took the book from his hands, and inquired which questions aroused his curiosity most.

"Tell me this one first: Why *don't* birds have teeth?"

I turned to the place, well pleased that Monsieur Pontier had a fair answer for that.

"It seems they lack teeth because the material out of which their teeth would be made is already used up in the making of their beaks; it is clear, therefore, that they cannot have both a beak and teeth at the same time."

"That's great!" exclaimed Monsieur Ware. But I knew that for some reason he was still making fun of Monsieur Pontier's book, although, after all, the answer of a modern scientist would not be much better, only put in more formidable language, with some such words as "adaptation," and "adjustment," and the like.

"Do you think that one's character is revealed by the nature of one's hair, Monsieur l'Abbé?"

This seemed a strange question, and then I remembered it was one of those in the book. I had forgotten the answer, so I looked it up.

The answer is, Yes. Monsieur Pontier mentions that animals with coarse hair are generally stronger and more courageous, such as lions and boars. On the other hand, the timid animals, like sheep and rabbits, have soft hair. As with animals, so with men—so says the book.

"Rather hard on me," laughed Monsieur Ware, running his fingers through his hair, which is fine, and of a light color. "But go on."

I then read what Monsieur Pontier says:

"Those who have the hair of another color at the head than at the beard are usually dangerous men. This diversity in them is an indication of the inequality of their humors, which makes them variable, hypocritical, and dissembling, if they do not correct their bad nature by good morals, as Socrates and others did."

At this, Monsieur Ware asked for the book, although I myself was really getting tired of the whole matter. I was hoping he would lay it down, when he pointed to the question which asks why God commanded Noah to make an ark to save himself from the waters of the Deluge, instead of a strong and high tower on the highest part of the world, so that he would not be forever in motion and within two fingers of being wrecked.

I was able to give the answer without the book. Monsieur Pontier points out rightly that God does not wish his servants to lead an easy life. So an ark was better, because then Noah could not guess certainly whither he was going, and thus he would more readily abandon himself to God's protection and guidance.

I also told Monsieur Ware how, it is said, the

beasts were called into the ark, for I was certain he had not heard of it. The tradition is that Noah used an instrument of wood, fourteen feet long. This was struck with two wooden mallets, producing a very loud and reverberating noise. Some Eastern Christians still call their worshipers that way, instead of using bells. So says Jerome Magius.

At this moment, my little Latin pupil arrived in the doorway with his last load of books from the garden-house. In very truth, it was a miscellaneous lot that his arms carried, an unwieldy lot, too, for as he tried to lay them down, they all tumbled in a motley heap on the floor. I hastened to pick up a cherished volume of Lamartine—ah, there is language which, as you read it, fills your eyes with dreams! Then a volume of Browning's poems, some of which I mentioned I had read and found a little cumbrous.

But it appears that Browning is one of Monsieur Ware's favorite poets, concerning whom he gives lectures, and at my mention of him he became enthusiastic at once.

"He may be cumbrous," he replied, "and when he woos Music, it is often with such whole-souled heroism that she is frightened to flight. Yet, when he sings, he sings deep things from a mighty spirit; and in her triumphal progress, Truth uses all weapons, the battering ram, as well as the lance. The sweet murmur of Apollo's lyre is ever godlike, but godlike, too, the thunder of Jove and the hammer of Thor!"

All this sounded a little grandiloquent to me. But

Monsieur Ware was welcome to his opinion. I, too, like all kinds of poets, each in his own way, but Browning's way is beyond me, I fear.

There were also some philosophical books in this last load. Some of them were not entirely orthodox, which led Monsieur Ware to remark that, in his opinion, I was inclined to be liberal in my religious views.

"It is a sort of proof," he added, smiling, "to see the infidel, Voltaire, over there on your shelf."

This made me a little vexed, for I hate most of the incredible things that Voltaire has written. There are some writers with thoughts that poison the blood; that make Hope cry aloud in the streets of reason. Such is Voltaire. But I only answered,

"The best of the philosophies of men may be good enough to defend, but not one of them is good enough to live by."

I know this, for have I not taught philosophy for forty years?

I could see, though, that Monsieur Ware himself put great trust in human reasoning; so I hastened to assure him that even some of the lower animals know some things better by instinct than we do by our boasted reason.

"But how about your beloved Montaigne that you quote so often? Why, Monsieur l'Abbé, you are liberal in spite of yourself. Your famous Gascon skeptic was not any too religious, to my thinking!"

Well, what if I do admire Montaigne and am proud of all my editions of him, especially that of Le Clerc, and the four volumes by Louandre, bound in blue and gold, with the leaves edged in gold all around?

I asked Monsieur Ware if he himself did not like Montaigne.

"Yes, I like him, so far as I have read him. Our Emerson mentions the tomb of somebody in the cemetery of Père-Lachaise, on which it is recorded that he lived to do right, and 'formed himself to virtue on the Essays of Montaigne.' In spite of that, I think Montaigne is sometimes disgraceful in his morals."

I felt like quoting what Montaigne himself once wrote about books—"no good without pains; no roses without prickles." But I forbore.

"If there are passages in Montaigne that are bad for one, well, one should not read them," I replied, smiling. "As for me," I continued, "if a man like Montaigne has written lines that are questionable, perhaps he has harmed himself enough through the very writing of them without our punishing him further by not reading him—besides depriving ourselves at the same time. Anyway, these questionable parts are the exceptions, and one need not look for them."

I might have added that we old people can read what the young cannot; and that if Montaigne sometimes antagonizes my faith, he has no other effect than to strengthen it, which is an excellent thing to accomplish, even if he did not intend it. Many times, too, he has set me to contriving how to combat opinions with which I do not coincide.

At any rate, there is no need for assailing Mon-

taigne. He has faults; but in spite of them, he is
our greatest Gascon writer. In Paris from the very
first, my fellow-scholars, especially the Abbé Rivoire,
expected me to know him, I being a Gascon; and so
I determined not to disappoint them.

It was not until Monsieur Ware had risen to go,
and had even got as far as the door, that I learned
the real reason of his visit. It was not the book
on Gascony that had brought him to my house after
all, although I had given it to him, and he held it in
his hand. No, he confessed that it was something
else, far more important, although he seemed
strangely hesitant about mentioning it.

Although Monsieur Ware's French has been improving, it is still very bad. Most of the time we
have conversed in English, for my English is better
than his French, if I may say so. But I was not prepared for what Monsieur Ware had to propose.

"I hesitate to ask you, Monsieur l'Abbé, but I was
wondering if you would not give me lessons in French
—if you can at all spare the time. You know how
wretchedly I speak, and I have many reasons for
wanting to do better!"

I could think of one reason, which I suspected to
be the principal one. In other words, Germaine
Sance cannot speak English. That was the reason,
no doubt! One did not require much subtlety to
guess that!

The trouble with Monsieur Ware's French is that
he knows chiefly nouns and a few adjectives, but is
very scant in verbs. One can't build successful sentences that way. I hold that the substantives of a

language are the stones, and the verbs the mortar. Monsieur Ware has no mortar. He sometimes makes ridiculous mistakes.

Incontestably, Monsieur Ware's French needed mending. But did I care to undertake it?

"You see, it is this way, Monsieur l'Abbé: I have full-fledged thoughts, but here in Gascony they cannot fly; they are enmeshed in the net of articulate ignorance," he added, laughingly. "One might become lyrical about it if it were not all such a pity, and say that here my thoughts are as seeds hidden in the dark ground, struggling for the light in vain. They are cries from a far-sunk cavern, that mock themselves with echoes, and never attain an understanding ear!"

I asked Monsieur Ware how long he was to remain here in Aignan.

"I do not know yet—perhaps for the rest of the summer. My sister does not want me to go away. I am willing to pay you whatever you ask, Monsieur l'Abbé."

"You need pay me nothing," I hastened to say. "You shall improve your French; and, in return, I will be improving my English. Come to-morrow afternoon. I shall be in my garden as usual. We can begin then."

So it was arranged. I saw Monsieur Ware down to the front door, and then returned upstairs to my chamber.

There have been three epochs in my acquaintance with Monsieur David Ware. The first was when I heard that he and Germaine had come to know

one another.   The second was on St. John's Eve,
when I began to feel that we were friends.   The
third was to-day, when I consented to teach him
French.

While I was thinking of this, the sun had been
setting, and my books were getting dim in the be-
ginnings of twilight.   All at once my Aunt Madeleine called up the stairs, *"A table!"* so I had to get
ready to go down to supper, for my Aunt Madeleine
does not encourage delays at such times.   I would
have to tell her that my books were not yet fully
put in order, after all.

"But I have a new pupil, anyway!" I said to myself, as Aunt Madeleine again called up the stairway,
much louder than before.

Chapter XXV: *The Road*

YESTERDAY was the last day of June. Of course, I could put it just as well by saying that to-day is the first of July, yet, after all, that would be saying something entirely different. For July is yet the veriest stranger; true, it is just as real as any unknowable future is real; still it is yet but a blank page for which I have hope, but not affection. On the other hand, June is recorded and done and has achieved a place in my life that nothing can change. This year's June has been filled with days worthy to keep in memory, some for their quiet joy, and some for that deeper thing than joy, which brings the sad notes into life's music. Perhaps that deeper thing which sings through all our thoughts like an infinite sigh speaks from the great heart of God; the same sad murmur of song that often whispers up through the winding ways of recollection and dims our eyes, we know not why.

So, yesterday was the last day of June. In the afternoon, Monsieur Ware came for his first lesson in French and stayed about an hour. I find much that satisfies me in this young American. Although I have known him so short a time, yesterday he asked me in his boyish, frank way to call him by his first name if I did not mind, since we were to be together so much. "David." I asked him just how his friends pronounced this name, but he said that in this instance he would prefer that I use the French pronunciation. Assuredly, I prefer it myself!

Later in the day, something happened that bothered me a little when I got to thinking about it. I was walking up the Street of the Church from my garden to my father's house, when I heard the raucous horn of the little doctor's automobile echoing along the street back of me. Just as I hastily stepped to one side by the covered poultry market, he caught up with me and, stopping suddenly with a shrill rasping of brakes, told me that he had just been out into the country to see a peasant family by the name of Massat. The mother had given birth to a child, which had died the second day, and while she was not dangerously ill, she needed looking after.

I said that I would inform the curé, whom I was to see a little later.

And now I come to the thing that bothered me. I had noticed the little doctor looking at me more closely than usual, and as he started to leave me, he called out above the terrific noise of his engine,

"You had better take care of yourself, Monsieur l'Abbé!"

To tell the truth, I had noticed for several mornings when I looked into the mirror that I did not appear as well as usual. Perhaps the reason is that I have not been getting enough out-of-door exercise. Although I have spent much of my time in my garden lately, it has been mostly in my garden-house, or, if not there, in my little pavilion, putting down these thoughts of mine, or perhaps reading on my bench under the fig tree. Then, too, I have been known to sit up late in my library at home, recording the events of the day, before I should forget them; indeed, my old Aunt Madeleine, seeing my lamp, has had to remind me several times that it was time to go to bed.

The fact is, I have kept from growing old, in spite of my sixty-five years, by three simple devices: plain food, regular sleep, and long walks. But I have been woefully neglecting those walks of mine lately. So, this morning, even as I was on the way to mass, I, Abbé Pierre Clément, made up my mind to reform. This very afternoon, I would begin by walking out the road into the country.

As I was ever telling my friend, the Abbé Rivoire, there is nothing in all the world like the roads of Gascony! Especially this part of Gascony. Golden threads they are of the rich tapestry that is our landscape; golden threads that weave in and out in random, graceful lines that hold together the confusion of hill, and valley, and village, and vineyard, and forest, lending them unity and figure. The roads of Gascony! How well my boyhood's feet knew every pleasant turn of them for miles around! How often, when far away in Paris, I dreamed of these same roads as of old friends, caring more for them than for all the glamour of those strange city streets, bordered by walls instead of smiling hedgerows; where the stone sidewalks (tombstones over dead Nature!) took the place of grasses and wild flowers.

If the roads of Gascony were all erased and a poet should build them again as he would like, he could do nothing better than to put them back just as they are.　Look at them—what more does one want?　Winding roads and straight; up hill and down; shady roads and sunny; lonely, peaceful roads, and roads friendly with red-roofed houses and barns; little roads, hardly wider than lanes, bordered with the encroaching grasses, and great, broad highways like that from Bayonne to Toulouse; roads arched by tall poplars, and roads arched by the sky; roads old and roads new, but mostly very old, and so not without their legends and stories; they have known the feet of countless peasants; they have known the carriages of kings.　Why, there is a little lane just beyond the house of Marie, the dressmaker, along which "our Henry" once went on his way from Nerac to his castle in Pau!　Ever since, they have called it the Lane of the King.

And all these roads are brave, indomitable roads, conquering every hill that comes in their way, however high, some of them stopping only at the Pyrenees, which is the wall of the world!　And all these roads are bordered by hedges, without which, in my opinion, a country is undressed and bare; hedges trimmed, and hedges uncut—ragged and wild and high, such as I like the best of all.　And all these roads lead somewhere—climb somewhere, descend somewhere—to a pleasant town, and then on through other pleasant towns, threading them like jewels along their winding ways—all except the littlest roads, that keep away from villages and dream their sequestered courses between vineyards and tiny farms, or lead to cool springs and quiet places in the heart of the woods.

But, after all, these roads are so interesting only because they belong intimately to the drama of life; only because men and women travel on them and build their houses by them. Beside some road in the world each man has a place that he calls home; and the road that leads home, that is the most blessed road of all!

I like to think of these homes of Gascony that nestle by the road, often so close that they seem to love it. Plain, honest, rectangular houses they are, most of them, but picturesque for all that, with their gabled roofs of red tile, and their plastered walls, and their weather-worn, wooden shutters, and over the door a grapevine growing against the light green stain left by the spraying. Those grapes, high in the sun, will be the first to ripen, too! And there are the barns, and, most likely, a covered archway somewhere between buildings, leading to an inner yard and affording shelter for a load of hay, or whatever one wants to keep from the rain. And perhaps a pond for the ducks and geese, and a stack of straw with a tall pole rising from the middle of it, and vineyards stretching beyond.

And then that great artist, Time, has touched so many of these homes and given them beauty. He works patiently on the tile roofs until they become saggy and delightfully undulating and irregular. He pulls at the plaster here and there with the eager help of the wind and the rain and the frosts, and it crumbles piecemeal, revealing the rough, yellow stone and clay, and the wooden beams underneath. I suppose people first put plaster on the outside of their homes to conceal these things; but now, even when a Gascon house is built of good, smooth stone, in blocks that would be fair to see, they cover it with plaster, too! Such is the power of custom over men!

In all these houses along the road there are human souls, living out the joys and sorrows of the mysterious thing we call life; and the homely signs of their presence are everywhere—a scythe hung neatly by the front door; a rough, round broom, for sweeping the yard, leaning by the step; a wild boar skin nailed up on the wall in the sun; newly-washed clothes spread over the clean, rain-cleansed hedges to dry; ridiculously simple things all these, but the miracle of love may have come along this road to dwell here and to give such common things their infinite meanings. Hark! one hears the swift patter of children's feet through an archway, and the laughter that makes a lyric of the humblest road that ever climbed a Gascon hill to the sun!

Look up that same road to the summit, and just as likely as not one will see one of our Gascon windmills, through whose desiccated roofs one can glimpse the sky. The old windmills of Gascony! They are the ancient troubadours of the landscape, that have sung their songs to the wind, and sing them no more, no more! One often sees them on the little hills, round in shape, builded of rough stone, about thirty-five or forty feet to the tip of their conical roofs, with one door, and a few square windows under the eaves, and the dilapidated framework of four huge arms, so long that when they turn they almost sweep the ground. In other days, it was a merry sight to see these long arms turning, their white canvas sails full spread, flashing in the sun.

But the canvas sails are gone now; only the broken skeletons on which they were stretched remain, vivid against red sunsets. The great arms turn no more, and the walls are in all stages of decay. Grasses and gorse and weeds grow long at their feet, and the old path that led to them is overgrown and lost. The long, slender ladder that led up to the roof at the back still leans there, perhaps, but its days are numbered. Ruined and lonely on their summits, the old mills look as if they had been worsted in a joust with some giant Don Quixote, who had stepped back across the Pyrenees and abandoned them to desolation and defeat.

It is so much easier now to send the wheat to the mill at Plaisance or at Bétous. The waters of the Arros and the Midour do the work the wind used to do. It is an improvement, they say.

But often, when I walk out the road, I wonder if what we call modern improvements will not take out of civilization all of its picturesque beauty. Gone are battlemented walls, and donjon-towers, and ancient brass lamps, and gilded coaches, and tapestries, and cloths of gold; and now our old windmills, too, are soon to mingle with the dust that was once the living heart of yesterday. After a time, what will be left for the poets to write about? Or are they, too, to vanish at last?

To me, walking out the road takes on the character of an adventure. The roadway is the greatest theater in the world. On it is staged a continuous drama, of which one knows neither the beginning nor the ending, so it is the more fascinating, since it gives the imagination free play. On our Gascon roads, everybody knows everybody, speaks to everybody. It is always, *"Bonjour, Monsieur!"* or *"Bonjour, Monsieur et Dame!"* spoken cordially. One meets many children on the way to or from school— sometimes they have to go far—with their bags of books and their wide-brimmed straw hats, covered with white cloths to shield their little heads from the sun. Nearly always respectful they are, and well-behaved, greeting one courteously and taking off their hats. One will meet boys with arbalests twenty-five feet long on their shoulders; they are on their way to hunt frogs. Two-wheeled carts rattle by, as the driver cracks his whip and calls out a greeting. One rarely sees an automobile, and then it is likely to be a large truck, loaded high with huge wine casks. At a turn of the road, one possibly hears shrill cries from peasants standing in a farmyard; they are looking up at the sky where great buzzards, whose home is in the forest, are circling nearer and nearer, threatening the chickens; the weird cries are to warn them off, and the dogs are aiding with their frantic barking till the buzzards reluctantly retire for a more favorable day.

Here comes a donkey hauling a cart; he is literally covered with green branches, for it is a hot day. The driver looks like an Arab of the desert, with that flowing white cloth of his draped over his hat and hanging down behind. From a lane, a team of oxen emerge into the road; the man who drives them has a long pole with which he guides them by touching them with its sharp point. Nets are over the oxen's faces to keep the flies off, and garlands of leaves are about their great necks; and on their backs are spread canvas cloths, gayly embroidered in purple and pink. "Name of a finger!" cries the driver as his oxen shy at my near approach.

Entering the road from some barnyard just ahead is a herd of slow-moving cows, or, perhaps, a flock of ducks, or geese. And what wonderful geese they are! Stately, portly, dignified, immense in size, strutting leisurely along the road in the sunshine, like aristocratic dowagers out for an afternoon walk. One could almost imagine them lifting their lorgnettes haughtily as they pass!

But to tell all the wonders of the road would require volumes. The tower of a church peeping over a rolling meadow; vast expanses of valley and hill from a height; the cool shades of poplars as one crosses a quiet stream in a tiny valley; a level field, carpeted in green velvet, with the great, spreading oak in the center; the geese, white and gray, resting in its gracious shade; the friendly trees, acacia and linden and walnut and alder and pine and plane and chestnut—the trees, some of them gracefully hung with mistletoe; and the flowers by the road's edge in the deep grasses, such as the delicate blue chicory blossoms, which pale to white a few hours after being picked.

Why is it that sometimes a softness steals over one so that one cannot pluck the wild flowers, swaying on their long stems by the sunny road, any more than one could mutilate a child? How often have I stood before such beauty, perhaps a spray of the golden blossoms of a weed, irresolute, trying to summon courage to sever it from its stem! The more I become acquainted with these little inhabitants of our world, the more I study into their wondrous texture, the more I feel that nothing should be wantonly destroyed. The true test of our love of nature is our respect for her creations. One who really loves nature will be as tender to a flower as he is to a friend. A weed studied is to the soul a weed no longer. It becomes hallowed—a living thing with a right to live, and plucked up, even when necessity calls, only with regret. I have seen flowers cast along the roadside to wither in the dust, and could not resist the impulse to rescue them as helpless and forsaken waifs.

Perhaps I am getting to be only a sentimental old man; but the world will be worth our leaving when sentiment dies.

So, then, I often hear the call of these Gascon roads, and sometimes heed it, to my soul's profit. For, as I travel them, I think thoughts that reach far out to distant horizons, to the dawns that never were. And if they wind and wind, well, perhaps through their leisurely windings one shall learn this blessed truth, that Time is not the most valuable thing we have! One shall pause at the crosses of wood or iron that are to be found where two roads meet—it is proper that these crosses should be there, for they serve to remind us that all roads are but tributaries of the long highway that leads beyond the crest of the farthest hill to the end of all journeying!

Chapter XXVI: *In Germaine's Garden*

I HAVE always said that one of the most delightful spots in all this Gascony of ours is
Germaine's garden.

Of course, it would be difficult to prove this to
any one who has not been there; to one who has been
there, no proof is necessary.

I renewed my faith in Germaine's garden to-day,
for I spent an hour in its quiet shades by the long
pond.

It came about in this way.

The longing for the road got into me, and I
walked all the way out to that poor family of the
Massats, which Dr. Dousset spoke to me about on
the street. They live east of our village, beyond the
high ridge we call the Bethaut, where the road descends to the level of a charming little valley.

It was just the day for a walk—not too warm, the
sky flecked with clouds, and a breeze blowing them
over the dome of the world. There was nothing to
keep me in the village, unless Monsieur Ware wanted
a French lesson; and he couldn't come to my garden
to-day, he said, because of an engagement he had.
So out the road I went, my steps keeping careless

rhythm with the harmony one finds in all things on a summer day like this.

It was past the middle of the afternoon when I again reached the summit of the Bethaut on the way back. For several minutes I stood there, contemplating our village a mile and a half away. The air was so clear that I even caught a glimpse of a corner of my garden-house through the trees—at least, I thought I did.

Descending the winding road toward the village, I soon came to the crossroads called the Tonkin—there is a story connected with that!

Several years ago, one of the finest girls of our village had a soldier for her sweetheart. He was suddenly ordered to the far-away Tonkin, in Indo-China. The name of that distant place came to be synonymous with calamity to the lovers.

In the long twilights, they often strolled out from the village to the crossroads and back. And to this same place so blessed in their memories, they took their last walk together.

Alas! like so many soldiers of our France, he never returned. And the crossroads, which, in jest, had been called the Tonkin by the close friends of the lovers, gradually acquired the name as a right; until now nobody thinks of calling the place anything else.

So human hearts have their geography, too — their crossroads, their valleys of dreams, their cities set on hills, each with its own name.

When one reaches the Tonkin, one is nearly home. A few steps further, the houses of the village begin.

One passes the white statue of the Madonna. Still further, the little house of old Marinette hugging the road. She was in her yard, calling her geese: "Sai! Sai! Sai!" (that is patois for "Come! Come! Come!") and "Balen! Balen!" ("Valiant! Valiant!"), which ought to bring them to her surely, if they are at all susceptible to flattery!

Next to Marinette's house, Germaine's garden begins. I have already jotted down something about the great old house.

But the garden!

From the road, it presents an enchanting sight. Just on the other side of the sunlit hedge that borders the road is the long, narrow pond, whose placid surface is dappled with sunshine sifted through the trees. By the edges, the long grasses droop gracefully down to it, their tips touching the water. Just the other side of the pond is a low fence of slender, iron palings, tumbled with ivy in wild disarray, and flanked by rosebushes that nestle close. (Oh, the roses, red and pink and white, that sway along the edge of the pond in May and early June!) But now it is the sweet-pea blossoms reaching their sprays over the pond to mirror themselves, and a row of stalwart hollyhocks of white and pink, which peer out over fence and pond and hedge to the road, to see what is going on in the world.

Then, beyond the pond, the real garden begins.

It may have been a formal garden once, but Nature has improved that! As you look at it from the road, you get the effect of restful, shady places, boldly touched with stretches of grass and patches of sunshine, for one of which you may at first mistake that vivid bed of yellow daisies. There are trees, trees, trees, in delightful disorder—tall pines, and firs, and fancy-trimmed yews, and acacias, and laurels, and live oaks, not to speak of the huge chestnut trees by the long wall that separates the garden from the drive, and, close to the pond, the great cypress tree that dominates all. In some places, the branches of the trees interlace with one another. There is one tree in a delightful corner that has become so crowded that it has bent itself away to one side, seeking the sun.

It is so restful in there as you look in from the sunny road! You get an impression of winding paths, not too carefully trimmed, strewn with pine needles and cones. Rich, green beds of periwinkle here and there, and a stump or two, overgrown with ivy and bridal-wreath. Through the trees you get a stray glimpse of the old-fashioned well, the pail resting on the edge; or, perhaps, a corner of the house, or the red roof of a barn; and then the sunlit fields beyond, and still beyond these the hills. And mingling with what you see, you detect the delicate fragrance of honeysuckle and jasmine in the air. And then you begin to think that the poetry of the road has been greatly over-rated; indeed, you wish that you were not in the road at all, but in the garden there.

From the moment I passed Marinette's house, I had heard the sound of voices in the garden; and now, looking across the hedge, I saw Germaine, as well as her sister, the doctor's wife, and Madame

Lacoste, seated on benches under the trees. Beyond, in a grassy, open space, Robert (the doctor's young son) was jumping by means of a pole over a high-stretched rope—and there, too, was none other than David Ware, joining in this sport like the veriest boy! Now I knew what that important engagement of Monsieur Ware's meant! Watching it all, Dick, the bird-dog, lay near by, luxuriously stretched on a cool bed of periwinkle.

I suppose that I must have unconsciously paused in the road looking at the pretty scene before me— at any rate, before I knew it, the doctor's wife was calling a greeting to me and inviting me to come in. Well, I was glad to do so. How often had I sat in that same garden with Germaine's father on long summer evenings! There is something besides trees and flowers and grasses beyond that hedge—there are memories, too!

I had to walk along the road the length of the hedge to the driveway that separates the house and the garden. From the driveway, one enters the garden by a path bordered with anemones, and then through a low gate in the garden wall, over which is a rustic archway covered with leafy vines. Robert hastened with a large garden chair he had been told to fetch from under the steps of the house. Monsieur Ware, too, came, hurriedly donning his coat and arranging his tie, finally seating himself on the grass, not far from Germaine, who was working on a square of filet.

As for Madame Lacoste, she is a frequent visitor here on summer afternoons. She it is who has the garden that I see from the back window of my father's house. Madame Lacoste is valuable. She knows all the gossip of the village, and can tell it well. She is really a wonderful woman. Although she is over seventy years old, she does not look a day over fifty, hearty and wholesome, and with the figure of a girl. She has had thirteen children, and they are all alive and prosperous. Her husband is dead—how regally they used to live in the great château on the hill to the east, before he lost all he had in that unfortunate speculation which loosened his hold on life! Madame Lacoste is the most devout woman in our canton. She goes to early mass every morning of the year, and is always at vespers; she is to be seen in all our religious processions —on St. John's Eve, she was there—and every year she makes several pilgrimages to Lourdes.

It is fascinating to hear—better still, to watch— Madame Lacoste talk. What animation! What infectious laughter! What gestures! She is a born actress, and to hear her tell the latest bit of news is like going to a play.

Just now, she has much to say of the approaching marriage of her handsome daughter, Henriette, to a soldier who has been courting her for a long time. But it was not of this she spoke as I seated myself. No, she was full of a new wonder—how Monsieur Ware had come to her rescue with his American genius in putting together a new, patent, sheet-iron oven that had come from Paris in so many pieces that it was simply impossible to tell which pieces belonged where. The hardware merchant had tried it; Lignac, the lame blacksmith, had tried it; and Monsieur Ware had not only tried it, but *voilà!* it was done within five minutes after he had looked at it!

When I was through telling them of my talk of the afternoon, Monsieur Ware hastened to relate an experience he had in the country a few days ago. He had encountered a half-witted and garrulous peasant on his rambles, who called him into his yard and insisted upon talking to him for over an hour in mingled French and patois, and showed him everything he had.

I then asked Monsieur Ware if, in his wanderings on our roads, he had found anything worth putting into poetry—besides the sabots, which had inspired him to that lyric outburst in my garden.

He said that, as a matter of fact, he had written some verses about this very peasant he had just been mentioning.

I don't much care to hear a person read his own poetry to me, even though he be a teacher of literature as ingenious as Monsieur Ware—it is often such an effort to keep interested. But, of course, I had to ask him to read his verses, if he had them with him. But he modestly declined to do this, saying, however, that he might do so later, if I really desired it.

All the time we had been sitting there conversing, I had been hearing the most weird sounds imaginable. They seemed to come from a group of trees at the extreme side of the garden bordering on old Marinette's chicken yard. First, one heard a run of mellow, flutelike notes, a birdlike melody, soft and plaintive. Then silence. Then a sudden blast of inharmonies from another instrument entirely, as if the spirit of music were sorely wounded and in intense agony. It was undoubtedly a saxophone, every note expressing a most painful and riotous distress. Then silence again. Then a human voice, a singing voice, tore wide open the peace of the garden—and then I knew what it all meant. I knew it was Germaine's brother, Henri, torturing his voice into an exaggerated tremolo by vibrating his larynx rapidly with his hand and running up and down the scale in a wild imitation of operatic passion. That is an old trick of Henri's.

"He has made himself a study over there among the trees," said Germaine, smiling. "He says he wants to be in a place where he can be quiet and undisturbed."

A little later, I told Monsieur Ware of a project I had in mind, namely, in a day or two I intended to walk out to Marius Fontan's, on account of the manuscript I have been wanting to see. I asked Monsieur Ware if he would like to go.

"He, too, is a poet," I said, "although he hardly ever writes in anything but patois."

He said that he would like very much to go, and laughingly added that he would wear his red sash and sabots. He said that when Marinette had seen him in his sabots, she had admired them immensely.

I could see that Monsieur Ware made this proposal in jest; but I noticed that Germaine glanced at him with a rebuke in her eyes, and I overheard her say,

"Please don't be ridiculous!"

I knew then that Monsieur Ware would not wear his sabots, or his sash, either!

I did not stay long after this. It was getting toward sunset. While the women were engaged in discussing a detail of Germaine's filet work, I tried to imagine this garden as it was when Jean-Louis Sance was alive. From the potato field beyond the barn came the sound of a hoe. My eye wandered over to a corner of the garden where the tall distaffs of St. Germaine flamed red against the syringa bushes—the distaffs of St. Germaine, whose blossoms burn to yellow as they open, and then finally die to a dull brown as their brief season ends. Near them were some long, rare grasses Germaine's father had planted. Above and beyond, I glimpsed the gable of a barn, under whose eaves were small openings he had made for his pigeons, in which he took delight.

Yes, the memories were here, just as I said. There were trees here that Germaine helped her father to plant; that myrtle yonder her baby hands held upright in its hole while her father packed the dirt around it.

In the midst of these reveries of mine, Germaine's mother appeared with a spray of fragrant jasmine, which she handed to Madame Lacoste.

"For you!" she said, her face lighted up with a look an angel might envy. Jasmine is her favorite flower.

We cast long shadows upon the road back of us as Madame Lacoste, David and myself—accompanied a short distance by Germaine and her sister —made our way toward the village.

At the beginning of the Street of the Church, we said, *"Bonsoir!"* and parted.

Chapter XXVII: *Monsieur Ware Turns Poet*

THESE are the verses Monsieur Ware referred to in Germaine's garden. He brought them to me to-day, when he came for his French lesson. He has entitled them:

THE FUNNY PEASANT MAN

Walking down a sunny road,
  In Gascony, in Gascony,
I spied a little peasant man,
Old, and toothless as a toad,
  A funny man to see!
"Trop chaud!" he called, "Come out of the
    road
  Into the shade with me!"

I stepped into his little yard,
  Where cooling shadows lay;
"Une chaise pour vous!" "Oh, no!" I said,
"The ground is not so very hard,
  I'll rest here, if I may."
So, there beside me, in his yard,
  We talked an hour away.

227

"I once was over in Spain!" he said,
  And waved his horny hand;
And then he burst into patois,
And laughed, and shook his ancient head,
  And often made demand,
"Vous comprenez?" "Un peu," I said—
  'Twas hard to understand.

Then, all at once, "Allons!" he cried,
  And toward the barn he went;
'Twas built of yellow, crumbling stone,
The battered door was open wide,
  The roof was torn and rent;
"Alors, Monsieur, entrez!" he cried;
  I followed, quite content.

My legs, they brushed a fat canard;
  Some pans hung overhead;
There was a wine-press by the wall,
Some barrels, and an earthen jar,
  And straw that made a bed;
He turned to this—"Pour les canards!"
  "That's French for ducks," I said.

He seized my coat, "A la cuisine!"
  And through a narrow door,
He led me, talking eagerly,
With laughter and with strange demean,
  Across the stony floor;
I knew the English for "cuisine,"
  So hastened all the more.

Glasses he fetched with many a word,
  And straightway filled up mine;
And, as I drank, he rattled on,

In the quaintest patois ever heard,
  With many an eager sign;
I could not understand a word—
  But I never tasted better wine!

The strange thing about it all is that I know exactly who Monsieur Ware means by his "funny peasant man." It is old Jules Michaud, who, as everybody knows, has been half crazed ever since the loss of his wife and only son over a year ago. He lives by himself, and talks nonsense to every one that comes out the road.

Chapter XXVIII: *I Call for David*

A T last I have been to see Marius Fontan. I
fully intended to go within a day or two after
I saw David Ware in Germaine's garden and
suggested to him that he accompany me. But a whole
week went by.

That is the way with me, although I am not quite
so bad as the Abbé Rivoire. He has a little book in
which he carefully puts down the things he ought to
do. Then, after they are once put down in the book,
he straightway forgets them. It is as if putting them
down in the book disposed of the whole matter.

According to an arrangement with David (I find
myself frequently calling Monsieur Ware by his first
name lately), I was to stop for him at the Château
de Lasalle, which is on the road we had to take. So,
after mass, and then breakfast, I started out, first
providing myself with a package of tobacco, which
I knew well enough Marius would be glad to have.

It was a wonderful morning, cloudless, and with
the sort of air that makes one feel younger and
ready for vast horizons. I even began to regret that
Marius lived only two miles away.

As one leaves the village, the road descends a

little. One passes the convent school, and then the
ox-market with its trees, where the fire was on St.
John's Eve. Then the little house of Marie, the
dressmaker—she was just opening her shutters upstairs; and after that, one can really feel that he has
left the village behind him. Then a gentle slope
on the left covered with vineyards, and, farther on,
at the top of the slope, a park of great trees, through
whose dark foliage one gets fugitive glimpses of the
round, white towers, ivy-grown, of the ancient Château de Lasalle.

When I got as far as the long avenue of plane
trees that leads up to the château, I heard a merry
shout, and saw David running down toward me with
no thought that this same sedate avenue has been
more than once dignified by the august retinues of
princes. I would no more think of running down
that stately avenue than of any other misdemeanor,
—but then, of course, it never occurs to me to run,
anyway!

"Just finished breakfast. Wait a moment, Monsieur l'Abbé!—I haven't had a chance to fill my pipe.
The main use of breakfast is to smoke afterwards!"

And then, when he had thrust a stem of broom
through the pipe to clear it, and was smoking con-
tentedly, we walked on.

"Tell me about this Marius Fontan, Monsieur
l'Abbé."

Now, I did not want to say too much about Marius yet, as I wished David to see him first and judge
him for himself. So I merely told him that he was
an old peasant of about seventy-five; that his wife

had died fifteen years before; that he had never had any children; and that he now lived alone in considerable poverty.

"But you said he was a poet."

"Not only that," I answered. "He also writes stories about the old days in Gascony—he knows all the ancient legends of this region better than any one else. These stories he writes in French. But his poems are in patois. You will see."

And then I learned the abyss of my young friend's ignorance. He had no idea what patois—our Gascon patois—is! He actually thought that it was some sort of corruption of the French tongue, spoken by peasants in the country, who knew no better.

That made me a little provoked. For I am proud of our Gascon language, which is no corruption of French at all, but is a language with its own rights, as old as French. It makes me sad, too, when I think of how, with the new generation being taught French in the schools, it is fast passing away. To be sure, some of the older peasants still speak it. Old Marinette talks nothing but Gascon patois; and Marius is one of the remaining few who can speak it purely.

"It is the most beautiful language in the world," I added. "It is more picturesque than French to my ear. It does not neglect so many vowels and consonants. Some say it is harsher; but to me its sound is like a swift brook running over many stones."

And now, at length we came to a narrow, shady road leading off to the left, up a hill. Grass-grown the road was, edged with blackberry bushes, the fluffy white of "old man's beard" showing in the hedges. And then, when we had descended the hill on the other side, long rows of slender alder trees grew in the ditches. All in all, it was a road such as one would choose to lead him to a poet's house.

Then we turned up a narrower lane, bordered by fields of daisies. And then another road came into view, rough and unkept; and there beside it, in its yard of barren clay, was a square house, its ancient plaster pealed off in places, showing the rough stone and clay and black timbers beneath.

It faced toward the east, as a poet's house should. The morning sun was shining on it, trying in vain to caress its poverty into something beautiful!

Chapter XXIX: *A Singer of Gascony*

AS David and I crossed the yard and came close to the front of Marius Fontan's house, a most striking picture met our view, framed in the open window. For square behind it was Marius, seated at a small table, writing. The sun shone full upon him; and, as he heard us and rose, and leaned forward to see who it was, the surprising apparition he made there affected the imagination strangely.

A tall, bent form, loosely hung with frayed clothes; a face covered with a close-cropped, gray beard; and dim, blue eyes, looking out from under the most ridiculous hat imaginable! Perhaps it was the hat that held one's attention most of all—a wide-brimmed hat of straw, all covered over with cloth, once white, but now soiled and tattered at the edges, with a narrow band of rusted black around the low crown—the sort of hat the children wear in summertime. I found out later it was a hat his little niece had thrown away.

When the tall form of Marius had hastily transferred itself to the open door, it was plain how happy he was to see me! He wrung my hand and exclaimed, "My good friend! My good friend!"

234

his face lit up with his delight at my unexpected coming. Then David, who had been lingering a little behind, came up and I introduced him, and we went into the room to the right of the narrow hall, in whose window we had surprised Marius.

It was pitiful, that room, or so it seemed to me. In a corner was a bed, unmade and tumbled, hidden partly by some cheap draperies covered with dingy, flowered figures. On the worn floor of red stone, loose bundles of fagots were lying in a disorderly way in front of the wide fireplace, a blackened coffee percolator standing in the ashes. Above, the large beams of the ceiling were smoked and dirty. On the wall, besides a few pans, were hung two or three cheap engravings—one, Our Savior on the cross, over the fireplace; another, a fanciful picture of the Resurrection above a rickety chest of drawers, which served also as a sort of buffet, for on it were a few onions and apples, a fragment of bread, and some bottles, one partly filled with red wine. At the window, where stood the writing table, were some yellow curtains drawn to one side, stained and wrinkled.

There were two chairs in the room—one that Marius had been using at his table by the window, and another heaped with clothes, which he hastened to cast into a corner. These two chairs he offered us, while he excused himself with many apologies to fetch another from upstairs.

It was quite clear that Marius was not accustomed to having visitors! I could not help thinking what a lonely life his must be, and remembered, with a pang of remorse, how I had postponed coming to see him.

While Marius was gone after that other chair, David could not resist glancing at the table where he had been writing. The ink-bottle was tilted up, as though the ink were about gone. Several pages of closely written manuscript lay there, very finely done in a small hand, surprisingly neat and regular, and altogether beautiful. Indeed, that manuscript was the only beautiful thing in the room—perhaps, too, I thought, it represented the only beautiful thing in Marius' life.

"He is copying all his best poems and stories in order that I may see if there is not a way to publish them," I told David. "But he actually had no writing paper for a long time, until one day I heard of it."

"Have you known him long, Monsieur l'Abbé?"

"I have known him always," I replied. "When I am here, he depends upon me as upon no one else. He is even dedicating his writings to me—'To my excellent friend, the Abbé Pierre Clément.'"

We had heard Marius rummaging about overhead, and now the clattering of his wooden shoes came from the stairs, and he entered with another chair.

When he was seated, I ventured to say that Monsieur Ware was much interested in his poetry.

"But can he understand patois?" Marius eagerly asked, scrutinizing David with new interest.

Of course, I had to tell him that David hardly understood even French, except to read it. But in spite of this, Marius began to explain to the young American about the Gascon language and why he wrote in it—he and others—so that it should not die.

"Only," he added sadly, "the peasants who speak patois cannot read it. If they read at all, it is apt to be French, for you see all the books and newspapers are written in French. So alas, we who write in patois are doomed to write only for scholars!"

While Marius was talking in this way to David, I was studying the picture he made as he sat there with his back to the door of the hallway, slightly ajar. He had taken off that ridiculous hat when we entered. I wished that I were an artist so that I might put on canvas that finely molded head, the hair cut very close, and darker than the short, white beard; the intellectual forehead, the strong nose, the high cheek-bones, the dim and filmed eyes of blue, the large, well-shaped ears, the loose-drawn skin of the throat, the old soiled shirt, collarless and open at the front, the black linen vest, the short, faded smock of gray, the shapeless trousers, pathetically ripped up one side, and the bare feet in huge sabots. One's eyes kept traveling back to that face—the face of a man of native refinement; the face of a scholar and a dreamer—it might be the face of a professor at the Sorbonne, but for his shabbiness!

Yes, I wished I were a painter!

But Marius broke in upon my musings by asking us if we would not have a glass of wine after our long walk. He asked it with as fine a courtesy as one could show who had a well-stocked cellar. And there

was Marius, with only yonder poor remnant of a
bottle left, I was sure. Of course, I refused as best
I could, and then mentioned something that had
been in my mind ever since I had thought to ask
David Ware to come with me.

I wanted Marius to sing us one of the ancient
folk-songs of Gascony—the songs that only the older
peasants know how to sing in patois—the songs that
are dying out and soon will be heard no more.

"Ah," said Marius, "the ones I know are always
sung in the fields, not indoors like this.—It is some
time since I have sung, Monsieur l'Abbé."

I saw that Marius was a little reluctant, perhaps
on account of the presence of my young friend. But
after some persuasion he consented, especially when
I told him that Monsieur Ware had never heard a
patois song, and had long desired to hear what one
was like.

And then, after a moment's silence, Marius began. It was then that I sensed the pathos of it all,
—Marius, old and poor, singing—actually singing—
here in this squalid room. One felt tears. Afterwards, David told me that it was something he would
never forget to his dying day—that strange picture
of Marius, singing the song of the reapers. After
the first few notes, it was plain he had forgotten his
surroundings and lived only in the song. His voice
rose strong and sonorous, though trembling at times
because of his age, and his face became transfigured
with the rapt, far-away look of one who sees the
happy things of long ago. Dramatic gestures he
made, too, that brought to the imagination the fields

of waving grain and the reapers of whom he sang; and sometimes his distant look vanished, and he turned his eyes to me, his face lighted up with a smile that brought back the Marius Fontan that once looked out on life as a glad adventure, before the pitiless years had mocked him, and bent his tall form, and touched his eyes to dimness.

At the long-sustained minor that ended the first stanza, I noticed that Marius' lips quivered a little. Like most of our patois songs, the effect was one of a haunting sadness, although I do not think that the words themselves were particularly sad:

There are nine wagons of fine wheat in yonder plain;
The heads are golden, and the stalks are silvery.
I know very well who it is that is aweary!
It is Jennie—yes, and everybody else!
Go down, beautiful sun, toward thy resting!
Go, beautiful sun, go!
Speedily go, as I bid you!

Suddenly, in the very midst of the second stanza, Marius' voice faltered and stopped, the sunlight died out in his face, and there was silence, and we three were sitting again in the midst of the dirty floor of a poverty-stricken room, and everything was common—for that dream of song that had changed all and made us forget was shattered.

"My throat—Monsieur l'Abbé." Then, turning to David, "Pardon, Monsieur, I cannot sing any more, as you can see—I forgot; I cannot sing any more."

I wanted to get Marius' thoughts away from sad

things, and I felt a little to blame, too, for insisting that he should sing; so I changed the subject by asking him to tell Monsieur Ware about some of the old legends of this part of Gascony.

It was then that he narrated what he knew about the last wolves of the Forest of Aignan—an absorbing tale, which even I had never heard, and which I strongly suspected was largely made up in Marius' imagination. This story served to take us out of ourselves, and so put us all in a happier mood.

When at last we rose to go, David noticed a large frame on the wall in which were medals Marius had received from time to time for his patois poetry and prose. Actually, one of them was from the famous and venerable Academy of Floral Games at Toulouse! Others were from societies modeled on this, to encourage writings in the Gascon language. The frame was upside down on the wall—Marius is so near-sighted he would never notice—and I had to right it so that David could examine these tributes the world had sent this singer of Gascony.

Oh, the hard, hard reality of it! This singer in rags and poverty, and the world brings not food or clothing in his need, but mocks him with medals!

I said something like this to Marius; but he only smiled and said that I need not worry about him at all.

"I have enough. A half loaf of bread is left me every week. You see, I am on the list of destitutes. Besides, I do not eat much, Monsieur l'Abbé."

But when I gave him the package of tobacco I had brought, his delight was good to see.

"It comes just at the right time, Monsieur l'Abbé! My store was almost gone."

I had seen a few grains spread upon a newspaper on the chest of drawers, and had guessed as much.

Marius went with us out into the yard, past a lone tamarind tree close to the path, and then through the gate, accompanying us a few steps along the road. In parting with us, David said he impressed him as having the indescribable courtliness of an old-fashioned gentleman. For, as he mentioned later, he felt, in spite of Marius' rags, a culture unmistakable and far above his station. I could see that Marius suddenly became conscious of his disreputable-looking smock and passed his hand over its front as though to smooth it and make it more presentable. We finally left him standing there in the road, with that wide-brimmed, tattered hat on his head—Marius Fontan, Officer of the Academy, *Félibre*, Laureate of many learned societies!

"What is more appropriate, after all," murmured David, as we turned into the lane—"the old poet, his heart forever young, crowned with the hat of a child!"

Chapter XXX: *The Last Wolves of Aignan*

THE story that Marius Fontain told us about the last wolves of the Forest of Aignan—I do not want to forget it; besides, I wish the Abbé Rivoire to have it; so, here I shall put it down, in Marius' own words, as nearly as I can remember them:

On the twenty-fourth of December, 1825, when the noonday meal was over, the mistress of the Château de Gaure said to her servants,

"Listen to me. This eve you must fetch a Christmas log as big as you can find; for, according to custom, it must burn all the night long. At sundown I shall light the fire; then, to-morrow, at sunrise, we shall gather from the hearth the embers that remain. We shall first let them go out, and then place some of them on the roof of the château and the barns, for, as you well know, these embers will serve to guard us from the fires of earth and of heaven. We shall spread the rest of the embers in the fields to protect the harvest from lightning, hail, and storm. Do not forget to put under the log a good lot of fagots as well as larger branches. This done, you will clean with care the stables of the horses and the cattle. And do not fail to make for them good litters of fresh straw, for this is Christmas eve, and everybody is aware that, while the mass will be going on, at the very moment of the consecration of the Host, the animals kneel down to adore the infant Jesus, and speak between themselves. And if they did not have a good litter, they might hurt their knees."

When evening came, the mistress of the château lit the fire, just as she said she would; and, after supper, the servants were allowed to lie down for awhile until the time to go to mass. As soon as they had retired, the mistress of Gaure sat herself down at one side of the huge fireplace, her feet on the bar of one of the great andirons; and, at the other side, there kept her company a fair young girl, eighteen years old, Jeanne Garbay by name.

A word about these two women.

The mistress of the château, Antoinette de Medrano, was born in Spain. Her brother, Duke Ramon de Medrano, had been lord of Mauser, Gaure and other places; this very château had been his. But the Revolution came, and he was guillotined. In order that she herself might not share the fate of her brother, she had fled to Spain, disguised as a goatherd, where she found refuge with her other brother, who was a Bishop. After the Restoration, she had returned to France to claim the estates inherited from her ill-fated brother, the Duke. She had settled in the Château de Gaure and had taken into her service as a shepherdess a little girl twelve years old. Later on, she kept her as a servant, and finally grew to love her as if she had been her own daughter. She it was—Jeanne Garbay—who sat on the other side of the fireplace this Christmas eve.

Now, Antoinette de Medrano was about fifty years old, tall, thin, and bony. She had the typical

Spanish features and complexion. Very pious and a fervent Christian, she was to be seen at mass every Sunday, went to confession, and took communion on all the holy days of the year. She was very charitable, too, and visited the sick, and helped the poor and needy.

In spite of all this, however, she was not liked in the neighborhood. To tell the truth, she was dreaded. The superstitious neighbors called her a sorceress and said that she had been known to ride astride a broomstick; that she had learned from her brother, the Spanish Bishop, the redoubtable secrets of necromancy; also that she was endowed with the evil eye, and knew how to weave spells. Not for anything in the world would the farmers' wives in the neighborhood let her count their broods of chickens, or turkeys, or goslings; for if she succeeded in counting them, they would die. When they met her on the road, they spoke to her politely enough; but after they had passed her, they made the sign of the cross, saying,

"May St. Simon sink her!"

"May the devil blow on her back!"

The fire was crackling on the hearth and the Christmas log was sending out a thousand sparks— the sign of severe cold weather. In a large earthenware pot, covered with a piece of oiled paper kept in place by a flat tile, bubbled and sang the customary Christmas *daube*. Soon Antoinette said,

"Go and get ready, Jeanne; we must start for mass."

Within a few minutes, Jeanne was ready. Her mistress handed her some matches and two long, resin torches. Then she wrapped herself up in a wide cape of black merino, adjusted the hood over her head, put under her arm a fine linen napkin, and together they left the château.

Antoinette double-locked the great château door and hid the key under a tile at the base of the wall nearby. The north wind was blowing sharp and biting, the ground was frozen, and threatening clouds were massing on the horizon toward the north.

"If I am not mistaken," said Antoinette, "we shall have a snowstorm."

To reach the village of Aignan from the Château de Gaure it was necessary to go through the forest for the distance of about two kilometers, along a wide path, called the path of Gaure. Arrived at the edge of the forest, Jeanne lighted a torch and the two women plunged into the woods. The wolves were howling in all directions; the crows, the jays, and the magpies, frightened from the trees by the light, flew away with confused cries; and with the beating of their wings they made fall a shower of icicles, which were hanging from the slender branches like stalactites of silver.

They arrived at the village of Aignan at the moment when the bell, with its three strokes, announced that the mass was about to begin. Antoinette entered a baker's shop, where she bought a long loaf of white bread, to be blessed according to the ancient religious custom; this she wrapped up in the napkin. Then they entered the church, which was lighted up with more than a thousand tapers. There were candles burning on the altar and in the great chandelier hanging in the middle of the nave. First they went to kneel down before the altar of the Holy Virgin, where was represented the manger of the infant Jesus, and then, having said a prayer, they went and knelt at their usual place in the church.

Jeanne took the loaf of bread to the communion table to have it blessed, and the mass began.

Young girls and boys sang canticles in the French and Gascon languages, including the canticle of *The Angels and the Shepherds,* composed by the good Abbé Daudigeon, priest of Lembeye. Then, after the mass was finished, Jeanne secured the loaf from the communion table, and they left the church.

By this time, the snow was whirling through the air in big flakes. The village, as well as all the country round, was covered with a thick layer of snow as the women took the road to the forest.

When they came to the edge of the forest, Jeanne relighted the torch; a few minutes later, she suddenly let it fall, uttering a cry.

"What are you doing, unhappy girl?" said Antoinette. "If your torch goes out, we shall be devoured by the wolves; the light is our safeguard— the flame frightens them away."

"But, Madame," replied Jeanne, "some burning drops of the melting resin fell on my hand."

"Hold the torch tilted a little forward, then; in that way, the drops won't fall on your hand."

Jeanne relit the torch. A few minutes later, when they had just crossed the path running from the Spring of Pichecrabe to Lespès, they heard plaintive wailings like those of a new-born baby. They stopped in great surprise.

"Do you hear those wailings, Jeanne? Where do they come from?"

"I believe, Madame, that they come from that juniper bush yonder."

"Give me the torch; let us see."

Antoinette lifted the lower branches of the juniper, and there she saw a baby wolf, which was trying to get up and run away; but his legs, benumbed by the cold, refused to support him, so that he fell down again.

Antoinette gave the torch back to Jeanne, gathered up the corners of her apron and tucked them in her belt, then took the little wolf and placed him in it.

When they arrived at the château, they found the log still burning, its uncertain light making fantastic shadows in the vast kitchen. Antoinette put the wolf in a basket and wrapped him up in a warm woolen blanket. Then she placed on the fire a dish of milk. When it was tepid, she put a few spoonfuls in the mouth of the wolf, who eagerly licked his lips. Then she dipped his nose in the milk and the little animal greedily lapped up the contents of the dish. After that, he sat up on his haunches before the fire and warmed his chest and nose.

Antoinette divided the blessed bread in halves, and then cut one of the halves into small pieces. She gave one piece to Jeanne and took one for herself, and they ate it, after having made the sign of the cross. This done, they filled two plates with *daube,* for the customary Christmas *réveillon,* and went to bed.

The next day, Antoinette gave a piece of the blessed bread to each of the servants, who ate it, after having made the sign of the cross; then she took the embers that remained of the log and went to spread them about, just as she had said. Then she put in the various wardrobes and linen closets pieces of the blessed bread; this bread never molds —it has the power to prevent the mice from gnawing the linen and clothing, and the moths from ruining them.

*   *   *   *   *   *

Five years later, the baby wolf had grown to be enormous. Antoinette had given him the name of Pharamond, and he had become her pet. She talked with him as with a child, and the wolf finally got so that he understood all that she said to him. During the daytime, he lay down under her bed; but during the night, he went to roam abroad with the other wolves that abounded in the forest of Aignan, and which considered him as their leader. He always returned to the château at daybreak.

Meanwhile, came the winter of 1830, one of the most severe ever known. The ground was frozen to the depth of more than a meter, and was hard as a rock. At the beginning of January, there fell a thick layer of snow, and the ground remained covered with it, without thawing, for seven weeks. The ditches, the ponds, the springs, and the streams froze to a great depth—indeed, the ice was so thick that you could cross the ponds of Poey and Chiberre with a yoke of oxen harnessed to a cart without breaking the ice.

Why, that winter the bread was frozen in the cupboards and the wine in the casks. The wild game, as well as the smaller birds, nearly all died from cold and hunger. The crows even ventured into the yards in front of the houses and fought there for the grain which the housewives threw to the chickens, and they were killed there with sticks. The wolves, famished by long fasts, committed frightful ravages. Nearly all the watch-dogs were killed by them and dragged behind the stacks of straw in the barnyards and devoured. Woe to the peasant whose sheepfolds, stables, and barns were not securely fastened! When he woke up in the morning, he found his cattle had been made away with in the night by the wild beasts. The wolves finally grew so bold as to attack human beings, and at length their depredations became such that the inhabitants of Aignan and the neighboring communes petitioned the prefect of the Gers that a general hunt be organized, with the object of destroying these *carnassiers*. The prefect sent this petition to the Minister of the Interior, who ordered Monsieur de Ruble, master of wolfhounds at Montauban, to go to Aignan to organize and direct a wolf hunt in the forest.

It was late in the month of February that Monsieur de Ruble arrived at Aignan, accompanied by three huntsmen with their bugles, nicknamed La Fleur, La Ramée, and La Jeunesse, and a pack of forty-eight magnificent hounds. He put up at the Hôtel Maulézun, and then consulted with the mayor concerning the plans for the hunt.

On the following Sunday, as the people were coming from mass, the village crier announced that there was to be a big wolf hunt in the forest. A similar announcement was made in the neighboring communes, and all the inhabitants, whether they could hunt or not, were asked to lend their aid. The gathering was to take place on the following Tuesday at daybreak, on the little elevation of La Papourre, which dominates all the forest.

Antoinette de Medrano, who had come to mass, heard this announcement. As soon as she returned to Gaure, she called Pharamond; and the wolf came and crouched submissively at her feet.

"Attend closely, Pharamond—listen well to what I am going to tell you."

The wolf lifted his pointed nose and pricked up his hairy ears in sign of attention. Antoinette went on,

"There has arrived in Aignan a master of wolf-hounds, accompanied by three huntsmen with their bugles, and a numerous pack of hounds, to organize a wolf hunt in the Forest of Aignan Tuesday morning at daybreak. They will kill the wolves with shots from their guns and carbines, *'Pan! Pan! Pan!'* "—and she accompanied her words with expressive mimicry. "This evening, you must induce the wolves of the forest to go away. You will lead them far, very far, through the communes of Bourrouillan and of Panjas, into the wooded heaths of Catalan and of Louvre. Then you will return alone here. The master of wolfhounds, not finding any wolves, will withdraw. As soon as he is gone, I will let you know; then you can go and get the wolves and bring them back to the forest. Do you understand, Pharamond?"

The wolf made assent by nodding his head and by howling three times, "Ah-oo! Ah-oo! Ah-oo!"

At nightfall, Pharamond went to the forest, to the plateau called Las Tachouères, and there began to howl in a peculiar and unwonted manner. These howls were a summons to the wolves to come together; and similar howls replied from all directions. The wolves arrived in numbers and formed a circle around their leader.

As soon as Pharamond, who knew them every one, saw that they all had arrived, he told them in their language of the danger which threatened them, and urged them to leave the forest immediately. He then arranged them in single file, put himself at their head, and thus they went through the communes of Loubédat, of Ste. Christie, and of Bourrouillan, and came to the wooded heaths of Catalan and Louvre, where they hid themselves. Pharamond made them understand that they must remain where they were until all danger had disappeared and he should come back to get them.

Then he returned to the Château de Gaure.

"Well," said Antoinette to him, "have the wolves gone?"

"Ah-oo! Ah-oo! Ah-oo!" replied the wolf, nodding his head.

On the following Tuesday, at daybreak, the huntsmen sounded their bugles from the elevation of La Papourre. The hunters arrived in force, to the number of about five hundred. The master of the wolf hounds made them form in a circle about him and said,

"I am going to send one of my huntsmen ahead with a hound in leash. He will keep on until the hound detects the scent of a wolf. This place will be noted carefully, for wolves have the habit of hiding together during the day. Wherever that wolf whose scent we find will be, there, also, will be the others. We will surround that place and let loose the dogs—and then, on with the music!"

As he was finishing this speech, Antoinette de Medrano came out of the crowd and stood in front of him and said,

"I had heard, Sir Captain, that they had sent to Montauban for you to organize a hunt for wolves in this forest of ours. But they got you here to no purpose; there is not a single wolf in the whole forest!"

"You lie, old sorceress!" interjected a peasant by the name of Mathieu de La Cahuse. "The wolves are in the forest in great numbers!"

"Well, Captain," rejoined Antoinette, "if you can

find a single wolf, I will make you the present of a white blackbird that will sing the livelong day!"

"Enough of this!" exploded the Captain. "Off with you, old hag, or I will loose my dogs and let them devour you!"

Antoinette slipped away.

He who was called La Fleur started out at once with a hound in leash and skirted the forest. Needless to say, he did not find the trace of a single wolf. He then went through the length and breadth of the woods with the same result. Finally he returned to the Captain, saying,

"There is not a single wolf in the forest; I have crossed it in all directions without finding the least trace."

The Captain thereupon returned to Aignan, followed by most of the hunters. He was in a very bad temper. One, Jean Monjeau, followed him to the inn and said to him,

"Sir Captain, if we have not found any wolves in the forest, I will, if you will allow me, venture an explanation and give you some good advice."

"Speak!" replied Monsieur de Ruble, in a haughty tone.

"Did you notice well the woman who told you this morning that there was not a single wolf in the forest?"

"Perfectly; what then?"

"Well, it is she who sent them away."

"What kind of a thing are you telling me?"

"The truth, Sir Captain; that woman is a most accomplished sorceress. She lives in the Château de Gaure at the edge of the forest, and possesses a monstrous wolf which is believed to be a devil in a wolf's form. She calls him Pharamond, and converses with him as with a person; and the wolf understands everything she says. Having heard of your arrival, and that you were going to organize a big hunt, she must have told Pharamond to warn the wolves away. Depend upon it, that is the reason why you haven't found a single wolf!"

"Nonsense!" blustered the Captain; "I do not believe in any of your silly stories about sorceresses and devils!"

"Well, Sir, in order that you may test the truth of what I say, I advise you to do as follows: Go tomorrow about the village with your huntsmen and let it be known that you are going to return to Montauban. You will then actually leave Aignan; but you will stop when you get as far as Lupiac, at the Hôtel Bajan. There you will wait quietly for five days. The sorceress will learn of your departure; she will tell her wolf to go and get his companions and bring them back into the forest. I live at the edge of the woods; as soon as the wolves are back, I shall hear their howls; I shall then come and warn you, and then you will return to Aignan at night, stealthily. Monsieur le Maire will then take measures to warn the hunters secretly, and you will be able to organize the hunt without drum or trumpet. I assure you, Sir Captain, you will find that there are plenty of wolves."

After a moment, Monsieur de Ruble made up his mind.

"In spite of the fact that I have not much confidence in what you tell me, I am inclined to try your plan out of curiosity."

Antoinette de Medrano, having duly heard of the departure of Monsieur de Ruble, went to Aignan to verify the report. It was confirmed for her by the innkeeper. She returned to Gaure, happy with the success of her stratagem. She called Pharamond and said to him,

"You may now go and get the wolves; the huntsmen have gone away and there is no more danger."

Two days after, just before dawn, Jean Monjeau went and climbed a tree at the edge of the forest and began to howl like a wolf. He imitated their howling with such perfection that it was impossible to tell that it was not a wolf. Howls replied to his from all directions in the forest. The wolves came and circled round the tree on which he had climbed without discovering him; for wild beasts always look horizontally and never upwards. He waited for the sun to appear, and then descended from the tree and proceeded immediately to Lupiac to tell Monsieur de Ruble that the wolves had returned.

Monsieur de Ruble waited for nightfall, and then went to Aignan. The next day, the mayor sent secret messengers to warn the hunters of Aignan and the neighboring communes and to invite them to come and lend their aid in the hunt, informing them that the gathering would take place two days later at daybreak, on the elevation of La Papourre.

At the appointed time, as soon as the hunters had gathered in full force, Monsieur de Ruble ordered La Fleur to skirt the woods as before, with a hound in leash, to find the scent. This time, the huntsman had gone hardly a hundred meters when the hound stopped, sniffed the ground and bayed; then he pushed into the brush, followed by La Fleur. At length, they came to the little gorge at the bottom of which runs the brook of Sarr-nau. There the dog stopped before a thick brush, gave a short and raucous bark, his eyes bloodshot, his hair bristling, and braced himself ready to leap.

La Fleur held the dog back, pulling at the leash; he noted the exact spot where the wolves were hidden, and straightway returned to the Captain and reported.

Without delay, Monsieur de Ruble led the hunters to the place and made them form themselves about it in a threefold circle, instructing them as follows:

"I am going to let loose my dogs. When the wolves are frightened from cover, be careful not to miss them; above all, take heed not to shoot each other."

Leaving the hunters, Monsieur de Ruble then took his hounds to the exact place where La Fleur had first come on the scent. The dogs were unleashed and put on the track of it. Into the woods they plunged with an infernal uproar. Coming to the place where the wolves were, they started them quickly from their hiding place, so that they fled in all directions. On arriving at the triple circle of the hunters, they were welcomed by a formidable volley of shots. Suddenly turning tail, they ran back and finally massed themselves together in a deep ravine in the midst of inextricable thickets, and, backing themselves up against a steep bank, offered aggressive and determined defiance to the hounds.

Now, when Pharamond, who all this time was lying down under Antoinette's bed, heard the uproar and the hunting bugles, he bounded toward the open door of the château to rush out; but Antoinette forestalled him and shut the door in his face. The wolf sprang to the window; with the impact of his huge body he smashed the panes into a thousand fragments and sped like an arrow toward the forest, howling.　The wolves, hearing the cry of their chief, replied to it and took courage.

When he came to the circle of the hunters, he was greeted with two shots; but he ran so very swiftly that he was not hit.　As soon as he reached the wolves, he formed them into two groups; in one, he placed all the adult males to the number of about a hundred; in the other, the she-wolves and the young ones.　This second group he made to understand that a terrible battle was about to take place, and that they must take advantage of it to run away in single file, proceeding in the direction of the Pyrenees mountains.　Then, at the head of the males, he rushed at the dogs.

The dogs withstood the assault bravely, and the gigantic struggle began.　The wolves and the dogs, rearing themselves on their haunches, embraced each other with their front legs, their jaws interlocked, and fought like grim wrestlers.　In the twinkling of an eye, Pharamond had strangled two hounds and had sprung upon a third; but the circle of the hunters closed in, and they began to kill the wolves right and left.　With a shot from his carbine, the huntsman, La Jeunesse, shattered Pharamond's thigh; the wolf rushed at him on three legs and leaped at his throat; but, impeded in his movements by his wound, he only reached the huntsman's shoulder, into which he planted his formidable fangs, throwing him to the ground.　La Jeunesse would certainly have been lost then and there had not his comrade, La Ramée, felled the wolf with a shot from his carbine, its muzzle pressed close against him, so that the shot went through his chest.　Pharamond let go, and rolled down the hill into the ravine.

After this the hunters made short work of the

wolves, until, at last, there remained not a single one. Of the superb pack of dogs, there were left only four, and these sorely crippled.

When Monsieur de Ruble surveyed the place of carnage and realized that his pack was reduced to nought, he was seized with a fit of anger which culminated in a veritable paroxysm of fury. His face became purple and the veins stood out on his forehead. While he was standing thus, suddenly Antoinette appeared before him. Her eyes were blazing.

"You are a barbarous monster," she hurled at him, to come thus and massacre these poor beasts that have never done you any hurt!"

"Ah, it is you, is it—wretched sorceress that you are!—I am going to have you shot!—La Fleur!" he shouted, "kill this woman with your carbine; I will answer for everything!"

Antoinette crossed her arms on her breast and spoke up,

"Very well, then; let us see if you will be coward enough to assassinate a defenseless Christian woman!"

La Fleur raised his gun, aimed at Antoinette in the breast and pressed the trigger; as the report resounded, the huntsman fell backward as if struck by a thunderbolt; his carbine had burst and a fragment of the metal had pierced his eye and penetrated his brain. While his companions rushed to him to pick him up, Antoinette disappeared into the thicket.

Monsier de Ruble had a stretcher improvised with branches to carry the body of La Fleur to Aignan. La Ramée with three others bore it and, followed by the master of the wolfhounds and a crowd of hunters, proceeded toward the village.

But the misfortunes of this memorable day had

only begun, and Monsieur de Ruble soon found out
that one cannot so lightly defy the powers of necromancy. When they had come to the edge of the
wood, La Ramée caught his foot under the root of
a tree and stumbled and fell so unhappily that he
broke his thigh bone in two places, and they had to
make another stretcher to carry him also.

It was in this pitiable state that Monsieur de Ruble
and his huntsmen arrived at the inn. The doctor
was sent for immediately; but, unfortunately, he
(whose name was Lafont) had just gone to make
a call in the country and would not be back until
evening. La Ramée was placed on a bed. As for
La Jeunesse, they put on his injured shoulder a lin-
seed plaster, for he was suffering unspeakably from
the bite of Pharamond. This soothed the wound a
little.

The innkeeper then approached Monsieur de
Ruble:

"Sir, dinner is ready; come to table." To which
Monsieur de Ruble replied that he did not wish to
eat anything.

"Oh, yes!" remonstrated the innkeeper, "you are
fatigued and hungry and it will do you good to take
something."

"Very well, be it so; but go and tell La Jeunesse
to come, if he is able, and keep me company."

In spite of his suffering, and out of deference to
his master, the huntsman joined him at table; but
neither of them scarcely touched the viands that
were spread before them. On the other hand, the
Captain drank generously, and toward the end of
the meal ordered two bottles of champagne with
some cakes. La Jeunesse hardly drank at all and
Monsieur de Ruble emptied the two bottles by him-

self. Then the coffee was served, and with it a liter of old Armagnac brandy. La Jeunesse took his coffee without the brandy; but Monsieur de Ruble poured it into his cup recklessly.

All of a sudden he seized the bottle, put the neck to his mouth and with one long draught imbibed the remainder of the contents. A few moments later his face became congested, he started up convulsively, tugged violently at his cravat and broke the buttons off his shirt, gasping,

"Air! Air! I am stifling!"

He beat the air with his two hands and then suddenly crumpled down and fell prone, his face against the floor and his arms outstretched in the form of the cross, dead.

When, after much excitement, the body of his master was disposed of, La Jeunesse, who was suffering more and more grievously from the deep wound Pharamond had inflicted, went and lay down on a bed. About four o'clock in the evening the doctor returned from his call and went immediately to the inn. He examined the thigh of La Ramée and said with considerable concern,

"The inflammation is spreading higher up; amputation is the only thing that can save him!"

"Operate on me if you like," replied the huntsman; "I am not a coward."

The doctor began his work at once; but alas! in the very midst of the operation the patient was taken with a fainting spell and expired before regaining consciousness.

Monsieur Lafont then went into the room in which La Jeunesse was lying down. Him he found in a fearful condition; his eyes were flaming like those of a maniac, and from his mouth came blood and foam

—evident signs of hydrophobia. With a hoarse and unnatural voice he cried out,

"Why do you come here?—Begone, or my teeth shall rend you!"

The doctor hastily retired from the room, locked the door securely, and sent for two of the most sturdy men in Aignan, Durban and Laclotte. When they came, he said to the former,

"Here is a mattress. Take it, enter the room of La Jeunesse quickly, cover him with it and hold him tight. Laclotte and I will bind his legs at the ankles and his arms at the wrists."

All this was soon accomplished.

Then the doctor had a warm bath prepared, in which they put La Jeunesse. This done, he mercifully opened the four arteries of the arms and the legs, and the huntsman died without feeling death, like a man who goes to sleep.

And now a word, and the rest of the story is told.

As soon as the hunters had left the forest, Antoinette went with Jeanne to the place of battle to look for Pharamond, if he was still alive, or to get his body, if he was dead. They found him at last, stretched at the bottom of the ravine, showing no signs of life. Antoinette called to him,

"Pharamond! Pharamond!"

The wolf, who was not quite dead, opened his eyes. Antoinette approached him, crouched down beside him, took his head on her knees and caressed him and kissed him several times on his nose, and the wolf feebly licked her hands. He made an effort to get up, but a jet of blood spurted from his wound. He had a convulsive spasm, his eyes became veiled, and he breathed his last.

Antoinette had his body carried to the Château de Gaure and ordered a grave dug near the front of the main door of the château, and here he was buried. From that day on, she shut herself up in her chamber and would see nobody save Jeanne Garbay, with whom she spent whole days speaking about Pharamond. She ate hardly anything and gradually wasted away.

Feeling her end near, she sent for the curé of Aignan and the notary. She confessed, received the last sacraments of the church and dictated her testament to the notary, directing him to sell her farms and to distribute the money to the most needy families of the parish of Aignan. She bequeathed the Château de Gaure with its dependencies to Jeanne Garbay.

Three days later, she died.

Since that time, no one has ever seen any more wolves in the Forest of Aignan. But the wild boars abound there to this day.

Chapter XXXI: *What One Gets for a Pair of Gloves*

I AM not improving my English by David's visits to my garden as much as I hoped, for when he talks, he much prefers to practice his French on me.

A few days ago, I became aware that he was using a certain phrase that stirred my memory vaguely; it was as if something of long ago spoke through him; a something familiar, which puzzled me greatly —that is, until yesterday. Then it suddenly flashed on my mind that this phrase he was repeatedly using was a favorite expression of Germaine's father. Thereupon, I thought I saw the solution: David had probably caught this trick of speech from Germaine herself, who unconsciously imitates her father in many things.

It appears, then, that I am not Monsieur Ware's only teacher of French!

What a pity that the soul has to be encumbered with words in order to convey its ideas! Why cannot our thoughts meet each other without the clumsy medium of language?—language that divides and confuses mankind and makes us forever misunderstand one another?

That is one thing in which the angels in heaven

have a great advantage over us. According to St. Jean Damascin, the angels have no need at all of tongues or ears, still less do they use signs and gesticulations, like the deaf mutes. On the contrary, it is likely, as this same author says, that they simply direct their thoughts toward each other by the exercise of their wills, somewhat as a child, with a fragment of a mirror, flashes the sun into the eyes of whomever he chooses. Perhaps they speak through music—the artists sometimes picture them with harps or trumpets; what delight to express one's thoughts through music, a language all of us can understand!

I like exceedingly a sentence I found lately in one of my old books; it expresses the entire matter as well as mere words can:

We say one thing, and often think another; the angels, on the contrary, reveal their hearts infallibly and manifest themselves plainly on the soul of the one to whom they speak, who sees into their substance as through a clear glass, discerning their thoughts in all their truth and candor.

But in whatever fashion the angels speak with one another, it is manifest that they do not need to speak to God, save, perhaps, for their own soul's sake. Their thoughts He knows before they ever think to bring them to His infinite beholding. And in this one thing, angels and men are alike.

David, much to his distress, lost some of Marius' story of the wolves just because it had to be told in language. So, to-day I cleared up the parts he had not quite understood. I also told him that the very inn at which the master of wolfhounds tarried—the Hôtel Maulézun—is still standing, and that from the window of my back chamber I can look across the alley through the crumbling archway of its ancient yard. He wanted to go at once to see the room where La Jeunesse was smothered with the mattress.

But I had something else in mind. I took him by the road that ascends the long hill on top of which is the beginning of the Forest of Aignan, where the wolves used to be. At last, we arrived on a sort of plateau at the edge of the woods, where there is a charcoal-burner's hut, and there we stopped to rest. Far below us, our little village dozed lazily in the afternoon sun.

"This," I said, "is that very elevation of La Papourre, where Monsieur de Ruble gathered all his men together on the fateful dawn of the big hunt. And there, just on the other side of the woods to the north, was the château where Antoinette lived."

David remarked how small the forest was, after all, and how it could hardly hide so many wolves.

Of course, compared with American forests, such as I once read about in Chateaubriand, this one is little enough. Yet, I remember a peasant who thought that he knew the Forest of Aignan well. He shot a bird while he was standing by a certain oak tree. He went to pick up his bird, and then wandered for two whole hours trying to find that oak again. He could recognize nothing. He was lost.

Over four hundred years ago, the Count of Armagnac presented this entire forest (much larger then) to the commune of Aignan, provided the latter furnished him annually with "one pair of plain, white gloves for the fête of La Toussaint." Those are the very words. The whole agreement, solemnly attested by notaries, and dated the 29th of September, 1481, is to be found in the archives of our village—or, rather, it was there until the old town hall burned down a few years ago. And to this day, the wood that is cut in the forest belongs to the families of the commune as their right, and it will be thus as long as the forest lasts.

We were seated on the slope just below the charcoal-burner's hut, looking out over the hills. After quite a silence, during which I was musing on the forest, its poetry, its legends handed down from long ago, there came into my head the episode of the Abbé Druilhet, which I proceeded at once to tell David, knowing his pleasure in such things.

It, too, belongs to Marius. He says it is true.

AN ANECDOTE OF THE ABBÉ DRUILHET

When the Revolution came and overturned the old order of things, the people of this region were not at all in sympathy with it. Indeed, they actively rebelled, and at length took up arms against the new régime. At their head was the Abbé Druilhet, priest of Margouet. a determined man, possessed of herculean strength. Among the leaders were also the three sons of the Sir Knight of Labourre, whose castle once rose on the very place now occupied in our village by the convent school.

The rebels were in the habit of gathering at night

in great numbers in the middle of the Forest of Aignan. The signal that brought them together was the hoot of the owl, which they imitated perfectly.

Naturally, it was not long before the rebellion got noised abroad. At length, Citizen Daubes, the magistrate of Nogaro, was forced to do something. He sent a company of the National Guard, commanded by one, Lieutenant Sarthe, to seize this Abbé Druilhet and take him to Nogaro, prisoner. The Abbé was hiding at Margouet, in the house of his friend, Laborde. It was in the afternoon, about four o'clock, when the guards surrounded this house and then violently forced their way inside. Before the Abbé could escape, Lieutenant Sarthe seized him by the collar, calling out in a loud voice,

"In the name of the law, I arrest you!"

But you may well believe that it was not to be so easy as all that! With an incredibly quick movement, the Abbé suddenly disengaged himself, and, with a thrust of his bull-like head into the very middle of Citizen Sarthe's chest, he sent him rolling on to the floor. Then the Abbé made a rush for the doorway. The guards barred his passage there and threw themselves upon him, and in spite of his great strength, he had to submit to their overwhelming numbers. Then, bound hand and foot, he was dragged along the road toward Nogaro.

Now, it happened that some peasants of Margouet, having been secret witnesses of all this, began to send forth the hoot of the owl from all directions. This signal was heard far and wide, through this and the neighboring communes. When the company of guards, sixty men strong, dragging the Abbé Druilhet along with them, came to the hollow at the foot of the Château Mauhic, they all at once found themselves surrounded by more than three hundred peasants, armed with guns, axes, and scythes, demanding the release of the prisoner if they did not want to be exterminated. Yielding to superior strength, and in order to avoid a bloody struggle, the Lieutenant gave in to them. The priest hastily returned to his parish and hid, sometimes in one house, and sometimes in another, and try as they would they could not succeed in retaking him.

After a moment, David looked at me in surprise, and said,

"Is that all?"

I had to tell him that this is the way Marius relates it, and that he always stops right here, probably because there is nothing more to recount.

By this time, the sun was low enough so that the shadow of the little charcoal-burner's hut had crept over close to us. Still, we sat there for a little while longer. All about us on the hillside the prickly gorse was growing in rank profusion, vivid with its little yellow flowers, the long stems bending gently to the breeze. I lazily reached out and plucked one of them, though the sharp needles hurt my hand.

This prickly gorse with its tiny yellow flowers— it is to me the symbol of my village and the country round about. I have known it since childhood, when it cruelly scratched my bare legs and caught in my clothes. It grows everywhere man will let it. One sees its grayish green, often mixed with the purple heather, rising above the rough hedges on the high banks of country roads, its long stems swaying in the wind. Sometimes carts go along the road, piled high with this same gorse—it makes an excellent bed for the oxen to lie on in their stalls; the needles cannot penetrate their tough hides.

It was near here, on this very hillside among the gorse, that a monastery was built away back in the night of time, Marius says a great deal more than a thousand years ago. And what did the monks call it? Well, the gorse grew everywhere around them, so what more natural than that they should name the monastery and the little cluster of thatched houses after the gorse—*agnas* was the Gascon name for it; and after awhile it became Aignan in our French, and Aignan my village is to this day. Anyway, that is what Marius says, and I would as soon believe him as anybody.

The monastery is gone now; but where it stood is a gabled house, up whose front the grapevines clamber. It is just there, where the forest tumbles over the top of the hill. It is still called Monjeau, which is patois for monastery; and there actually lived the Jean Monjeau that climbed the tree that dawn of the big hunt and howled so successfully at the wolves to call them together.

I like to think of the monks as they lived, and prayed, and sang, and labored on that hillside thirteen centuries ago, there in their wilderness of gorse. The gorse, with its prickly needles and its tiny blossoms of yellow—fit symbol, is it not, of the lives of God's saints here on earth! Oh, there are thorns that pierce the flesh; but amid the thorns, yes, praise God, amid the thorns, grow the little golden flowers of our immortal faith!

Chapter XXXII: *The Pipes of Pan*

THIS morning I was awakened very early by some liquid notes of birdlike sweetness that drifted through my partly open shutter from the street beneath. Up and down the scale the capricious melody scampered, now thin and plaintive, now rippling down a cadence like the fall of a woodland stream.

It was the goat-man. He had stopped in front of the house across the way, his ten or fifteen goats straggling along the street, ready to be milked should any one desire it. For my part, his music was more precious than his milk; and as I lay there half in dream, it seemed as though the pipes of Pan were echoing from some cool depth of forest. I knew, though, that if I looked out, the illusion would quickly vanish; I should find on my goat-man no hoofs and horns, and nothing resembling the great Pan except the good-nature of the goatherd's face. Even his rapturous pipe is not the least like Pan's syrinx, being of one piece like a flageolet, rather than that row of reeds with which the grotesque god was wont to woo his nymphs in ancient woods.

What luck one has on some days! This day was one of the fortunate ones, not because it was the 14th of July, but for two other reasons: first, because it commenced with the music of the pipes of Pan; and next, because when I got to my garden after mass and stood on the highest point and looked across the valleys away to the south—why, there were the Pyrenees, plainly visible along the horizon as far as one could see.

The Pyrenees furnish the dominant note of the symphony that is our landscape—that is, sometimes they do, for they are by no means a constant note, being invisible for days at a time, or so slightly visible that one can hardly distinguish their dim peaks from the clouds.

But this morning! Lofty, deep-furrowed, and patched with snow, they gave themselves to the smile of the sun, an apocalypse of sudden beauty. Their foothills were hidden by a gray-blue haze, so that their higher portions mounted into the upper air as though resting on nothing—a miracle let down from heaven, giving the impression of impossible heights.

They have a rollicking song they sing about the Pyrenees. One hears it when companies of youths pass along the road on the way to some fête. It is really the song of a mountain shepherd, who is urged by a stranger to forsake his mountains and follow him to the lowlands and cease to be a shepherd more. But the loyal shepherd sings,

> *Never, never! That were folly!*
> *Happy, happy is my life.*
> *My sash I have and my béret,*
> *My joyous songs,*
> *My sweetheart and my chalet.*

When I was in the Pyrenees last summer, after a visit to Lourdes, I heard this self-same song echoing down a winding pass, blending with the rushing music of the mountain stream by whose side I was musing.

What I was musing about then is what I have been thinking about to-day—of the note of beauty that transfigures our lives, especially here in this southern reach of the world. The way of Truth leads to God; the way of Goodness leads to God, and the way of Beauty leads to God, too. And the great Church, knowing this, has made God's temples beautiful with the glory of arch and high-flung roof, and windows rich with splendor, and spires that search the stars, and deep-toned bells that call. And she has graced His praise with the beauty of music and sculpture, and swinging censers, and altar lights, and processions, that bring to men's hearts the stately beauty of God's service. As my wise friend, the Abbé Rivoire, used to say, without beauty, goodness is not complete, and truth is not true. Yes, the way of Beauty leads straight to the heart of the good God—oh, not carnal beauty, not that, but the spiritual beauty of which all physical things, be they the peaks of the Pyrenees or the pipes of Pan, are but poor symbols.

But I once had a friend—he was an artist, a painter—who said that he preferred what was beautiful to what was true. As if the two things could rightly be separated!

"It is glorious," he said once, "to have a mission

in life so beautiful that one is even willing to lie for it."

He said that when he painted a picture, he never painted things as they really were, but as they ought to be. And this was the lie he was talking about and which he thought art required for beauty's sake!

"How worthless mere facts are!" he used to say. "It is the imagination that builds the dream!"

Truly, how stupid he was! Could he not see that one is not contorting facts into a lie when one paints the dream that they suggest? The sunset across the hills is a fact; but the dream it suggests is a fact, too—not a lie—nay, it is the very truest fact of all, for it gives all facts a glorious meaning, and makes all lesser truth worth while! My friend did not falsify nature, as he said; he transfigured it! And in this transfiguration of nature, he was feeling after God, though he knew it not.

I am glad that my own life is touched by this note of beauty; would that every hour of it had been! They used to tell me at our school in Paris that we Gascons are too practical to care for beautiful things. At first I believed it, but I know better now. Though we Gascons do not furnish the world with many great artists and poets, the very same beauty such geniuses create is in our lives instead. It is not put in the form in which beauty is sold in the market, but it is there, unobtrusive as you please. Marius feels that note of beauty and actually sings it in his verses. One can hear it in the patois of the songs that echo across our fields and vineyards. There is Marinette, simple and crude, perhaps—yet, in spite of the fact that she has very little land, and that she must use it to raise her vegetables for the market, she grows flowers there, too, all the year round, for beauty's sake—what roses those were she gathered for Germaine on her fête-day! And Germaine herself—that dainty filet lace she makes in her garden is just as much a poem as any melody a poet ever sang his heart into! And Germaine's mother—I have seen some tapestry of her own fingers' weave that made a whole room charming just by being there!

The other day, I went to a peasant's house out in the country near Dému, where I stayed to dinner. They were not wealthy peasants either, and the husband wore his *béret* at table, which in Paris would be considered very bad manners indeed! But what fine embroideries on the tables, at the windows and on the beds! The wife had embroidered those sheets while watching the cattle in the fields, and had done the embroidery of the curtains while walking to Aignan on market-days. This very noon I saw some farm machinery going by—a huge engine of some sort—with a bouquet of daisies stuck in the whistle; and the driver actually had a rose in his mouth—his hands were busy with driving his oxen.

Of all things beautiful that man creates, music is best. It expresses the mysterious depths of the soul that mere words never fathom. When I have heard the music of the organ surge down the nave of Notre Dame, the infinite has caught me up and I seemed to be close to things to which death alone opens the gates.

To-night, being the night of the 14th of July, we had some great music in the public Place by the village band. How thrilling to hear them! They played under the arcades of the town hall, which was hung with paper lanterns all over its long façade; and the music stormed the fronts of the close-built houses surrounding the Place, flowed up the side streets, and sent its harmonies out over the hills beyond, till I am sure that they heard it as far as Margouet. Our band has twenty men in it, and not one of them but taught himself how to play; the note of beauty struggled in them for expression and our splendid band is the result. Henri plays in it, the postmaster plays in it, the mayor's secretary plays in it—he it is that beats the drum—and little Paul Sarrade, the sabot-maker, leads it exactly as he has seen the leader of the great band over in Tarbes do it. That Paul Sarrade can do almost anything with music. He sometimes sings tenor in the church, and he performs upon the saxophone and the clarinet equally well. And if there is music in wooden shoes, well, he puts music into them—I don't refer to the clatter, but to the carvings he puts on them when he has a mind to do his best.

When the band had finished playing the Marseillaise, I rambled down the narrow street past the post office. The gendarmerie, too, was brightly illuminated with paper lanterns; but I found the most beautiful decorations of all at the edge of the village, in front of the little house in which the guardian of the forest lives. There is a tree across the road, and he had transformed this tree into a thing of wonder for the glory of France and the day she celebrates. It was hung with gorgeous lanterns, and not only that—colored glass containers were suspended from the tree with oil wicks burning inside them. No wonder people went in crowds after the music to see what the guardian of the forest had done with his tree, on which it was appropriate that he should hang his lanterns rather than on anything else, considering his office. One sees that the note of beauty is in his soul, too.

On my way back, while I was crossing the Place toward home, I passed a young man who is a member of the band. He had under his arm a horn, and was walking along with all the importance of one who can thrill men's hearts with songs that never die.

Yet I happen to know that he cannot play a note. He is, indeed, a member of the band as I say, pays his dues regularly, and is always present when they play, pretending to blow his alto saxophone; but if one should get quite close to him and listen, he would perceive that no sound ever comes forth. When he first joined the band, they stuffed his horn with paper because he was always out of tune. Still, he remained, and now he is taken as a matter of course by every one, although everybody knows that his contribution to the music is a blessed silence.

His name is Soucaret. He is a baker's helper in Sabazan. He has written plays that were never acted and never will be acted. But the note of beauty in him gropes for utterance, though in vain.

I cannot laugh at him. Strange to say, he reminds me of my own life. Don't we all fail? Isn't it all a matter of degree? The ineffable beauty that we seek—did the pipes of Pan ever express it, has poet, sculptor, painter, ever found it?

But oh, the glimpses of its wonder that we find by day and night—they strengthen our faith in God, and change life's failure into that exquisite yearning which is brave enough to mock at death, and to seek its vision until it finds it at some far corner of the everlasting years!

Chapter XXXIII: *Madame Sance Asks Advice*

MY Aunt Madeleine has very strong likes and
dislikes. I do not always trust her dislikes
—I have observed that women tend to have
aggressive prejudices without sufficient reasons; but
when I hear my Aunt Madeleine speaking highly of
any one, I know the praise is probably deserved, possibly because she is extremely cautious about praising
anybody at all.

Now, my Aunt Madeleine insists that Madame
Sance, the mother of Germaine, is the finest woman
in Aignan. In this, she does not except even
Madame Lacoste, who, she says, talks too much.
And yet if there is any woman that talks as much
as Madame Lacoste, it is my Aunt Madeleine herself. True, she does not talk quite so fast, but that
is probably a matter depending largely on the nature
of the tongue itself, which is a purely physical organ,
the speed of which does not determine how much
one really says in a given time, any more than the
fastness of a clock can be measured by the mere
speed of its pendulum—no, you have to consider its
length as well! I have listened to them both and
I have concluded that, while Madame Lacoste uses

more words, still, give them both an hour, the tongue of each will cover about the same amount of gossip and accomplish about the same harm.

But one cannot get my Aunt Madeleine to say the slightest word against Madame Sance. She has known her for forty years, and still admires her.

My Aunt Madeleine appeared in the doorway of my study this morning, interrupting me as I was writing an important letter to none other than the Archbishop at Auch. She said that while she was watering her potted geraniums on the sidewalk, Madame Sance had stopped and talked with her, and had finally left word that if I should be passing by her house in the afternoon, she would like to speak with me.

"She has something on her mind. I think I know what it is; you must go."

But nothing more could I get out of my Aunt Madeleine.

Starting from the church at the head of my street, it is not far out the Road of the Madonna to Madame Sance's house. It was toward four o'clock when I went that way.

"My Aunt Madeleine is right about Madame Sance," I said to myself. "One of the best things that one can say of our village is that Madame Sance was born in it."

One is sure to see Madame Sance in the village on Monday afternoons, when we have our market. She is a little woman, always dressed in black; up to seven or eight years ago, she still had a girlish figure and was more robust than she is to-day. Now she is bowed a little, her face is thinner, and sorrow has left its traces there; her hair has grown from brown to gray, and her eyes are getting dim. But when she smiles!—it is the same wonderful smile of her girl-hood, which makes one forget that there are such things as years and age and grief and loneliness! And her voice is like her smile—how sweetly she used to sing!—and both remind one somehow of the dainty, fragrant, jasmine flowers she loves so well.

Madame Sance is still marvelously energetic. She has not lost her vivacious temperament, although lately she is inclined to look more on the sad side of things. In her heart are two visions that com-fort each other: the memory of her husband, and the hope that lives in her children.

When I arrived at the house and turned in at the driveway, nobody was in sight, although I half ex-pected to find some of the family in the garden. The wide-open doors of the ground floor, which serves as the little doctor's garage, showed that he had gone out in his automobile, no doubt to visit patients in the country. Dick, the bird-dog, lay sprawled in the sun by the chicken yard, a favorite spot of his, where he has made quite a collection of bones, which he will let no one molest. Just as I had mounted the steps to the entrance, outside of which several chairs were invitingly arranged, Madame Sance appeared, carrying her fancy-work basket.

"Good afternoon, Monsieur l'Abbé! I was just coming out here to sew. I hope you have not been waiting. Will you not be seated here where it is cool? It is kind of you to come."

It was only after a while that Madame Sance could bring herself to reveal what she had wished to see me about. I never hurry people in such matters, least of all an old friend. At length, though, after we had been silent for a few moments, she asked in a very hesitating way,

"You know Monsieur Ware well, do you not, Monsieur l'Abbé?"

Then, that was it! I knew it would come some day. And thereupon she told me all about it. How she had watched the tall American's increasing interest in her daughter; how she had suspected that it meant more than a mere passing friendship, especially when Monsieur Ware began coming almost every day. At first it was to ask for Henri; but now she knew it was Germaine he most wished to see. He had taken no pains to hide it. And Germaine herself—well, yesterday she had been surprised into a confused admission that Monsieur Ware meant more to her than any casual acquaintance. Germaine had not said much, but her looks had betrayed a great deal.

"What is to become of my little Maimaine!—I need your advice, Monsieur l'Abbé. Will Monsieur Ware be here much longer?—How I wish he would go away!"

It was difficult for me to say anything. None of all this was any surprise to me. Still, I wanted to know more. So I took the liberty of asking Madame

Sance if Monsieur Ware had ever spoken to her about Germaine.

"Not directly, Monsieur l'Abbé. These Americans—perhaps I do not understand them; but he has said things that make me afraid. Why does he take care to tell me of his family, and of his prospects, and of the school in America where he is going to teach, and even what his salary will be, and other personal things which he seems to want me to know, as if I had a right to know them? Ah, Monsieur l'Abbé, I am afraid!"

"Have you never thought that Germaine might marry some day?"

"But not a foreigner! Not Monsieur Ware! It is impossible—you must know it is impossible! When my Angèle married Maurice, it was hard enough; but he is a Frenchman, one of us. But an American! That is different! Besides, Germaine is only a baby! She is too young to think of marriage yet.—No, no, no, it cannot be!"

After a little I said,

"But Monsieur Ware—since you appeal to me—he is a very good kind of American. He is not at all like the Americans we sometimes find traveling in our country. He is a gentleman; he is kind; he is an idealist; he loves beautiful things; he is sane and good; he is healthy in mind and body. At first I did not like him; now I find great comfort in his friendship. There is one great defect, though, one very grievous defect—he is outside the Church. That is the serious thing. That has disturbed me from the very first. That is bad. That he is a foreigner might be overlooked. But to be outside the fold of the Church—that is different."

I knew what this meant to Madame Sance, too—she who is so devout, who goes to communion often, and to vespers, and who would never even think of missing mass on Friday, and who is an example of piety to the whole village.

So I was distressed over the whole matter. Yet I tried to be fair in speaking of David, mentioning the good things about him, hoping that if the worst happened in spite of everything, this would reconcile her a little.

But for the moment, I had no advice to give, and told her so. I wanted to think it over. And so I left her, promising to see her again soon.

As I went through the gates, I glanced back along the driveway and saw a girlish figure in the distance nearing the sunlit barns from the orchards, a basket on her arm. It was Germaine.

To tell the truth, now that I am here alone, I am at a loss. There is one insuperable objection to the suit of Monsieur Ware: he is a Protestant. I wish I could think of other objections. I do not want Germaine to marry him. Yet, after all, forgetting his religion, who will ever come into Germaine's life so good, so suited to her in so many ways— that is, if she is to marry at all? No youth in this commune can equal David; that I know.

If only he were within the Holy Church! There is Germaine's soul to think of.

As I was walking back to my garden, it came over me how desolate our little village would be without

Germaine. I could see that her mother's underlying sorrow was the thought of Germaine's going away to far-off America, across the seas those thousands and thousands of miles. And Madame Sance is getting old. It would be cruel. To lose Germaine like that!

I wonder what David really thinks of the unseen things of the spirit. I have never heard him speak of his religion. I must discover this, if I can without offending him.

Chapter XXXIV: *The Church on the Hill*

IN the undulating tapestry that is our landscape, the church towers, crowning the hills, are the recurrent figures, lending it special character and distinction.

All kinds of towers they are, but mostly square towers, sturdy and strong, like those of a rugged fortress. Plain, square towers, up which the ivy creeps, covering with masses of dark green the crumbling stone, working its way into all the crevices it can find; enlarging them, loosening them with fingers subtle and sure, hastening the time when tower and ivy shall tumble back to the earth together.

These churches on our hills! The hands of many generations have left their traces on nave and roof and choir and belfry, repairing a little here, a little there, as the centuries have rolled by, until no man can surely tell which stones are the oldest, although it is easy to see which are the newest. The weather has done its part, too—I maintain that the weather is the most skillful decorator an architect can find, and that, until the winds and suns and rains have done their full and transforming part, the most beautiful building ever made by men is barren and unfinished.

But the weather has done its splendid best with all the towers that one sees from my garden. And if you but climb the hills and enter the little villages that nestle about their churches as if for protection, you will see if God's good fortresses, whose towers you saw against the sky, are not far more than so much mere stone and mortar! If a Gascon village can be said to have a heart, a soul, it is to be found in its church. I know a little village on its hill south of here, where the homes hug the church so close that one can get to the gothic portal only by the tiniest of paths between the houses, which seem like happy children gathered about their ancient mother!

I like to enter the peaceful silence of such a church, suddenly to find myself shut away from the world. There, in front of the altar, suspended from the roof, is the sanctuary lamp, its flame forever burning. Like the love of God, it burns there night and day. The sun fades daily from those stained windows, and on dark nights the stars cease to send their tiny shafts of light through them; and yet this lamp burns on—like the love of God, it never fails!

If our villages have souls, they have voices, too— the sweet-toned bells that speak across the valleys every day from these ancient towers. How often have I stood in my garden watching the sun sink behind the far-away hills; then, when the afterglow spread itself along the western rim of the world, and the tower of the high-roofed church at Sabazan was vivid against a curtain of old rose and silver—then the soft-toned Angelus drifted across the valleys from towers near and far, the nearer bells loud and courageous, and some of them faint and far away, like the sigh of an angel, or the whisper of a forgotten hope. Morning, noon, and night, the bells talk to each other across the hills. Sometimes they toll slowly and solemnly, and then one knows that there is one whose soul shall never hear their music any more. Sometimes they speak fast, and in as merry tones as a bell can have, when the ringer strikes it rapidly with a little rock in his hand; it is a christening, and new ears shall learn to listen for and love these voices from our towers. And sometimes when storm-clouds bank themselves dark and terrible against the sky, and the lightning begins to flash, and the hail threatens, one hearkens for the valorous clangor of the bells that call to God to protect His children and their harvests from the desolating armies of the air. Then it is, that, as the clamor of the bells mingles with the crash of thunder and the howling of winds, the priest is before the altar praying for his people. But be they bells of alarm, or joy, or sadness, or the peaceful bells that daily call to mass, they come to mean something more than the mere sounds of earth; heaven speaks through them, and their music seems to give the soul a glimpse through spiritual gates.

Our church in Aignan is not at all beautiful or graceful at first sight; but, truly, there is no church just like it anywhere in the world! From one side, it looks like one church, from another side it looks like another church, and so on for all four sides. Changeful history has built itself into those rough, time-worn stones so many times and in so many circumstances that art long ago succumbed in despair. It is like an old warrior, wounded and crippled from many battles, but the more interesting for all that, and unconquerable still. High up under the eaves are traces of a line of battlements, and a place where the village wall of defense once joined. But the tower! *That* is the thing that spells Aignan to those who look from the surrounding valleys. Heavy and square, flanked by a thick buttress, surmounted by a bulbous dome, with a slender cupola on top—there is only one other like it in all Gascony, that at the town of Eauze, across the hills to the north. All these years, when I have been away from my native village, the first thing that came to my mind when I thought of it—oh, so often!—was this tower rising in its midst. And to show how capricious memory is, dwelling even on the homely things, the next thing I was quite likely to picture was the narrow Street of the Balustrade, which leads up to the church, with somebody's washing ever hung up to dry on the low, wrought-iron fence that gives the street its name.

Inside our church, we have a treasure. It came about thus.

It is said that hundreds and hundreds of years ago, a peasant was plowing a field somewhat beyond where Germaine's garden is. Suddenly, the oxen stopped and would not go on any farther; some say they knelt down. Taking it as an omen, the peasant, with several others, procured shovels and dug into the earth, and behold! they found a beautiful statue of the Virgin, in an almost perfect state of preservation! It is now in our church, in the Chapel of the Holy Virgin.

All the roads in Gascony really lead to the churches on the hills. One might claim that they lead to the villages, just as much as to the churches; but if that is so, of what meaning are the crosses all along the roadsides, reminding the traveler of his debt to God? Crosses of many kinds: immense, rough-hewed wooden crosses, like the actual cross on which Our Savior was crucified; iron crosses of all sizes, some with the Virgin wrought in the center, some with cherubs at the base, some inwrought with the sad implements of the crucifixion—the hammer, the spear, the sponge—and many with the cock at the very top. David asked me the other day why the image of the cock surmounts our wayside crosses and the steeples of our churches, and I quoted from Monsieur Pontier's book where it says that this cock, which is the image of the very cock that crowed at the passion, signifies the conscience which speaks to us and arouses us when we have offended God.

Then, there are the life-size images of the Holy Virgin, golden-crowned. Ours is just beyond Marinette's house, on the other side of the road. Just now, lilies are in bloom in the ground before her, and always an offering of flowers is at her feet.

Since he came, David has watched every procession that has gone to this place from the church, including the one we had on Corpus Christi Sunday, when the roads were strewn with rose-petals and ferns, and the fronts of the houses were hung with sheets richly decorated with flowers and branches, and a chorus of girls sang as they passed along, and the old priest walked under the golden canopy with the Host, and little girls, dressed in white, carried baskets containing more rose-petals and leaves to strew before the wayside altars. David is not used to such things in his country. Why, every Sunday morning before mass, we have a procession through our streets! In some towns, even in France, the authorities do not allow them any more; there was a great disturbance over the Corpus Christi procession in Montauban this year.

My conversation with Madame Sance was three days ago. It was only to-day, when David came to my garden, that I found a chance to talk with him about religion, as Madame Sance had charged me to do just as I was leaving her. We had finished the French lesson, and were sitting out under the fig tree. To my immense surprise I soon discovered that David is not a Protestant at all.

"No, Monsieur l'Abbé, I am neither a Protestant, nor am I a Catholic. Not that I am irreligious. Only, I am afraid no church would admit me. There is always something in every church's creed I cannot believe."

"But that college in America where you go to be a professor, is it not Protestant?"

"No, it is not Protestant; it is supported by the State; many Catholic students go there, too."

I found out many astonishing things about David. Although he is not a Catholic, he believes in God, the soul, and immortality; only, he has reasoned these things all out for himself. He knows St.

Thomas d'Aquin very well, and respects his philosophy very highly. And he spoke of the beauty of many of the teachings of the Holy Church. Indeed, he went so far as to say that he would as soon belong to the Catholic Church as to any church, only he felt he could belong to none.

"It is my reason, Monsieur l'Abbé. I have to reason everything out before I can believe."

I told him of the dangers of free-thinking in spiritual things, of the extreme peril of a man supposing that he can make his own religion out of his poor finite reason.

"Most men," I said, "when they undertake to reason about the great truths of the Church, think only just far enough to doubt them and to destroy their faith in them. That is a pity."

"But, Monsieur l'Abbé," David remonstrated, "that is not the way it is with me. It may be hard to reason one's way into religion, but it can be done. Some men believe first in order to understand, as your St. Augustine advises; but I am one of those who must understand first in order to believe. And most of the great truths of religion I believe in now, although my reason led me to doubt them all once. You and I are not so far apart, Monsieur l'Abbé, even though you are in the Church and I am outside of it!"

I could not help asking David just why he was not a Catholic then.

"You have too many superstitions, or what I call superstitions; and your miracles, beautiful as some of them are, I cannot accept, although I have nothing to say against those who can believe in them. Let me show you what I mean.   When my sister and I were coming down here from Paris, we stopped a few days at Poitiers.   There is a very old church there, the church of St. Radegonde, with its curious clock tower.   Well, in the middle of the crypt is the tomb of the Saint herself.   The walls are covered with crutches of those said to be cured by petitions to the Saint.   Why, on those walls are hung letters written to her by people in distress.   There was one like this: 'Dear St. Radegonde, please have my husband cured from his sickness.'   Then, to the right of the nave, there is the Chapelle du Pas-de-Dieu, and in this chapel a stone in which is something that looks like a footprint about fifteen inches long.   It is said to be the footprint of Christ, and was brought from the convent of the Saint, where Christ appeared to her.   This precious stone is protected by iron bars. There is no use talking, Monsieur l'Abbé, I cannot believe in such things.   Surely, it is absurd."

David confuses such matters as these with the great verities of the Church!   Who knows?   It may be that there is hope for my young friend if I can but explain to him things I am certain he does not now understand.   I feel this all the more when I remember that after a short silence he remarked smilingly,

"After all, God's footprints are to be found everywhere!"

I could not have said that better myself.

David has told me of how the villages in America, even the small ones, have many churches, all differing in their beliefs. That must be a very bad thing. There can be only one true Church, as there can be only one true religion. Here in France, it is so much better. One Church, the true Church, that unites the souls of the village in one worship! In other things, the people who live here may be divided; but God unites them all as children of the same family, with the same eternal hope and the same everlasting faith.

At least, that is the ideal. Yet what indifference there is, after all, even in my village!

I communicated some of these thoughts to David. He finally said,

"In one thing I agree with you; the Church gives these peasants of yours a far better religion than they could ever think out for themselves. Perhaps in your country it is best as it is."

In *my* country? It is best in *any* country! The great Church is for all times and places. O Holy Church of the blessed God! We learn to come to Thee as to the Mother of all souls that seek Thy rest! Thy infinite heart shields us from every sorrow, and teaches us the mysteries that reason never finds, and that faith alone can fathom. Embattled by the centuries, Thou hast never known defeat, and Thy every triumph marks the progress of the spirit through the everlasting years. Thy splendid towers are fortresses that guard against all evil; they point to that unseen world to which the blessed sacraments of death lead all those who are steadfast in Thy faith. By Thee, all that is of worth that man achieves becomes transfigured toward God's service; in Thee, the struggles of heart-weary ages find their goal at last; for through Thee, and Thee alone, are to be reached all the glories that we vainly seek on earth!

Chapter XXXV: *I Seek a Parish*

TO-DAY, I got out a long ladder and after some trouble put it up against the front of my garden-house, so that the top of it just reached the grapevine that grows high over the door. My garden-house faces south; so day in and day out the warm sun has been working on the clusters of grapes hanging up there just below the eaves. Their little green jackets have steadily swelled themselves out during these long summer days, turning first to a dull, reddish brown, and then, slowly, to the deepest of purples. When I reached the top of the ladder, I plucked several of the ripest.

I had just put one of them in my mouth when I heard a sudden call from very near at hand; in truth, I nearly lost my balance. However, I had presence of mind enough to grasp the ladder with both hands; and then I cautiously turned about and looked down. There was David laughing a hearty *"Bonjour!"* up to me and asking me to throw down some of the grapes to him.

"These are my first Gascon grapes," he said, as he ate them.

I explained to him that grapes as favorably exposed to the sun as these are get ripe much sooner than those in the vineyards. Last year I did not have to wait until the last of July, as I have had to this time; no, last year, I remember, some of them were good enough to eat as early as July 17; but that was unusual.

David held the ladder steady while I climbed down. He was just taking a walk down the road, he said, and, catching sight of me, had turned in. I am always glad to see him, but at this particular time I would have preferred he had not come, since I had plans of my own for the morning. I had in mind to walk to Sabazan on a very important errand, and wanted to go alone.

Still, I wished some one to talk to, for I was about to take a serious step—so serious, indeed, that it will mean more or less of a turning point in my life. If Germaine's father were alive, I would have confided in him weeks ago and sought his sound advice.

I sometimes feel very lonely and apart. I know so many people, and yet there are so very few with whom I would care to talk about the matters that concern me most. Although I have known David for so short a time, I actually find myself telling him things that usually I would not think of telling anybody.

It was for this reason that at length I proposed to David that he walk to Sabazan with me.

Just as we two were leaving my garden and I was locking the gate, my neighbor across the road—the one I often hear singing—was plowing in his vineyard and shouting lustily at his oxen.

*"Mascaret!   Ha! — Prou! — Millet!   Arrè!
Arrè—Doucement!"*

And then, instead of getting a chance to tell David
what was on my mind, I had to answer a score of
questions about our oxen.   I had to explain to him
how they are trained in pairs from the time when
they are young; how they always keep on the same
side of each other; and how, if one dies, the other is
at a loss and ceases to eat, and sometimes pines
away; how one is usually named Mascaret, and the
other Millet.

"Or sometimes Lauret and Mulet," I added,
"which means 'little mule.'"

"But why don't you use horses, as we do in America?"

I told him it was because of the heavy, clay soil.
We must plow deeply and slowly.   Horses would
be too light and fast.

If David keeps on asking his innumerable questions, he will soon know as much about Gascony as
I do.   I wonder if all Americans are as curious about
the reasons of things.   I frequently have to think up
reasons for our commonest customs—reasons that I
become doubtful of myself, when I get to thinking
them over!

We took the short way to Sabazan, a narrow,
winding road, going uphill and down, somewhat too
rough for carts, so that we had it to ourselves.   It
is a picturesque road, bordered with high shrubbery
and trees on both sides, so that much of the time we
were in the shade.   Every little while, as we reached
an eminence, we could get a glimpse of the heavy,

square tower of the Sabazan church peeping over the fields.

It was when we were about half way that I finally mentioned to David the thing I had told nobody else but my old associate, the Abbé Rivoire, to whom I wrote only yesterday; it was this: I had decided, after a great deal of thought, to look for a place as curé of some parish.

There, it was out!

"It is not to be repeated to anybody just now," I said. "But since I am teaching no longer, and have come back home here to spend the remainder of my days, I have been thinking that I can make better use of them than by merely studying books and writing down thoughts that will never do a single person any good but myself. When I came back to Aignan this time, I was very tired, and I thought it was time for me to rest. But now I begin to be anxious for some labor that is of service to God and my fellow creatures. And what better way to such service than to be curé in one of the villages near my native place —near enough, I am hoping, that I may come as often as I like to see my old father and the people and things that have ever been so close to my life that they are a part of me!"

I am not so old yet. I am only sixty-five. Perhaps there is still much worth while for me to do before I die.

"What parish is there about here, Monsieur l'Abbé? Is there a vacancy?"

I explained to David that there is no vacancy

now, but that I had written to the Archbishop at Auch and that yesterday I had an answer.

"I had thought of Fustérouau," I went on. "That is not very far away; and then, it has other advantages. The church is close to the railroad station, which makes it easier to go to Lourdes, or, perhaps to Paris once in a long while."

David remembered Fustérouau well, because he had first come to Aignan that way. He added that it was not much of a village.

That is true; but if all goes well, I shall not go to Fustérouau after all. For the Archbishop's letter gives me a hope far beyond any I dared to entertain. I did not even venture to hope for the parish of Sabazan—Sabazan, whose church I see so clearly from my garden; whose tower is forever associated in my mind with the sunsets against whose glory it works its daily miracle; the tower that has made me feel the beauty of these towers on our hills as no other has—why, I made that square window in my little pavilion in the garden just so that I could look out across the valleys to Sabazan, and dream of Sabazan! And now the Archbishop suggests Sabazan! Although nobody knows it, the young curé there is going to be changed. Well, the Archbishop has always been friendly to me. We went to the same seminary. Even then, I am sure, I talked to him of Sabazan. Perhaps he remembers it!

It is possible that if David had known enough about the history of France, I might have reminded him of what they once called certain abbés that sought attractive preferments several hundreds of years ago, the *abbés de Sainte Espérance*—the abbés of St. Hope, he would say in English. But truly, no one can rightly maintain that I am like them, for they sought a sinecure and an easy life, while I seek only a chance to serve God in the best way I can, even though it means something of labor and hardship.

When at last we reached the top of the hill and entered the village, with its winding, irregular streets, David was surprised that everybody we passed seemed to be acquainted with me and greeted me cordially. David was struck, too, with the peace and charm of the place—it is very small; there are not more than two hundred souls in the entire commune.

We made our way toward the church, in the center of things. Near the church portal is a huge cross made of the trunk of a tree, very rough, its knots protruding, on which hangs the image of the Divine Redeemer.

If I had been alone, I would have entered the church and remained awhile, thinking the thoughts that come to one only in God's sanctuary. Instead, we kept on past the tiny cemetery in front of the great tower and skirted the pond that follows the road in a crescent—it may have been the moat of an ancient château once—and took our way toward the curé's house, which is down the hill on the other side of the village.

Now, this is just what I had come to Sabazan for, —to see the priest's house and garden, even though I had seen it so many times before. For when one looks at a place, thinking of it for the first time as the one spot in the world where he is to spend the rest of his days—where he is to live and work, and at last to die—he looks at it with new and appraising eyes.

It is charming—the little two-storied house, set back from the road, with a lawn and flower garden sloping down from the front of it. As we entered the iron gates, painted a dull claret color, we saw the priest's cart under a tree. He was probably home then. When we sounded the big, iron knocker, the tall form of the Abbé Bousquet almost immediately appeared.

The Abbé Bousquet is well-built and vigorous; an out-of-doors man, who loves to hunt and is very skillful with the partridge and quails. He is young, being only thirty-five. He is very dark, having black, crisping hair and an olive complexion. His face is unusually intelligent. His voice is rich and deep, and his smile is worth seeing; indeed, that frank, honest smile of his made David like him at once.

They say that one can read the soul of a man by the surroundings he makes for himself. One could tell much about the soul of the Abbé Bousquet by looking at the room at the back of the house where he reads and studies. It is as simple and direct as he is. The floor is of red stone, and the furniture is plain, most of it home-made—I am sure that the Abbé Bousquet made the bookcases himself. The table where he writes is of the commonest sort, made of pine and unpainted, such as people use in kitchens. There is a brass candelabra on it.

But there is one very unusual thing about this

room, which takes away from its bareness, contradicts its simplicity, and reveals another side of the soul of the Abbé Bousquet.

A priest's study with an organ in it is not very common; and one with a piano in it is still rarer; but the Abbé Bousquet actually has both in his—an organ with eight stops on one side of the room, and a piano on the other! And the wonder of it is he can play both well. I have heard that he used to be the organist at the seminary in Auch. Every Thursday in the year, without fail, the Abbé Préchac drives over from Margouet in his cart; and these two spend the long afternoon playing duets together.

I knew that David would like to hear the Abbé Bousquet play, so I asked him; at which his face lit up with pleasure, for the Abbé Bousquet would rather play music than eat, holding rightly that music is not only the food of the soul, but that it so affects the body that it suffices to take away hunger. Seating himself at the organ, he played several of the preludes of Bach; and then, opening the piano, he gave us two of his favorite Haydn sonatas. How the little room thrilled with the music his soul put into the sweet-toned keys! I love the music of nature and the music of man. I have listened to the whisper of myriads of leaves on a cloudy day, when the wind began to rise; once, when I was in the Pyrenees, I heard the long roll of the full-throated thunder shouting tumultuously from the deeps and crashing down from imperious heights; and I have heard the Abbé Bousquet play at his best this very day. And I do not know which affects me the more.

And while my friend played, I looked out through the wide-open door at the sunshine flooding the quiet vineyard and the rich field beyond. It is thus that the music of sight and sound sometimes blend into one.

On the road home, I was descanting to David upon the innocent pleasures that the life of a priest like the Abbé Bousquet may hold; pleasures that do not corrode, as do the pleasures of worldly men, but rather, strengthen and ennoble.

But David was not attending to me. He evidently had something else on his mind. After awhile he cleared his throat and said,

"I want your help, Monsieur l'Abbé. I need your friendship and your help very badly—that is why I came to you this morning; to see if you would do something very important for me."

"What is it?" I asked, as unconcernedly as I could.

"It is very serious. It affects my whole life. I may as well tell it all to you, just as it is!"

But, strange to say, David all at once became silent and could say nothing further, until we came to the turn of the road where the steeple of our Aignan church came into sight through the trees. Then he went on with considerable effort,

"You know how I have learned to love your country, Monsieur l'Abbé. But I have found something here that means infinitely more to me. You must have seen what I mean; you must have guessed it weeks ago.—They tell me you have known Germaine from the time when she was a little child."

Suddenly, David stopped again. I put my hand gently on his shoulder—I had to reach up a little to do that—and said to him,

"How can I help you, David?"

"I have no friends here—no one that really knows me—except you.—Will you speak favorably of me to Madame Sance? That is what I wanted to ask you. Perhaps I am asking too much. She does not know what to say to me. I think she is very unhappy. The other day when I spoke to her of my wish to marry Germaine, she burst into tears and had to leave me. Of course, she does not wish Germaine to go from her. I can understand that. But she trusts you, Monsieur l'Abbé, more than anybody else. Your word has great weight with her. I suppose, though, it is asking too much of you!"

We were climbing the hill at the top of which is our village.

"And what about Germaine herself, David?"

"If it depended only upon Germaine and me, all would be well, Monsieur l'Abbé, and we two would be the happiest people in Gascony!"

I reached over by the side of the road and idly plucked a few slender stems of *brins d'amour*— "bits of love"—with their exquisitely dainty little flowers. I handed them to David, saying,

"These were Germaine's favorite wild-flowers when she was a little girl. Her soul is like them— exquisite, and delicate, and fine."

We said nothing more until we arrived in the middle of the Place, in front of the old arcades. There we stopped before parting, and David asked,

"Then you will speak to Madame Sance for me?"

I could not answer.   All I could say after awhile was,

"Come to my garden to-morrow."

Chapter XXXVI: *Have Pity, O God!*

I COULD not write for these last ten days. I could not, I could not!

Marius Fontan is dead.

By his own hand.

The shutters of his room were closed, save where a narrow shaft of morning sun fell on him where he hung.

It touched his face when they laid him on the bed.

There was a half loaf of bread on the chest of drawers, brought him the day before. It was untouched.

Some of his manuscripts lay on the table.

The last time I saw him—his voice broke suddenly in the midst of that song. His life's song has suddenly ceased just that way!

They buried him in that part of the cemetery where the grass is long and unkept.

The bell did not toll.

In that part of the cemetery, there are no crosses on the graves.

The life-size image of Jesus on the great wooden cross in the center faces the other way.

I cannot adjust myself to it.

How can such things happen?

Have pity, O God!

Chapter XXXVII: *The Inevitable*

I DO not know what I should have done during these difficult days without David. Most of the time, I have wanted to be alone. But when I wished to talk over things with some one, I sent for him.

One can forget one's sorrow a little by thinking of the happiness of others.

And David has found happiness.

Love and death—are they not the themes of the best things ever written or sung by mere men? Love and death, death and love! Between these two realities life's ceaseless pendulum swings. Love and death—how they answer one another, purge one another, transfigure one another! After all, may they not be joined together in some great and wonderful way we know not now? May they not be one and the same thing in the mystery of God?

I, an old man, saddened with the grief of death, find comfort in thinking of the love of Germaine and David. For, looking at the matter without prejudice, I now perceive that these two have it in them to fulfill in many respects the ideal of a perfect, earthly love. Both these young hearts are unsullied and true, and their love is likely to be of the kind that endures and ennobles. Each will find in the other a suggestion of that divine love which is beyond them and all earthly things.

In Germaine, David has found a fortune above all else this world could bring him. The strongest, sweetest virtues of earth will be with him constantly in her daily presence; more and more he will discover how natural, and simple, and direct she is, with no shadow of deceit; how the glory of the health of her body is expressed in the glory of the health of her mind. In her he will find cheerfulness that knows the dear content that is in common things made beautiful by a touch; large-heartedness and sympathy; faith in the triumph of all good hopes such as are born of valiant souls; the will to achieve without boasting—and all these virtues mirrored in a face that he will treasure as the dearest sight his eyes will ever see.

I now see that it was inevitable that such a man as David should have been drawn to Germaine from the first. One might put it this way: If David loves Gascony, how could he help loving Germaine? For she is the beauty and glory of Gascony expressed in a soul and a body.

Some days ago, I spoke with Madame Sance. Perhaps I did not raise as many objections as I should. I had had another long talk with David about the Church. He will respect Germaine's religion as a sacred thing. He will not discourage her loyalty to the things she has been taught, and will sometimes go to mass with her. It will be a solace to both

Madame Sance and myself to know this. Then, too, their children will be brought up within the Church. I have a secret hope that perhaps, some day, Germaine will be able to lead David to share her high faith and kneel with her before God, their souls made one in a new and blessed way.

Madame Sance has consented. The wedding will be soon—too soon, alas! It is not long now before David must go back to America. His college, which is in the Department of Ohio, opens in September he tells me. He wants to take Germaine with him.

America is far; but surely, they will come back again! That is the comfort. These Americans are great travelers. David's passion for Gascony will not die; and, besides, for Germaine's sake alone he will surely come. Then, his own sister may remain here at the château; certainly she will be here summers. Yes, I know David will come back!

There are some things in this world that are inevitable. And it is good to think that where the inevitable is, God has something in mind which He wishes to accomplish.

That we do not understand it is a matter of minor importance.

Chapter XXXVIII: *Compromises*

THE devil has been about to enter our little village—I speak figuratively—in the form of a cinema theater. It was all the idea of the little doctor.

"Nothing ever happens in this village," he had said. "There are no amusements."

So he and Rigot, the proprietor of the café, put their heads together and decided to have a theater for moving pictures.

But where was a hall big enough? The poultry market is not walled in, so it would not do in cold weather. The little doctor had a happy thought; he would use the old winery back of his house.

For a number of days they have been clearing it out, leveling the dirt floor and moving away loads of earth with an ox-cart. They even started to make a few benches.

As for myself, I was most thoroughly against it all. I may be wrong, but I like our village as it is, and do not want its simple charm destroyed by the intrusion of what they call modern improvements, which, to my mind, often do not improve at all. If our village has a decided individuality, it is partly because it has preferred to retain the good old customs, rather than to adopt questionable new ones. I do not believe in this particular kind of amusement anyway. I went to a cinema theater in Paris once, and the pictures I saw were the very opposite of uplifting. Whenever a traveling cinema has come to Aignan, I have advised people not to go. But they have gone just the same, which is additional proof of what a temptation such things are.

I had not yet talked to the little doctor about this project of his, hoping hat he would find some reason to abandon it. But this morning he came to bring me that bottle of armagnac which Madame Sance had promised me, so I took occasion to ask him how it was progressing.

And then I heard something that cheered my whole day.

"I am afraid it is all over," he said. "Yesterday, Marthe"—that is his wife—"went out and saw what was being done in the winery. I was in the country at the time. Since talking with her last night, I have changed my mind. I had never been sure that Marthe liked it. She had said nothing much, and when she says nothing—well, one is not certain."

After all, life is full of compromises like that. We never get exactly what we want; or, if we do, we lose something else that we want just as much or more. One might say that by this compromise, the doctor got nothing; but that would be a mistake. He had the pleasure of carrying his project up to a certain point; and then, when it came to the choice of fulfilling it, on the one hand, or of having peace with

Marthe on the other, he chose the latter, which was the far greater thing to have.

At my age, I have come to the conclusion that the little doctor's case is not exceptional; that most of our problems have to be settled by compromises. There is Mauser, that little hamlet just the other side of the forest. It is just between the communes of Aignan and Averon, and belongs to neither. How does it settle its problem? When its babies are brought into the world, they are baptized here in Aignan; and when its old die, they are buried in the little cemetery over in Averon.

It is only God that never compromises.

The real reason why we human beings have to solve so many problems that way is that we are limited in two things, our knowledge and our power. Either we are not sure of what is the best thing, so we do the next best; or, the best thing can't be done, because we have not the power to do it—circumstances baffle us.

In his very last letter to me, the Abbé Rivoire put it in this way:

"Our human intellects are like lamps of various degrees of intensity; some are brighter than others, but they all cast shadows."

There is Henri's hunting-dog, Dick. They often tie Dick at the end of a long rope fastened to a tree. Sometimes he wanders around and around the tree, until the rope gets very short. Dick never quite understands what has happened. He tries in every way but the right way to unwind his line. Finally, the solution of his problem is a compromise; he lies down, or, perhaps he howls or barks, knowing that if he waits long enough, Henri will notice him and release him from his predicament. His reason is limited. I, who look on, would know what to do, but Dick doesn't.

So, God would know what to do, but I don't.

Therefore, I do the best I can. The beauty of it all is that I can at least do something. I have wisdom enough for that. I am never utterly defeated. There is even a measure of victory in the compromise my poor reason makes.

Old age is the time when one realizes all this most. Our ideals—those of this world—are every one of them compromised by that time. But every such compromise means some compensation, for which it is our business to thank God.

For instance, we old men—when the living have left us, we can at least commune with the dead and find our solace there!

I do not know what it was that led my steps thither, but when the little doctor was gone, I strolled down the road from my garden, opened the creaking, iron gates of our cemetery close by and entered, closing the gates behind me.

On every side, the high stone wall, covered with moss and ivy, shut me out from the world.

How peaceful it was!

I was the only one there—and yet so many were there!

I sat down on a low stone wall shutting in the

graves of an ancient family of our region, and looked about me.

The sunshine lay over everything, save where the tall cypresses cast their brooding shadows; it rested lingeringly on rows and rows of crosses, large and small; crosses of stone, of wood, of iron, hung with wreaths and rosaries—the sun lay over them all, till they seemed emblems of life, not of death; of joy, not sorrow. Yes, this morning, the sunshine had penetrated into this little world, and was different from the sunshine anywhere else. The flowers in bloom over the graves here and there were glorious with it, and even the faded bouquets in their vases did not look so pitiful; touched by its delicate miracle, the motionless grasses were caught in some dream of such subtle beauty that the least footfall might have destroyed it. In the distance, yellow butterflies floated between the trees—golden memories come back from days the dead once knew. And no sound at all except the occasional call of a bird, exquisitely clear, or the strident and monotonous note of a *cigale,* or faint footsteps passing outside along the road, and once the muffled rattle of a cart, which, when it was gone, made the silence more apparent than before.

I thought to myself, "It is as I have often said, death is more friendly here, more gentle here than anywhere else in the world!"

While I was still sitting there, thinking such things, I heard the creak of the iron gates at the entrance, and I knew I was no longer alone. I got up and turned slowly toward the east wall, by which is the grave of Jean-Louis Sance, a grave to which I often go, musing over the old days when this splendid man filled a place in my heart that has never been filled since.

His grave is surrounded by a low iron fence, delicately wrought, green with moss. Back of it is the stone wall of the cemetery, over which the ivy tumbles in richer profusion than anywhere else. Over the grave is a large cross of wrought iron, hung with wreaths. If you stand farther back in the middle of the cemetery, you see this cross rising above the wall and outlined against the tower of the village church just beyond. The bell of the town hall, striking the hours, can be heard here very clearly; he himself put that bell in its tower when he was our mayor.

I heard soft footsteps on the path coming nearer and nearer, and, turning, was surprised and pleased to find it was Germaine. In her arm was a large bouquet of dahlias and asters.

"They are more beautiful than ever this year," she remarked as she opened the little gate and prepared to arrange them in the large vase she always keeps filled with fresh flowers at the head of the grave.

"The rosebush here at the foot—did it bloom this year?" I asked.

"Yes, it bloomed early; it was beautiful in May— large red roses; and the pinks and violets, they all came out."

"In spite of these cypresses," I went on, "I have noticed that the sun gets to this place three times a day; once in the morning, once early in the afternoon, and again toward sunset."

Germaine was clearing the grave of some of the longer grasses and was casting aside the withered flowers she had brought several days before. Her face was turned away from me. Then for a long time she stood silent, looking away over the cemetery wall, past that cross; oh, I am sure she was not seeing the church tower at all! Finally, she turned to me, saying,

"It is quiet here."

Yes, thank God, it is quiet here where the dead sleep. But the silence of death, what a terrible silence it is for the heart of a child like this! Love and death! Here they were again, an infinite joy and an infinite pathos, struggling together in one soul.

Ah, what a compromise life is, indeed!

Yet the love that has newly come into her life, it will possess her more and more; and when she is far away, this little grave among the cypress trees will gradually become one of those memories that bless us—cherished more than any joy she ever knew.

After Germaine had gone, I went over and stood long by the newly-made grave of Marius Fontan.

He would not compromise with life.

There were no flowers anywhere near. But I had noticed that Germaine had thrown aside a large, red dahlia from her bouquet, because it was a little withered.

I went back and got it.

It made that rough, barren, lonely mound look less forsaken.

Chapter XXXIX: *The Wedding*

THE great event—it has happened!

For three weeks before the wedding, people read the bans posted on the bulletin board in the arcades of the town hall, the dispensation having arrived. And for three Sundays, our old curé had to announce the coming marriage in the church, in spite of the fact that he plainly thinks that Madame Sance is making a mistake. I am afraid that our curé holds me responsible for it. I was glad that he did not mind when I was asked to officiate.

"It is but natural," he said. "You are such an old friend of the family."

If it had been the young vicar, I am sure he would not have been so graceful about it. But nothing can harm the friendship of the old Abbé Castex and myself, for reasons we both know.

Any one passing the house on the Road of the Madonna the day before the wedding would easily notice that something very unusual was going on. Back in the big kitchen, four or five extra cooks were busy with the preparations for the wedding dinner; and little Renée, the kitchen girl, was running hither and thither on a hundred errands. Even old Marinette was in to help, although later, being a lifelong neighbor, she was to assume the dignity of an invited guest. Robust, red-faced, jovial Marinette!— she was present when Germaine was born, and she can hardly bring herself to think of her as anything more than a baby still; several times she stops in her work in a bewildered way and delivers herself of some trifling incident of Germaine's childhood, which she has long cherished, but which seems so impossible now.

But the others have very little time to listen to her. There are the soups to make, and the pastries to be baked, and the chickens and turkeys and guinea-hens to get ready—there are at least thirty of them in a row on the long table; and then there are so many other things that it would make one's head dizzy to enumerate them. Old Marinette's task it is to get ready the galantine of chicken, a task which she knows how to do best, and which has to be done with patience and tact. As I understand it, you first perform the feat of getting all the bones out of the chicken without taking it apart, except you do remove the ends of the wings and the feet before you begin. Then you fill up the places where the bones were with stuffing made of chopped pork and veal and other things; then, after you have sewed up the skin again, you wrap a cloth around it and boil it for hours in some rich stock, including calves' feet; when it is done you have something not far short of concentrated goodness. You serve it cold in its own jelly—and above all things you must not have forgotten the truffles.

Outside the house, too, important things are happening. The little doctor himself is busily directing some peasants who have just arrived from the forest, their ox-carts laden with tall, young trees. One by one they are being set up along the driveway on both sides, two even rows of them, stretching from the great iron gates at the entrance clear back to the barns. On these will be hung strings of gay, paper lanterns—they are in that big box from Auch, standing on end by the cellar door.

Also, back in one of the two large barns, at the end of the driveway, mysterious preparations are going on. Even at this moment Angèle—Germaine's sister from Bordeaux—and Juliette, her pretty cousin from St. Sever de Rustan, are going in through the wide-open doors, the one with an armful of white cloth, and the other with branches and flowers.

Relatives old and young, from near and far, are arriving all day long, and Madame Sance is continually being called to the front door to greet them. One thing is certain, they cannot all be accommodated in this one house, immense as it is; it would require a good-sized inn to take care of them all! But the homes of many neighbors are open to them, so everybody is happily placed; and by evening our village has taken on new life, and everybody is talking about the event of the morrow—especially about this young American, concerning whom there are many opinions. Not one of the new arrivals, however, can deny that the groom is a handsome fellow —those who went at five o'clock to the civil ceremony at the town hall are unanimous about that!

And how well he and Germaine looked together as they stood before Rigot, the deputy mayor, in the long council room! Of course, although the little doctor is mayor, it would hardly have been fitting for him to have officiated, since Germaine is in his own family.

It is clear that David does not even yet understand our customs very well. In the first place, he did not know that there had to be two ceremonies, this one at the town hall, and the other at the church. Of course, I explained to him that while the former was necessary, the really important ceremony was the one that would occur at the church the following day. And then he made the most extraordinary suggestion; he wanted to know if the religious ceremony could not be arranged at Germaine's home instead!

They actually have wedding ceremonies in the houses in America!

We do not do things that way. It is unthinkable. How could the marriage ceremony be anywhere but in God's sanctuary, and how can people be truly made man and wife except before His holy altar?

I was afraid it would be bad weather the day of the wedding. For late the night before there was a terrible storm, with high wind and hail; the trees the little doctor had set up by the driveway were all blown down. But the next morning when I looked out my window, the sun was brighter than ever, and the Pyrenees could be seen rising above the haze to the south—I think I never saw them look more beautiful; there was something sad about their beauty this time, but they looked wonderful and majestic for all that.

When I went up to the church to say mass, it was very early; but already young girls and boys were strewing the Street of the Balustrade with green branches and flowers.

It was about half-past ten when the wedding procession started from Madame Sance's house. My Aunt Madeleine saw it and told me about it; and when my Aunt Madeleine tells anything, nothing at all is left out. Two by two it slowly made its way along the Road of the Madonna toward the village: first, Germaine, on the arm of the little doctor; then David and his sister; then the bridesmaids and their escorts; then Madame Sance, on the arm of Maurice, Angèle's husband; and then the other relatives of the family. On the procession went, up the Street of the Balustrade to the church door, the whole way strewn with flowers, the bell from the church all the while sending its echoes out over the valleys and hills.

Ah, when will Germaine ever hear that bell again? I remember when it rang at her christening!

My Aunt Madeleine said that the bride was most entrancing, with her dress of soft, white silk, glistening in the sunshine, and her long, white veil, and the crown of orange blossoms on her head, orange blossoms, too, in her hand, sent all the way from Nice, and two tiny girls bearing her train, and she herself looking fresher and sweeter than she ever did before.

I suppose that the church was never more wonderfully decorated. My Aunt Madeleine had taken charge of that, and it is the first time that I had ever observed anything of an artistic nature in her. One never knows.

In front of the altar, beautiful with flowers from our best gardens and lit with numerous candles, two low *prie-Dieu* had been placed for the bride and groom. As the little doctor escorted Germaine up the aisle, Sarrade, the sabot-maker, put all the music he could into the little organ, until it sounded almost like the pipe-organ we have always been hoping to have some day. Then the music became very quiet and hushed as Germaine and David knelt before the altar, waiting for the service to begin.

I did my very best to say the ceremony as it should be said, but it was with an aching heart. Who that was there will ever forget the aria Angèle sang from Massenet's *La Vierge?* I never heard such singing in our church before—so exquisite!—it almost seemed as if through it the heart of Germaine was saying its farewell to all of us in notes that had that pure mingling of sadness and joy which thrills through all the songs that are truly great.

When the bride and groom had led the procession back to the house, the festivities of the day began; festivities that were to continue into the early hours of the next morning. The wedding dinner—everybody was looking forward to that, for it was to be something quite out of the ordinary, especially, on account of the place where it was to be held, in one of the spacious barns at the end of the driveway, where the cask-making and repairing used to be done.

You would never know it was a barn when once you got inside. The walls were covered up with sheets, decorated all over with flowers and greenery. Two long tables ran from end to end, and the doors at the front and rear were thrown wide open so that the breezes played through, making it deliciously cool, although it was a warm day, as everybody who had just marched down the hot road from the church could well attest. It was a fine idea to have this wedding dinner in the barn; the little doctor, who is exceedingly fertile in ideas, told me he thought of it first. There was no use trying to have it in the house; how could one hundred and fifty people ever have been put into one dining room?

As one went in, one noticed that at the table on the left all the young people were being seated, while the one on the right was for the older people, with the bride and groom in a place of honor at the middle. I was put very near them, across from David's sister. I observed that the old Abbé Castex was there, away down toward the end of the table. He was not sure he would be able to come, but he came after all, and was even in good spirits, already talking almost amiably with his neighbor, Madame Lacoste, thoroughly innocent of her well-known opinion of him. Down toward the other end, I saw Marinette and a few other neighbors who had known Germaine all her life.

While I was looking over at Germaine and her mother, who sat by her—Germaine had removed

her veil, but still kept her crown of orange blossoms
—David's sister spoke to me across the table in English (so that no one else understood),

"It is not our custom in America to wear evening
dress-suits in the daytime; my big brother remonstrated vigorously when I told him he would have
to."

It would have been unusual if David had appeared
in anything else. He looked handsome and even distinguished in it, too. All the men guests except one
or two had them.

There were many people there who had never
eaten a dinner such as they sat down to this day.
Even the Abbé Castex, who used to be an expert in
such matters, confided to me afterwards that it was
the most marvelous dinner he had ever experienced.
True, he had to stop after the fifth or sixth course,
which was only about halfway through, as he could
have known beforehand if he had only read the menu
each one had by his plate, especially printed for this
occasion at Auch. But plainly, he did not realize
how things were going and reached the limits of his
powers sooner than he otherwise should. However,
since the dinner lasted about three hours, and since
there was no hurry between courses, he was able to
rally again toward the end, and finished with some
show of valor.

As for me, I ate rather sparingly. Try as I would,
I could not enter fully into the gayety that was all
about me, even though I was truly glad that these
two souls were looking forward to such happiness.
Besides, I thought that I would propose a toast later

on, and I was considering what kind of a speech I should make. For I am like Montaigne in this, that "occasion, company, draws more from my mind than I can find therein when by myself I endeavor to employ the same."

At length, when the time for champagne came, I perceived my opportunity, and rose in my place. Very soon everybody was quiet, and I began,

"It is fitting that old age should drink a toast to youth; for old age was once young, wishes that it were still young, and sees the glory of youth as youth itself never can.

"Our little village has been neglected by the historians, although interesting things have often happened in it. Perhaps Americans who never yet heard of this place, which to us means all that makes our lives dear, will ask, 'Where and what is this Aignan, that such a bride as Monsieur Ware's may be found in it?'

"Through these open doors, I can just get a glimpse of the garden yonder. It may well occur to you that the best flower it ever knew is now being taken far away. May Monsieur Ware cherish this flower of our Gascony always; may God give His sunshine to their days; and may they never forget this little corner of the world, and may it so call to their hearts that they cannot resist its call and will soon come back to us!"

I could not say any more, for, although I smiled,

I felt a catch in my throat which I am glad nobody noticed.

After the dinner, everybody went out-of-doors and strolled about the cool garden, or gathered in intimate groups under the trees, the men smoking, and the women exchanging endless gossip—oh, of a harmless kind, for after such a dinner, everybody felt good and at peace with all the world.

I overheard old Marinette trying to tell David in part patois and part French that "Germaine was a good catch!" her ruddy face beaming with homely good-nature. A little later, he joined me where I was standing for a moment in a corner of the garden, under a chestnut tree. Germaine had gone into the house. Later, I learned that she could not resist going up to the attic to take a last look at some old things that were stored up there, things associated with her childhood, such as a tiny chair that was once her favorite, some picture-books, and toys of various kinds, including an old doll which I well remember seeing her play with in this very garden when she was a little girl.

While I was standing there with David, I heard the most remarkable thing. Monsieur Rigot came up and told David that he wished to give him several bottles of a very rare champagne he had, to take to America with him.

"I hear you will not come back to us for two years; when you drink this, you will think of us."

But David informed him that in America they were not allowed to drink champagne, no, nor wines of any kind!

"But this is good wine," I remonstrated, somewhat at a loss, "not wine such as any law could object to."

And then I found out that it did not make any difference how excellent the wine was, Americans would not be permitted to drink it if the government found out about it. Indeed, they would be punished very severely.

I cannot understand it, especially since America has no king, whose whim could be made into a law. I have seen a number of Americans here in France, and they never refused wine, or even cognac and liqueurs; in fact, I have sometimes thought that they drank more than was good for them.

The event of the day toward which the young people most looked forward was the grand ball. By six o'clock, when it was beginning to get cool, most of the women had changed to their evening dresses; and soon people were again taking their way toward the barn, only this time they went up the staircase that had been erected on the outside, leading to the big loft. Everything there had been moved out to make room. The floor had been waxed; here, as downstairs, the walls were covered with sheets decorated with flowers; potted plants were artistically arranged here and there; chairs were set all around the wall; and from the rafters hung gasoline lamps, very primitive in looks, fetched from the winery. The piano had been moved up from the house; the musicians came clear from Mont de Marsan; besides the piano, there was a violin and a cornet.

A moment after David had escorted his bride out

into the middle of the floor and opened the ball with the first dance, the space was filled with happy couples moving rhythmically to the music of a waltz.

For my own part, during the long evening I wandered about in the garden and chatted now and then with some of my old friends; but much of the time I was alone. After awhile, the moon came out, very bright through the trees, and though the garden and driveway were hung with strings of gay lanterns, which everybody thought beautiful, I liked the lights in the sky best. Much laughter and talk were wafted across the garden, at pauses in the music, from those who were partaking of refreshments, served on a wooden platform gay with red cloth, which had been built between the two barns, at a level with the dancing floor. Right where the platform was, there was once an old archway, now vanished, where Germaine's swing used to be.

So the old things go one by one; and then, after awhile, the memories go, too; or is any memory ever entirely dead?

I had no desire to stay very late. I remained to the supper that was served at ten o'clock and then went home. They would be dancing there until daylight. I knew that David and Germaine intended quietly to withdraw about eleven o'clock, and go to Riscle for their train.

The last wedding I attended was out in the country. Of course, peasants conduct such things differently. I was telling David of their custom of going to the chamber of the bride and groom about midnight to bring food and wine—I have known of the door being broken down if they were not admitted.

After I had gone home, I did not immediately go to bed. My shutters were wide open. As I sat there, my lamp unlit, musing over many things, the stars looked into my window from across the roofs of the houses on the other side of the street.

Suddenly, I heard the sound of horses' hoofs and the rolling of a carriage rounding the corner and coming my way down the Street of the Church. I leaned out the window. It went rapidly by and then rattled out across the Place, awakening a thousand echoes from the sleeping houses; and then the sound of the wheels gradually faded away down the long road toward Riscle.

And I sha'n't see them for two years!

Chapter XL: *Sunsets*

I AM sitting alone in my garden-house.

The day is nearly done. Through the open door, I look out now and then at the church tower near by, its heavy, windowless wall softened by the glow of the setting sun.

How old and crumbling our tower is, after all! I never quite realized it before. I wonder how long it will be standing there!

This whole village of ours is getting old and falling into ruin, and the number of people in it is becoming less and less. For one thing, it is away from any railroad; then, there is no river running through it, so there are no factories, and the young men do not stay here any more. There is no chance for them here.

The summer—this wonderful summer—is passing away. The leaves of the grapevine over the door have turned red. The fields are no longer green. The wheat has been reaped.

It is not merely that the summer has gone; but so much else has gone with it!

Germaine and David—they have been gone three days now.

329

I heard this morning that my young friend, Henri, Germaine's brother, is ordered to Algiers to commence his military service. So he goes also.

Marius is gone.

My poor, brave friend, the Abbé Rivoire—his sister writes from Paris that he was too weak to read my last letter. She had to read it to him, little by little.

As I muse in this place of many memories, I hear the silvery bells of the oxen along the road in the distance; one notices them most at sunset.

It occurs to me that toward this same sunset David and Germaine are at this moment sailing!

Two years is not so very long. That is the time that David said. Well, it is right that an old man should not be compelled to live entirely in his memories; he should have his hopes, too.

And then, I am to be appointed curé at Sabazan—yes, it is at last decided! So my old age—it may become a strength, not a weakness, with its own achievements, and its own beauty, too, I hope.

Old age should be to a life what the sunset is to a day.

Of all the things that pass into the night of death, the day knows how to die beautifully.

Just now, a last gleam of sun lit up some yellow flowers on tall stalks, as yet unopened, that grow over there near the cemetery wall. "Beauties of the night" they are called, since they open only after sunset; then they unfold so fast that one can almost detect the large petals in the very act of pushing themselves apart.

I think that as the twilight opens the hearts of these flowers, so the twilight of a man's life may make his soul to put forth blooms that his youth never knew—blooms that reach up through the darkness toward heaven!

(4)

THE END